Isaac Asimov has always been recognized as the most brilliant of science-fiction writers, but even he has never before produced such an imaginative, compelling story of the future as *The End of Eternity*.

Andrew Harlan is an Eternal, a man whose job it is to range through past and present centuries, monitoring and, where necessary, altering time's myriad cause-and-effect relationships. It is when Harlan meets a non-Eternal woman and falls victim to a timeless phenomenon – love – that he seeks to use the awesome techniques of the Eternals to twist time to suit his purpose . . .

This magnificent story deserves to stand with the very best in science fiction – a gripping and thoroughly absorbing book.

Also by Isaac Asimov

Isaac Asimov

The End of Eternity

PANTHER
GRANADA PUBLISHING
London Toronto Sydney New York

Published by Granada Publishing Limited
in Panther Books 1959
Reprinted 1964, 1965, 1968, 1969, 1971, 1973, 1974, 1976,
1978

ISBN 0 586 02440 9

Granada Publishing Limited
Frogmore, St Albans, Herts AL2 2NF
and
3 Upper James Street, London W1R 4BP
1221 Avenue of the Americas, New York, NY 10020, USA
117 York Street, Sydney, NSW 2000, Australia
100 Skyway Avenue, Toronto, Ontario, Canada M9W 3A6
Trio City, Coventry Street, Johannesburg 2001, South Africa
CML Centre, Queen & Wyndham, Auckland 1, New Zealand

Made and printed in Great Britain by
Richard Clay (The Chaucer Press) Ltd
Bungay, Suffolk
Set in Linotype Plantin

To Horace L. Gold

CHAPTER ONE

TECHNICIAN

ANDREW HARLAN stepped into the kettle. Its sides were perfectly round and it fitted snugly inside a vertical shaft composed of widely spaced rods that shimmered into an unseeable haze six feet above Harlan's head. Harlan set the controls and moved the smoothly working starting lever.

The kettle did not move.

Harlan did not expect it to. He expected no movement; neither up nor down, left nor right, forth nor back. Yet the spaces between the rods had melted into a grey blankness which was solid to the touch, though nonetheless immaterial for all that. And there *was* the little stir in his stomach, the faint (psychosomatic?) touch of dizziness, that told him that all the kettle contained, including himself, was rushing upwhen through Eternity.

He had boarded the kettle in the 575th Century, the base of operations assigned him two years earlier. At the time the 575th had been the farthest upwhen he had ever travelled. Now he was moving upwhen to the 2456th Century.

Under ordinary circumstances he might have felt a little lost at the prospect. His native Century was in the far downwhen, the 95th Century, to be exact. The 95th was a Century stiffly restrictive of atomic power, faintly rustic, fond of natural wood as a structural material, exporters of certain types of distilled potatoes to nearly everywhen and importers of clover seed. Although Harlan had not been in the 95th since he entered special training and became a Cub at the age of fifteen, there was always that feeling of loss when one moved outwhen from "home". At the 2456th he would be nearly two hundred forty millennia from his birthwhen and that is a sizeable distance even for a hardened Eternal.

Under ordinary circumstances all this would be so.

But right now Harlan was in poor mood to think of anything but the fact that his documents were heavy in his pocket and his plan heavy on his heart. He was a little frightened, a little tense, a little confused.

It was his hands acting by themselves that brought the kettle to the proper halt at the proper Century.

Strange that a Technician should feel tense or nervous about anything. What was it that Educator Yarrow had once said:

"Above all, a Technician must be dispassionate. The Reality Change he initiates may affect the lives of as many as fifty billion people. A million or so more of these may be so drastically affected as to be considered new individuals. Under these conditions, an emotional make-up is a distinct handicap."

Harlan put the memory of his teacher's dry voice out of his mind with an almost savage shake of his head. In those days he had never imagined that he himself would have the peculiar talent for that very position. But emotion had come upon him after all. Not for fifty billion people. What in Time did he care for fifty billion people? There was just one. One person.

He became aware that the kettle was stationary and with the merest pause to pull his thoughts together, put himself into the cold, impersonal frame of mind a Technician must have, he stepped out. The kettle he left, of course, was not the same as the one he had boarded, in the sense that it was not composed of the same atoms. He did not worry about that any more than any Eternal would. To concern oneself with the *mystique* of Time-travel, rather than with the simple fact of it, was the mark of the Cub and newcomer to Eternity.

He paused again at the infinitely thin curtain of Non-Space and Non-Time which separated him from Eternity in one way and from ordinary Time in another.

This would be a completely new section of Eternity for him. He knew about it in a rough way, of course, having checked upon it in the *Temporal Handbook*. Still, there was no substitute for actual appearance and he steeled himself for the initial shock of adjustment.

He adjusted the controls, a simple matter in passing into Eternity (and a very complicated one in passing into Time, a type of passage which was correspondingly less frequent). He stepped through the curtain and found himself squinting at the brilliance. Automatically he threw up his hand to shield his eyes.

Only one man faced him. At first Harlan could see him only blurrily.

The man said, "I am Sociologist Kantor Voy. I imagine you are Technician Harlan."

Harlan nodded and said, "Father Time! Isn't this sort of

8

ornamentation adjustable?"

Voy looked about him and said tolerantly, "You mean the molecular films?"

"I certainly do," said Harlan. The *Handbook* had mentioned them, but had said nothing of *such* an insane riot of light reflection.

Harlan felt his annoyance to be quite reasonable. The 2456th Century was matter-oriented, as most Centuries were, so he had a right to expect a basic compatability from the very beginning. It would have none of the utter confusion (for anyone born matter-oriented) of the energy vortices of the 300's, or the field dynamics of the 600's. In the 2456th, to the average Eternal's comfort, matter was used for everything from walls to tacks.

To be sure, there was matter and matter. A member of an energy-oriented Century might not realize that. To him all matter might seem minor variations on a theme that was gross, heavy, and barbaric. To matter-oriented Harlan, however, there was wood, metal (subdivisions, heavy and light), plastic, silicates, concrete, leather, and so on.

But matter consisting entirely of mirrors!

That was his first impression of the 2456th. Every surface reflected and glinted light. Everywhere was the illusion of complete smoothness; the effect of a molecular film. And in the ever-repeated reflection of himself, of Sociologist Voy, of everything he could see, in scraps and wholes, in all angles, there was confusion. Garish confusion and nausea!

"I'm sorry," said Voy, "it's the custom of the Century, and the Section assigned to it finds it good practice to adopt the customs where practical. You get used to it after a time."

Voy walked rapidly upon the moving feet of another Voy, upside down beneath the floor, who matched him stride for stride. He reached to move a hair-contact indicator down a spiral scale to point of origin.

The reflections died; extraneous light faded. Harlan felt his world settle.

"If you'll come with me now," said Voy.

Harlan followed through empty corridors that, Harlan knew, must moments ago have been a riot of made light and reflection, up a ramp, through an anteroom, into an office.

In all the short journey no human being had been visible. Harlan was so used to that, took it so for granted, that he would have been surprised, almost shocked, if a glimpse of a human figure hurrying away had caught his eyes. No doubt the news had spread that a Technician was coming through. Even Voy kept his distance and when, accidentally, Harlan's hand had brushed Voy's sleeve, Voy shrank away with a visible start.

Harlan was faintly surprised at the touch of bitterness he felt at all this. He had thought the shell he had grown about his soul was thicker, more efficiently insensitive than that. If he was wrong, if his shell had worn thinner, there could only be one reason for that.

Noÿs!

Sociologist Kantor Voy leaned forward towards the Technician in what seemed a friendly enough fashion, but Harlan noted automatically that they were seated on opposite sides of the long axis of a fairly large table.

Voy said, "I am pleased to have a Technician of your reputation interest himself in our little problem here."

"Yes," said Harlan with the cold impersonality people would expect of him. "It has its points of interest." (Was he impersonal enough? Surely his real motives must be apparent, his guilt be spelled out in beads of sweat on his forehead.)

He removed from an inner pocket the foiled summary of the projected Reality Change. It was the very copy which had been sent to the Allwhen Council a month earlier. Through his relationship with Senior Computer Twissell (*the* Twissell, himself) Harlan had had little trouble in getting his hands on it.

Before unrolling the foil, letting it peel off onto the table top where it would be held by a soft paramagnetic field, Harlan paused a split moment.

The molecular film that covered the table was subdued but was not zero. The motion of his arm fixed his eye and for an instant the reflection of his own face seemed to stare sombrely up at him from the table top. He was thirty-two, but he looked older. He needed no one to tell him that. It might be partly his long face and dark eyebrows over darker eyes that gave him the lowering expression and cold glare associated with the caricature of the Technician in the minds of all Eternals. It might be just his own realization that he was a Technician.

But then he flicked the foil out across the table and turned to the matter at hand.

"I am not a Sociologist, sir."

Voy smiled. "That sounds formidable. When one begins by

expressing lack of competence in a given field, it usually implies that a flat opinion in that field will follow almost immediately."

"No," said Harlan, "not an opinion. Just a request. I wonder if you won't look over this summary and see if you haven't made a small mistake somewhere here."

Voy looked instantly grave. "I hope not," he said.

Harlan kept one arm across the back of his chair, the other in his lap. He must let neither hand drum restless fingers. He must not bite his lips. He must not show his feelings in any way.

Ever since the whole orientation of his life had so changed itself, he had been watching the summaries of projected Reality Changes as they passed through the grinding administrative gears of the Allwhen Council. As Senior Computer Twissell's personally assigned Technician, he could arrange that by a slight bending of professional ethics. Particularly with Twissell's attention caught ever more tightly in his own overwhelming project. (Harlan's nostrils flared. He knew *now* a little of the nature of that project.)

Harlan had had no assurance that he would ever find what he was looking for in a reasonable time. When he had first glanced over projected Reality Change 2456-2781, Serial Number V-5, he was half inclined to believe his reasoning powers were warped by wishing. For a full day he had checked and re-checked equations and relationships in a rattling uncertainty, mixed with growing excitement and a bitter gratitude that he had been taught at least elementary psycho-mathematics.

Now Voy went over those same puncture patterns with a half-puzzled, half-worried eye.

He said, "It seems to me; I say, it *seems* to me that this is all perfectly in order."

Harlan said, "I refer you particularly to the matter of the courtship characteristics of the society of the current Reality of this Century. That's sociology and your responsibility, I believe. It's why I arranged to see *you* when I arrived, rather than someone else."

Voy was now frowning. He was still polite, but with an icy touch now. He said, "The Observers assigned to our Section are highly competent. I have every certainty that those assigned to this project have given accurate data. Have you evidence to the contrary?"

"Not at all, Sociologist Voy. I accept their data. It is the development of the data I question. Do you not have an alternate tensor-complex at this point, if the courtship data is taken properly into consideration?"

Voy stared, and then a look of relief washed over him visibly. "Of course, Technician, of course, but it resolves itself into an identity. There is a loop of small dimensions with no tributaries on either side. I hope you'll forgive me for using picturesque language rather than precise mathematical expressions."

"I appreciate it," said Harlan dryly. "I am no more a Computer than a Sociologist."

"Very good, then. The alternate tensor-complex you refer to, or the forking of the road, as we might say, is non-significant. The forks join up again, and it is a single road. There was not even any need to mention it in our recommendations."

"If you say so, sir, I will defer to your better judgement. However, there is still the matter of the M.N.C."

The Sociologist winced at the initials as Harlan knew he would. M.N.C. – Minimum Necessary Change. There the technician was master. A Sociologist might consider himself above criticism by lesser beings in anything involving the mathematical analysis of the infinite possible Realities in Time, but in matters of M.N.C. the Technician stood supreme.

Mechanical computing would not do. The largest Computaplex ever built, manned by the cleverest and most experienced Senior Computer ever born, could do no better than to indicate the ranges in which the M.N.C. might be found. It was then the Technician, glancing over the data, who decided on an exact point within that range. A good Technician was rarely wrong. A top Technician was never wrong.

Harlan was never wrong.

"Now the M.N.C. recommended," said Harlan (he spoke coolly, evenly, pronouncing the Standard Intertemporal Language in precise syllables), "by your Section involves induction of an accident in space and the immediate death by fairly horrible means of a dozen or more men."

"Unavoidable," said Voy, shrugging.

"On the other hand," said Harlan, "I suggest that the M.N.C. can be reduced to the mere displacement of a container from one shelf to another. Here!" His long finger pointed. His white, well-cared-for index nail made the faintest mark along one set of perforations.

Voy considered matters with a painful but silent intensity.

Harlan said, "Doesn't that alter the situation with regard to

12

your unconsidered fork? Doesn't it take advantage of the fork of lesser possibility, changing it to near-certainty, and does that not then lead to –"

"– to virtually the M.D.R.," whispered Voy.

"To *exactly* the Maximum Desired Response," said Harlan.

Voy looked up, his dark face struggling somewhere between chagrin and anger. Harlan noted absently that there was a space between the man's large upper incisors which gave him a rabbity look quite at odds with the restrained force of his words.

Voy said, "I suppose I will be hearing from the Allwhen Council?"

"I don't think so. As far as I know, the Allwhen Council does not know of this. At least, the projected Reality Change was passed over to me without comment." He did not explain the word "passed", nor did Voy question it.

"*You* discovered this error, then?"

"Yes."

"And you did not report it to the Allwhen Council?"

"No, I did not."

Relief first, then a hardening of countenance. "Why not?"

"Very few people could have avoided this error. I felt I could correct it before damage was done. I have done so. Why go any further?"

"Well – thank you, Technician Harlan. You have been a friend. The Section's error which, as you say, was practically unavoidable, would have looked unjustifiably bad in the record."

He went on after a moment's pause. "Of course, in view of the alterations in personality to be induced by this Reality Change, the death of a few men as preliminary is of little importance."

Harlan thought, detachedly: He doesn't sound really grateful. He probably resents it. If he stops to think, he'll resent it even more, this being saved a downstroke in rating by a Technician. If I were a Sociologist, he would shake my hand, but he won't shake the hand of a Technician. He defends condemning a dozen people to asphyxiation, but he won't touch a Technician.

And because waiting to let resentment grow would be fatal, Harlan said without waiting, "I hope your gratitude will extend to having your Section perform a slight chore for me."

"A chore?"

"A matter of Life-Plotting. I have the data necessary here

13

with me. I have also the data for a suggested Reality Change in the 482nd. I want to know the effect of the Change on the probability-pattern of a certain individual."

"I am not quite sure," said the Sociologist slowly, "that I understand you. Surely you have the facilities for doing this in your own Section?"

"I have. Nevertheless, what I am engaged in is a personal research which I don't wish to appear in the records just yet. It would be difficult to have this carried out in my own Section without –" He gestured an uncertain conclusion to the unfinished sentence.

Voy said, "Then you want this done *not* through official channels."

"I want it done confidentially. I want a confidential answer."

"Well, now, that's very irregular. I can't agree to it."

Harlan frowned. "No more irregular than my failure to report your error to the Allwhen Council. You raised no objection to that. If we're going to be strictly regular in one case, we must be as strict and as regular in the other. You follow me, I think?"

The look on Voy's face was proof positive of that. He held out his hand. "May I see the documents?"

Harlan relaxed a bit. The main hurdle had been passed. He watched eagerly as the Sociologist's head bent over the foils he had brought.

Only once did the Sociologist speak. "By Time, this is a small Reality Change."

Harlan seized his opportunity and improvised. "It is. Too small, I think. It's what the argument is about. It's below critical difference, and I've picked an individual as a test case. Naturally, it would be undiplomatic to use our own Section's facilities until I was certain of being right."

Voy was unresponsive and Harlan stopped. No use running this past the point of safety.

Voy stood up. "I'll pass this along to one of my Life-Plotters. We'll keep this private. You understand, though, that this is not to be taken as establishing a precedent."

"Of course not."

"And if you don't mind, I'd like to watch the Reality Change take place. I trust you will honour us by conducting the M.N.C. personally."

Harlan nodded. "I will take full responsibility."

Two of the screens in the viewing chamber were in operation

14

when they entered. The engineers had focused them already to the exact co-ordinates in Space and Time and then had left. Harlan and Voy were alone in the glittering room. (The molecular film arrangement was perceptible and even a bit more than perceptible, but Harlan was looking at the screens.)

Both views were motionless. They might have been scenes of the dead, since they pictured mathematical instants of Time.

One view was in sharp, natural colour; the engine room of what Harlan knew to be an experimental space-ship. A door was closing, and a glistening shoe of a red, semi-transparent material was just visible through the space that remained. It did not move. Nothing moved. If the picture could have been made sharp enough to picture the dust motes in the air, *they* would not have moved.

Voy said, "For two hours and thirty-six minutes after the viewed instant, that engine room will remain empty. In the current Reality, that is."

"I know," murmured Harlan. He was putting on his gloves and already his quick eyes were memorizing the position of the critical container on its shelf, measuring the steps to it, estimating the best position into which to transfer it. He cast one quick look at the other screen.

If the engine room, being in the range prescribed as "present" with respect to that Section of Eternity in which they now stood, was clear and in natural colour, the other scene, being some twenty-five Centuries in the "future", carried the blue lustre all views of the "future" must.

It was a space-port. A deep blue sky, blue-tinged buildings of naked metal on blue-green ground. A blue cylinder of odd design, bulge-bottomed, stood in the foreground. Two others like it were in the background. All three pointed cleft noses upward, the cleavage biting deeply into the vitals of the ship.

Harlan frowned. "They're queer ones."

"Electro-gravity," said Voy. "The 2481st is the only Century to develop electro-gravity space-travel. No propellants, no nucleonics. It's an aesthetically pleasing device. It's a pity we must Change away from it. A pity." His eyes fixed themselves on Harlan with distinct disapproval.

Harlan's lips compressed. Disapproval of course! Why not? He was the Technician.

To be sure, it had been some Observer who had brought in the details of drug addiction. It had been some Statistician who

15

had demonstrated that recent Changes had increased the addiction rate until now it was the highest in all the current Reality of man. Some Sociologist, probably Voy himself, had interpreted that into the psychiatric profile of a society. Finally, some Computer had worked out the Reality Change necessary to decrease addiction to a safe level and found that, as a side effect, electro-gravitic space-travel must suffer. A dozen, a hundred men of every rating in Eternity had had a hand in this.

But then, at the end, a Technician such as himself must step in. Following the directions all the others had combined to give him, he must be the one to initiate the actual Reality Change. And then all the others would stare in haughty accusation at him. Their stares would say: *You*, not we, have destroyed this beautiful thing.

And for that, they would condemn and avoid him. They would shift their own guilt to his shoulders and scorn him.

The "things" were people, dwarfed by the space-ship, as Earth and Earth's society is always dwarfed by the physical dimensions of space-flight.

They were little puppets in clusters, these people. Their tiny arms and legs were in raised, artificial-looking positions, caught in the frozen instant of Time.

Voy shrugged.

Harlan was adjusting the small field-generator about his left wrist. "Let's get this job done."

"One minute. I want to get in touch with the Life-Plotter and find out how long this job will take. I want to get that job done, too."

His hands moved cleverly at a little movable contact and his ear listened astutely to the pattern of clicks that came back. (Another characteristic of this Section of Eternity, thought Harlan – sound codes in clicks. Clever, but affected, like the molecular films.)

"He says it won't take more than three hours," said Voy at length. "Also, by the way, he admires the name of the person involved. Noÿs Lambent. It is a female, isn't it?"

There was a dryness in Harlan's throat. "Yes."

Voy's lips curled into a slow smile. "Sounds interesting. I'd like to meet her, sight unseen. Haven't had any women in this Section for months."

Harlan didn't trust himself to answer. He stared a moment at the Sociologist and turned abruptly.

If there was a flaw in Eternity, it involved women. He had known the flaw for what it was from almost his first entrance into Eternity, but he felt it personally only that day he had first met Noÿs. From that moment it had been an easy path to this one, in which he stood false to his oath as an Eternal and to everything in which he had believed.

For what?

For Noÿs.

And he was not ashamed. It was that which really rocked him. He was not ashamed. He felt no guilt for the crescendo of crimes he had committed, to which the latest addition of the unethical use of confidential Life-Plotting could rank only as a peccadillo.

He would do worse than his worst if he had to.

For the first time the specific and express thought came to him. And though he pushed it away in horror, he knew that, having once come, it would return.

The thought was simply this: That he would ruin Eternity, if he had to.

The worst of it was that he knew he had the power to do it.

CHAPTER TWO

OBSERVER

HARLAN stood at the gateway to Time and thought of himself in new ways. It had been very simple once. There were such things as ideals, or at least catchwords, to live by and for. Every stage of an Eternal's life had a reason. How did "Basic Principles" start?

"The life of an Eternal may be divided into four parts . . ."

It all worked out neatly, yet it had all changed for him, and what was broken could not be made whole again.

Yet he had gone faithfully through each of the four parts of an Eternal's life. First, there was the period of fifteen years in which he was not an Eternal at all, but only an inhabitant of Time. Only a human being out of Time, a Timer, could become an Eternal; no one could be born into the position.

At the age of fifteen he was chosen by a careful process of elimination and winnowing, the nature of which he had no conception of at the time. He was taken beyond the veil of Eternity after a last agonized farewell to his family. (Even then it was made clear to him that whatever else happened he would never return. The true reason for that he was not to learn till long afterward.)

Once within Eternity, he spent ten years in school as a Cub, and then graduated to enter his third period as Observer. It was only after that that he became a Specialist and a true Eternal. The fourth and last part of the Eternal's life: Timer, Cub, Observer and Specialist.

He, Harlan, had gone through it all so neatly. He might say, successfully.

He could remember, so clearly, the moment that Cubhood was done, the moment they became independent members of Eternity, the moment when, even though un-Specialized, they still rated the legal title of "Eternal".

He could remember it. School done, Cubhood over, he was standing with the five who completed training with him, hands clasped in the small of his back, legs a trifle apart, eyes front, listening.

Educator Yarrow was at a desk talking to them. Harlan could remember Yarrow well: a small, intense man, with ruddy hair in disarray, freckled forearms, and a look of loss in his eyes. (It wasn't uncommon, this look of loss in the eyes of an Eternal – the loss of home and roots, the unadmitted and unadmittable longing for the one Century he could never see.)

Harlan could not remember Yarrow's exact words, of course, but the substance of it remained sharp.

Yarrow said, in substance, "You will be Observers now. It isn't a highly regarded position. Specialists look upon it as a boy's job. Maybe you Eternals" (he deliberately paused after that word to give each man a chance to straighten his back and brighten at the glory of it) "think so, too. If so, you are fools who don't deserve to be Observers.

"The Computers would have no Computing to do, Life-Plotters no lives to plot, Sociologists no societies to profile; none of the Specialists would have anything to do, if it weren't for the Observer. I know you've heard this said before, but I want you to be very firm and clear in your mind about it.

"It will be you youngsters who will go out into Time, under the most strenuous conditions, to bring back facts. Cold, objective facts uncoloured by your own opinions and likings, you

18

understand. Facts accurate enough to be fed into Computing machines. Facts definite enough to make the social equations stand up. Facts honest enough to form a basis for Reality Changes.

"And remember this, too. Your period as Observer is not something to get through with as quickly and as unobtrusively as possible. It is as an Observer that you will make your mark. Not what you did in school, but what you will do as an Observer will determine your Speciality and how high you will rise in it. This will be your post-graduate course, Eternals, and failure in it, even small failure, will put you into Maintenance no matter how brilliant your potentialities now seem. That is all.'

He shook hands with each of them, and Harlan, grave, dedicated, proud in his belief that the privileges of being an Eternal contained its greatest privilege in the assumption of responsibility for the happiness of all the human beings who were or ever would be within the reach of Eternity, was deep in self-awe.

Harlan's first assignments were small and under close direction, but he sharpened his ability on the honing strap of experience in a dozen Centuries through a dozen Reality Changes.

In his fifth year as Observer he was given a Senior's rating in the field and assigned to the 482nd. For the first time he would be working unsupervised, and knowledge of that fact robbed him of some of his self-assurance when he first reported to the Computer iin charge of the Section.

That was Assistant Computer Hobbe Finge, whose pursed, suspicious mouth and frowning eyes seemed ludicrous in such a face as his. He had a round button of a nose, two larger buttons of cheeks. He needed only a touch of red and a fringe of white hair to be converted into the picture of the Primitive myth of St. Nicholas.

(or Santa Claus or Kriss Kringle. Harlan knew all three names. He doubted if one Eternal out of a hundred thousand had heard of any one of them. Harlan took a secret, shamefaced pride in this sort of arcane knowledge. From his earliest days in school he had ridden the hobbyhorse of Primitive history, and Educator Yarrow had encouraged it. Harlan had grown actually fond of those odd, perverted Centuries that lay, not only before the beginning of Eternity in the 27th, but even before the invention of the Temporal Field, itself, in the 24th. He had used old books and periodicals in his studies. He had even travelled far downwhen to the earliest Centuries of Eternity, when he could get permission, to consult better sources. For over fifteen years he had managed to collect a remarkable library of his own, almost all in print-on-paper. There was a volume by a man called H. G. Wells, another by a man named W. Shakespeare, some tattered histories. Best of all there was a complete set of bound volumes of a Primitive news weekly that took up inordinate space, but that he could not, out of sentiment, bear to reduce to micro-film.

Occasionally he would lose himself in a world where life was life and death, death; where a man made his decisions irrevocably; where evil could not be prevented, nor good promoted, and the Battle of Waterloo, having been lost, was really lost for good and all. There was even a scrap of poetry he treasured which stated that a moving finger having once written could never be lured back to unwrite.

And then it was difficult, almost a shock, to return his thoughts to Eternity, and to a universe where Reality was something flexible and evanescent, something men such as himself could hold in the palms of their hands and shake into better shape.)

The illusion of St. Nicholas shattered when Hobbe Finge spoke to him in a brisk, matter-of-fact way. "You can start in tomorrow with a routine screening of current Reality. I want it good, thorough, and to the point. There will be no sickness permitted. Your first spatio-temporal chart will be ready for you tomorrow morning. Got it?"

"Yes, Computer," said Harlan. He decided as early as that that he and Assistant Computer Hobbe Finge would not get along, and he regretted it.

The next morning Harlan got his chart in intricately punched patterns as they emerged from the Computaplex. He used a pocket decoder to translate them into Standard Intertemporal in his anxiety to make not even the smallest mistake at the very beginning. Of course, he had reached the stage where he could read the perforations direct.

The chart told him where and when in the world of the 482nd Century he might go and where he might not; what he could do and what he could not; what he must avoid at all costs. His presence must impinge only upon those places and times where it would not endanger Reality.

The 482nd was not a comfortable Century for him. It was not like his own austere and conformist homewhen. It was an era without ethics or principles, as he was accustomed to think of such. It was hedonistic, materialistic, more than a little matriarchal. It was the only era (he checked this in the records in the most painstaking way) in which ectogenic birth flourished and, at its peak, 40 per cent of its women gave eventual birth by merely contributing a fertilized ovum to the ovaria. Marriage was made and unmade by mutual consent and was not recognized legally as anything more than a personal agreement without binding force. Union for the sake of childbearing was, of course, carefully differentiated from the social functions of marriage and was arranged on purely eugenic principles.

In a hundred ways Harlan thought the society sick and therefore hungered for a Reality Change. More than once it occurred to him that his own presence in the Century, as a man not of that time, could fork its history. If his disturbing presence could only be made disturbing enough at some key point, a different branch of possibility would become real, a branch in which millions of pleasure-seeking women would find themselves transformed into true, pure-hearted mothers. They would be in another Reality with all the memories that belonged with it, unable to tell, dream, or fancy that they had ever been anything else.

Unfortunately, to do that, he would have to step outside the bounds of the spatio-temporal chart and that was unthinkable. Even if it weren't, to step outside the bounds at random could change Reality in many possible ways. It could be made worse. Only careful analysis and Computing could properly pin-point the nature of a Reality Change.

Outwardly, whatever his private opinions, Harlan remained an Observer, and the ideal Observer was merely a set of sense-perceptive nerve patches attached to a report-writing mechanism. Between perception and report there must be no intervention of emotion.

Harlan's reports were perfection itself in that respect.

Assistant Computer Finge called him in after his second weekly report.

"I congratulate you, Observer," he said in a voice without warmth, "on the organization and clarity of your reports. But what do you really think?"

Harlan sought refuge in an expression as blank as though chipped painstakingly out of native 95th Century wood. He said, "I have no thoughts of my own in the matter."

"Oh come. You're from the 95th and we both know what

that means. Surely this Century disturbs you."

Harlan shrugged. "Does anything in my reports lead you to think that I am disturbed?"

It was near to impudence and the drumming of Finge's blunt nails upon his desk showed it. Finge said, "Answer my question."

Harlan said, "Sociologically, many facets of the Century represent an extreme. The last three Reality Changes in the aboutwhen have accentuated that. Eventually, I suppose the matter should be rectified. Extremes are never healthy."

"Then you took the trouble to check the past Realities of the Century."

"As an Observer, I must check all pertinent facts."

It was a standoff. Harlan, of course, did have the right and the duty to check those facts. Finge must know that. Every Century was continually being shaken by Reality Changes. No Observations, however painstaking, could ever stand for long without rechecking. It was standard procedure in Eternity to have every Century in a chronic state of being Observed. And to Observe properly, you must be able to present, not only the facts of the current Reality, but also of their relationship to those of previous Realities.

Yet it seemed obvious to Harlan that this was not merely unpleasantness on Finge's part, this probing of the Observer's opinions. Finge seemed definitely hostile.

At another time Finge said to Harlan (having invaded the latter's small office to bring the news), "Your reports are creating a very favourable impression with the Allwhen Council."

Harlan paused, uncertain, then mumbled, "Thank you."

"All agree that you show an uncommon degree of penetration."

"I do my best."

Finge asked suddenly, "Have you ever met Senior Computer Twissell?"

"Computer Twissell?" Harlan's eyes widened. "No, sir. Why do you ask?"

"He seems particularly interested in your reports." Finge's round cheeks drew downward sulkily and he changed the subject. "To me it seems that you have worked out a philosophy of your own, a viewpoint of history."

Temptation tugged hard at Harlan. Vanity and caution battled and the former won. "I've studied Primitive history, sir."

22

"*Primitive* history? At school?"

"Not exactly, Computer. On my own. It's my – hobby. It's like watching history standing still, frozen! It can be studied in detail whereas the Centuries of Eternity are always changing." He warmed up a trifle at the thought of it. "It's as though we were to take a series of stills from a book-film and study each painstakingly. We would see a great deal we would miss, if we just scanned the film as it went past. I think that helps me a great deal with my work."

Finge stared at him in amazement, widened his eyes a little, and left with no further remark.

Occasionally, thereafter, he brought up the subject of Primitive history and accepted Harlan's reluctant comments with no decisive expression on his own plump face.

Harlan was not sure whether to regret the whole matter or to regard it as a possible way of spending his own advancement.

He decided on the first alternative when, passing him one day in Corridor A, Finge said abruptly and in the hearing of others, "Great Time, Harlan, don't you *ever* smile?"

The thought came, shockingly, to Harlan that Finge hated him. His own feeling for Finge approached something like detestation thereafter.

Three months of raking through the 482nd had exhausted most of its worth-while meat and when Harlan received a sudden call to Finge's Office, he was not surprised. He was expecting change in assignment. His final summary had been prepared days before. The 482nd was anxious to export more cellulose-base textiles to Centuries which were deforested, such as the 1174th, but were unwilling to accept smoked fish in return. A long list of such items was contained in due order and with due analysis.

He took the draft of the summary with him.

But no mention of the 482nd was made. Instead Finge introduced him to a withered and wrinkled little man, with sparse white hair and a gnomelike face that throughout the interview was stamped with a perpetual smile. It varied between extremes of anxiety and joviality but never quite disappeared. Between two of his yellow-stained fingers lay a burning cigarette.

It was the first cigarette Harlan had ever seen, otherwise he would have paid more attention to the man, less to the smoking cylinder, and been better prepared for Finge's introduction.

Finge said, "Senior Computer Twissell, this is Observer Andrew Harlan."

Harlan's eyes shifted in shock from the little man's cigarette to his face.

Senior Computer Twissell said in a high-pitched voice, "How do you do? So this is the young man who writes those excellent reports?"

Harlan found no voice. Laban Twissell was a legend, a living myth. Laban Twissell was a man he should have recognized at once. He was the outstanding Computer in Eternity, which was another way of saying he was the most eminent Eternal alive. He was the dean of the Allwhen Council. He had directed more Reality Changes than any man in the history of Eternity. He was – He had –

Harlan's mind failed him altogether. He nodded his head with a doltish grin and said nothing.

Twissell put his cigarette to his lips, puffed quickly, and took it away. "Leave us, Finge. I want to talk to the boy."

Finge rose, murmured something, and left.

Twissell said, "You seem nervous, boy. There is nothing to be nervous about."

But meeting Twissell like that was a shock. It is always disconcerting to find that someone you have thought of as a giant is actually less than five and a half feet tall. Could the brain of a genius actually fit behind the retreating, bald-smooth forehead? Was it sharp intelligence or only good humour that beamed out of the little eyes that screwed up into a thousand wrinkles?

Harlan didn't know what to think. The cigarette seemed to obscure what small scrabble of intelligence he could collect. He flinched visibly as a puff of smoke reached him.

Twissell's eyes narrowed as though he were trying to peer through the smoke haze and he said in horribly accented tenth-millennial dialect, "Will you petter feel if I in your yourself dialect should speak, poy?"

Harlan, brought to the sudden brink of hysterical laughter, said carefully, "I speak Standard Intertemporal quite well, sir." He said it in the Intertemporal he and all other Eternals in his presence had used ever since his first months in Eternity.

"Nonsense," said Twissell imperiously. "I do not bother of Intertemporal. My speech of ten-millennial is over than perfect."

Harlan guessed that it had been some forty years since

Twissell had had to make use of localwhen dialects.

But having made his point to his own satisfaction, apparently he shifted to Intertemporal and remained there. He said, "I would offer you a cigarette, but I am certain you don't smoke. Smoking is approved of hardly anywhere in history. In fact, good cigarettes are made only in the 72nd and mine have to be specially imported from there. I give you that hint in case you ever become a smoker. It is all very sad. Last week, I was stuck in the 123rd for two days. No smoking, I mean, even in the Section of Eternity devoted to the 123rd. The Eternals there have picked up the *mores*. If I had lit a cigarette it would have been like the sky collapsing. Sometimes I think I should like to calculate on great Reality Change and wipe out all the no-smoking taboos in all the Centuries, except that any Reality Change like that would make for wars in the 58th or a slave society in the 1000th. Always something."

Harlan was first confused, then anxious. Surely these rattling irrelevances must be hiding something.

His throat felt a little constricted. He said, "May I ask why you've arranged to see me, sir?"

"I like your reports, boy."

There was a veiled glimmer of joy in Harlan's eyes, but he did not smile. "Thank you, sir."

"It has a touch of the artist. You are intuitive. You feel strongly. I think I know your proper position in Eternity and I have come to offer it to you."

Harlan thought: I can't believe this.

He held all triumph out of his voice. "You do me great honour, sir," he said.

Whereupon Senior Computer Twissell, having come to the end of his cigarette, produced another in his left hand by some unnoted feat of legerdemain and lit it. He said between puffs, "For Time's sake, boy, you talk as though you rehearsed lines. Great honour, bah. Piffle, Trash. Say what you feel in plain language. You're glad, hey?"

"Yes, sir," said Harlan cautiously.

"All right. You should be. How would you like to be a Technician?"

"A Technician!" cried Harlan, leaping from his seat.

"Sit down. Sit down. You seem surprised."

"I hadn't expected to be a Technician, Computer Twissell."

"No," said Twissell dryly, "somehow no one ever does. They

25

expect anything but that. Yet Technicians are hard to find, and are always in demand. Not a Section in Eternity has what it considers enough."

"I don't think I'm suited."

"You mean you're not suited to take a job with trouble in it. By Time, if you are devoted to Eternity, as I believe you are, you won't mind that. So the fools will avoid you and you will feel ostracized. You will grow used to that. And you will have the satisfaction of knowing you are needed, and needed badly. By *me*."

"By you, sir? By you particularly?"

"Yes." An element of shrewdness entered the old man's smile. "You are not to be just a Technician. You will be my personal Technician. You will have special status. How does that sound now?"

Harlan said, "I don't know, sir. I may not qualify."

Twissell shook his head firmly. "I need you. I need just you. Your reports assure me you have what I need up here." He tapped his forehead quickly with a ridge-nailed forefinger. "Your record as Cub is good; the Sections for which you have Observed reported favourable. Finally, Finge's report was most suitable of all."

Harlan was honestly startled. "Computer Finge's report was favourable?"

"You didn't expect that?"

"I – don't know."

"Well, boy, I didn't say it was favourable. I said it was suitable. As a matter of fact, Finge's report was *not* favourable. He recommended that you be removed from all duties connected with Reality Changes. He suggested it wasn't safe to keep you anywhere but in Maintenance."

Harlan reddened. "What were his reasons for saying so, sir?"

"It seems you have a hobby, boy. You are interested in Primitive history, eh?" He gestured expansively with his cigarette and Harlan, forgetting his anger to control his breathing, inhaled a cloud of smoke and coughed helplessly.

Twissell regarded the young Observer's coughing spell benignly and said, "Isn't that so?"

Harlan began, "Computer Finge had no right –"

"Now, now. I told you what was in the report because it hinges on the purpose I need you most for. Actually, the report was confidential and you are to forget I told you what was in

26

it. Permanently, boy."

"But what's wrong with being interested in Primitive history?"

"Finge thinks your interest in it shows a strong Wish-to-Time. You understand me, boy?"

Harlan did. It was impossible to avoid picking up psychiatric lingo. That phrase above all. Every member of Eternity was supposed to have a strong drive, the stronger for being officially suppressed in all its manifestations, to return, not necessarily to his own Time, but at least to some one definite Time; to become part of a Century, rather than to remain a wanderer through them all. Of course in most Eternals the drive remained safely hidden in the unconscious.

"I don't think that's the case," said Harlan.

"Nor I. In fact, I think your hobby is interesting and valuable. As I said, it's why I want you. I want you to teach a Cub I shall bring to you all you know and all you can learn about Primitive history. In between, you will also be my personal Technician. You'll start in a few days. Is that agreeable?"

Agreeable? To have official permission to learn all he could about the days before Eternity? To be personally associated with the greatest Eternal of them all? Even the nasty fact of Technician's status seemed bearable under those conditions.

His caution, however, did not entirely fail him. He said, "If it's necessary for the good of Eternity, sir –"

"For the *good* of Eternity?" cried the gnomish Computer in sudden excitement. He threw his cigarette butt from him with such energy that it hit the far wall and bounced off in a shower of sparks. "I need you for the *existence* of Eternity."

CHAPTER THREE

CUB

HARLAN had been in the 575th for weeks before he met Brinsley Sheridan Cooper. He had time to grow used to his new quarters and to the antisepsis of glass and porcelain. He learned to wear the Technician's mark with only moderate shrinking and to refrain from making things worse by standing so that the insigne was hidden against a wall or was covered by the interposition of some object he was carrying.

Others smiled disdainfully when that was done and turned colder as though they suspected an attempt to invade their friendship on false pretences.

Senior Computer Twissell brought him problems daily. Harlan studied them and wrote his analyses in drafts that were four times rewritten, the last version being handed in reluctantly even so.

Twissell would appraise them and nod and say, "Good, good." Then his old blue eyes would dart quickly at Harlan and his smile would narrow a bit as he said, "I'll test this guess on the Computaplex."

He always called the analysis a "guess". He never told Harlan the result of the Computaplex check, and Harlan dared not ask. He was despondent over the fact that he was never asked to put any of his own analyses into action. Did that mean that the Computaplex was *not* checking him, that he had been choosing the wrong item for the induction of Reality Change, that he did not have the knack of seeing the Minimum Necessary Change in an indicated range? (It was not until later that he grew sufficiently sophisticated to have the phrase come rolling off his tongue as M.N.C.)

One day Twissell came in with an abashed individual who seemed scarcely to dare raise his eyes to meet Harlan's.

Twissell said, "Technician Harlan, this is Cub B.S. Cooper."

Automatically Harlan said, "Hello," weighed the man's appearance, and was unimpressed. The fellow was on the shortish side, his eyes an indefinite light brown, his ears a little large, and his fingernails bitten.

Twissell said, "This is the boy to whom you will be teaching Primitive history."

"Great Time," said Harlan with suddenly increased interest. "*Hello!*" He had almost forgotten.

Twissell said, "Arrange a schedule with him that will suit you, Harlan. If you can manage two afternoons a week, I think that would be fine. Use your own method of teaching him. I'll leave that to you. If you should need book-films or old documents, tell me, and if they exist in Eternity or in any part of Time that can be reached, we'll get them. Eh, boy?"

He plucked a lit cigarette out of nowhere (as it always seemed) and the air reeked with smoke. Harlan coughed and from the

28

twisting of the Cub's mouth it was quite obvious that the latter would have done the same had he dared.

After Twissell left, Harlan said, "Well, sit down" – he hesitated a moment, then added determinedly – "Son. Sit down, son. My office isn't much, but it's yours whenever we're together."

Harlan was almost flooded with eagerness. This project was *his*! Primitive history was something that was all his own.

The Cub raised his eyes (for the first time, really) and said stumblingly, "You *are* a Technician."

A considerable part of Harlan's excitement and warmth died. "What of it?"

"Nothing," said the Cub. "I just –"

"You heard Computer Twissell address me as Technician, didn't you?"

"Yes, sir."

"Did you think it was a slip of the tongue? Something too bad to be true?"

"*No*, sir."

"What's wrong with your speech?" Harlan asked brutally, and even as he did so, he felt shame nudge him.

Cooper blushed painfully. "I'm not very good at Standard Intertemporal."

"Why not? How long have you been a Cub?"

"Less than one year, sir."

"One year? How old are you, for Time's sake?"

"Twenty-four physioyears, sir."

Harlan stared. "Are you trying to tell me that they took you into Eternity at twenty-three?"

"Yes, sir."

Harlan sat down and rubbed his hands together. That just wasn't done. Fifteen to sixteen was the age of entrance into Eternity. What was this? A new kind of testing of himself on the part of Twissell?

He said, "Sit down and let's get started. Your name in full and your homewhen."

The Cub stammered, "Brinsley Sheridan Cooper of the 78th, sir."

Harlan almost softened. That was close. It was only seventeen Centuries downwhen from his own homewhen. Almost a Temporal neighbour.

He said, "Are you interested in Primitive history?"

"Computer Twissell asked me to learn. I don't know much about it."

"What else are you learning?"

"Mathematics. Temporal engineering. I'm just getting the fundamentals so far. Back in the 78th, I was a Speedy-vac repairman."

There was no point in asking the nature of a Speedy-vac. It might be a suction cleaner, a computing machine, a type of spray painter. Anything. Harlan wasn't particularly interested.

He said, "Do you know anything about history? Any kind of history?"

"I studied European history."

"Your particular political unit, I take it."

"I was born in Europe. Yes. Mostly, of course, they taught us modern history. After the revolutions of '54; 7554, that is."

"All right. First thing you do is to forget it. It doesn't mean anything. The history they try to teach Timers changes with every Reality Change. Not that they realize that. In each Reality, their history is the only history. That's what's so different about Primitive history. That's the beauty of it. No matter what any of us does, it exists precisely as it has always existed. Columbus and Washington, Mussolini and Hereford, they all exist."

Cooper smiled feebly. He brushed his little finger across his upper lip and for the first time Harlan noticed a trace of bristle there as though the Cub were cultivating a moustache.

Cooper said, "I can't quite – get used to it, all the time I've been here."

"Get used to what?"

"Being five hundred Centuries away from homewhen."

"I'm nearly that myself. I'm 95th."

"That's another thing. You're older than I am and yet I'm seventeen Centuries older than you in another way. I can be your great-great-great-and-so-on-grandfather."

"What's the difference? Suppose you are?"

"Well, it takes getting used to." There was a trace of rebellion in the Cub's voice.

"It does for all of us," said Harlan callously, and began talking about the Primitives. By the time three hours had passed, he was deep in an explanation concerning the reasons why there were Centuries before the 1st Century.

("But isn't the 1st Century *first*?" Cooper had asked plaintively.)

30

Harlan ended by giving the Cub a book, not a good one, really, but one that would serve as a beginning. 'I'll get you better stuff as we go along," he said.

By the end of a week Cooper's moustache had become a pronounced dark bristle that made him look ten years older and accentuated the narrowness of his chin. On the whole, Harlan decided, it would not be an improvement, that moustache.

Cooper said, "I've finished your book."

"What did you think of it?"

"In a way –" There was a long pause. Cooper began over again. "Parts of the latter Primitive was something like the 78th. It made me think of home, you know. Twice, I dreamed about my wife."

Harlan exploded. "Your *wife*?"

"I was married before I came here."

"Great Time! Did they bring your wife across, too?"

Cooper shook his head. "I don't even know if she's been Changed in the last year. If she had, I suppose she's not really my wife now."

Harlan recovered. Of course, if the Cub was twenty-three years old when he was taken into Eternity, it was quite possible that he might have been married. One thing unprecedented led to another.

What was going on? Once modifications were introduced into the rules, it wouldn't be a long step to the point where everything would decline into a mass of incoherency. Eternity was too finely balanced an arrangement to endure modification.

It was his anger on behalf of Eternity, perhaps, that put an unintended harshness into Harlan's next words. "I hope you're not planning on going back to the 78th to check on her."

The Cub lifted his head and his eyes were firm and steady. "No."

Harlan shifted uneasily, "Good. You have no family. Nothing. You're an Eternal and don't ever think of anyone you knew in Time."

Cooper's lips thinned, and his accent stood out sharply in his quick words. "You're speaking like a Technician."

Harlan's fists clenched along the sides of his desk. He said hoarsely, "What do you imply? I'm a Technician so I make the Changes? So I defend them and demand that you accept them? Look, kid, you haven't been here a year; you can't speak Inter-

31

temporal; you're all misgeared on Time and Reality, but you think you know all about Technicians and how to kick them in the teeth."

"I'm sorry," said Cooper quickly; "I didn't mean to offend you."

"No, no, who offends a Technician? You just hear everyone else talking, is that it? They say, 'Cold as a Technician's heart,' don't they? They say, 'A trillion personalities changed – just a Technician's yawn.' Maybe a few other things. What's the answer, Mr. Cooper? Does it make you feel sophisticated to join in? It makes you a big man? A big wheel in Eternity?"

"I said I'm sorry."

"All right. I just want you to know I've been a Technician for less than a month and I personally have never induced a Reality Change. Now let's get on with business."

Senior Computer Twissell called Andrew Harlan to his office the next day.

He said, "How would you like to go out on an M.N.C., boy?"

It was almost too apposite. All that morning Harlan had been regretting his cowardly disclaimer of personal involvement in the Technician's work; his childish cry of: I haven't done anything wrong, yet, so don't blame me.

It amounted to an admission that there *was* something wrong about a Technician's work, and that he himself was blameless only because he was too new at the game to have had time to be a criminal.

He welcomed the chance to kill that excuse now. It would be almost a penance. He could say to Cooper: Yes, because of something I have done, this many millions of people are new personalities, but it was necessary and I am proud to have been the cause.

So Harlan said joyfully, "I'm ready, sir."

"Good. Good. You'll be glad to know, boy," (a puff, and the cigarette tip glowed brilliantly) "that every one of your analyses checked out with high-order accuracy."

"Thank you, sir." (They were analyses now, thought Harlan, not guesses.)

"You've got a talent. Quite a touch, boy. I look for great things. And we can begin with this one, 223rd. Your statement

32

that a jammed vehicle clutch would supply the necessary fork without undesirable side effect is perfectly correct. Will you jam it?"

"Yes, sir."

That was Harlan's true initiation into Technicianhood. After that he was more than just a man with rose-red badge. He had handled Reality. He had tampered with a mechanism during a quick few minutes taken out of the 223rd and, as a result, a young man did not reach a lecture on mechanics he had meant to attend. He never went in for solar engineering, consequently, and a perfectly simple device was delayed in its development a crucial ten years. A war in the 224th, amazingly enough, was moved out of Reality as a result.

Wasn't *that* good? What if personalities were changed? The new personalities were as human as the old and as deserving of life. If some lives were shortened, more were lengthened and made happier. A great work of literature, a monument of Man's intellect and feeling, was never written in the new Reality, but several copies were preserved in Eternity's libraries, were they not? And new creative works had come into existence, had they not?

Yet that night Harlan spent hours in a hot agony of wakefulness, and when he finally drowsed groggily, he did something he hadn't done in years.

He dreamed of his mother.

Despite the weakness of such a beginning a physioyear was sufficient to make Harlan known throughout Eternity as "Twissell's Technician," and, with more than a trace of ill-humour as "The Wonder Boy" and "The Never-Wrong."

His contact with Cooper became almost comfortable. They never grew completely friendly. (If Cooper could have brought himself to make advances, Harlan might not have known how to respond.) Nevertheless they worked well together, and Cooper's interest in Primitive history grew to the point where it nearly rivalled Harlan's.

One day Harlan said to Cooper, "Look, Cooper, would you mind coming in tomorrow instead? I've got to get up to the 3,000's sometime this week to check on an Observation and the man I want to see is free this afternoon."

Cooper's eyes lit up hungrily, "Why can't I come?"

"Do you want to?"

33

"Sure. I've never been in a kettle except when they brought me here from the 78th and I didn't know what was happening at the time."

Harlan was accustomed to using the kettle in Shaft C, which was, by unwritten custom, reserved for Technicians along its entire immeasurable length through the Centuries. Cooper showed no embarrassment at being led there. He stepped into the kettle without hesitation and took his seat on the curved moulding that completely circled it.

When Harlan, however, had activated the Field, and kicked the kettle into upwhen motion, Cooper's face screwed up into an almost comic expression of surprise.

"I don't feel a thing," he said. "Is anything wrong?"

"Nothing's wrong. You're not feeling anything because you're not really moving. You're being kicked along the temporal extension of the kettle. In fact," Harlan said, growing didactic, "at the moment, you and I aren't matter, really, in spite of appearances. A hundred men could be using this same kettle, moving (if you can call it that) at various velocities in either Time-direction, passing through one another and so on. The laws of the ordinary universe just don't apply to the kettle shafts!"

Cooper's mouth quirked a bit and Harlan thought uneasily: The kid's taking temporal engineering and knows more about this than I do. Why don't I shut up and stop making a fool of myself?

He retreated into silence, and stared sombrely at Cooper. The younger man's moustache had been full-grown for months. It drooped, framing his mouth in what Eternals called a Mallansohn hairline, because the only photograph known to be authentic of the Temporal Field inventor (and that a poor one and out of focus) showed him with just such a moustache. For that reason it maintained a certain popularity among Eternals even though it did few of them justice.

Cooper's eyes were fixed on the shifting numbers that marked the passing of the Centuries with respect to themselves. He said, "How far upwhen does the kettle shaft go?"

"Haven't they taught you that?"

"They've hardly mentioned the kettles."

Harlan shrugged. "There's no end to Eternity. The shaft goes on forever."

"How far upwhen have you gone?"

34

"This will be the uppest. Dr. Twissell has been up to the 50,000's."

"Great Time!" whispered Cooper.

"That's still nothing. Some Eternals have been up past the 150,000th Century."

"What's *that* like?"

"Like nothing at all," said Harlan morosely. 'Lots of life but none of it human. Man is gone."

"Dead? Wiped out?"

"I don't know that anyone exactly knows."

"Can't something be done to change that?"

"Well, from the 70,000's on –" began Harlan, then ended abruptly. "Oh, to Time with it. Change the subject."

If there was one subject about which Eternals were almost superstitious, it was the "Hidden Centuries", the time between the 70,000th and the 150,000th. It was a subject that was rarely mentioned. It was only Harlan's close association with Twissell that accounted for his own small knowledge of the era. What it amounted to was that Eternals couldn't pass into Time in all those thousands of Centuries. The doors between Eternity and Time were impenetrable. Why? No one knew.

Harlan imagined, from some casual remarks of Twissell's, that attempts had been made to Change the Reality in the Centuries just downwhen from the 70,000th, but without adequate Observation beyond the 70,000th not much could be done.

Twissell had laughed a bit one time and said, "We'll get through someday. Meanwhile, 70,000 Centuries is quite enough to take care of."

It did not sound wholly convincing.

"What happens to Eternity after the 150,000th?" asked Cooper.

Harlan sighed. The subject, apparently, was not to be changed. "Nothing," he said. "The Sections are there but there are no Eternals in it anywhere after the 70,000th. The Sections keep on going for millions of Centuries till all life is gone and past that, too, till the sun becomes a nova, and past that, too. There isn't any end to Eternity. That's why it's called Eternity."

"The sun *does* become a nova, then?"

"It certainly does. Eternity couldn't exist if that weren't so. Novo Sol is our power supply. Listen, do you know how much power is required to set up a Temporal Field? Mallansohn's first Field was two seconds from extreme downwhen to extreme

35

upwhen and big enough to hold not more than a match head and that took a nuclear power plant's complete output for one day. It took nearly a hundred years to set up a hair-thin Temporal Field far enough upwhen to be able to tap the radiant power of the nova so that a Field could be built big enough to hold a man."

Cooper sighed. "I wish they would get to the point where they stopped making me learn equations and field mechanics and start telling me some of the interesting stuff. Now if I had lived in Mallansohn's time –"

"You would have learned nothing. He lived in the 24th, but Eternity didn't start till late in the 27th. Inventing the Field isn't the same as constructing Eternity, you know, and the rest of the 24th didn't have the slightest inkling of what Mallansohn's invention signified."

"He was ahead of his generation, then?"

"Very much so. He not only invented the Temporal Field, but he described the basic relationships that made Eternity possible and predicted almost every aspect of it except for the Reality Change. Quite closely, too – but I think we're pulling to a halt, Cooper. After you."

They stepped out.

Harlan had never seen Senior Computer Laban Twissell angry before. People always said that he was incapable of any emotion, that he was an unsouled fixture of Eternity to the point where he had forgotten the exact number of his home-when Century. People said that at an early age his heart had atrophied and that a hand computer similar to the model he carried always in his trousers pocket had taken its place.

Twissell did nothing to deny these rumours. In fact most people guessed that he believed them himself.

So even while Harlan bent before the force of the angry blast that struck him, he had room in his mind to be amazed at the fact that Twissell could display anger. He wondered if Twissell would be mortified in some calmer aftermath to realize that his hand-computer heart had betrayed him by exposing itself as only a poor thing of muscle and valves subject to the twists of emotion.

Twissell, said, in part, his old voice creaking, "Father Time, boy, are you on the Allwhen Council? Do you give the orders around here? Do you tell me what to do or do I tell you what to do? Are you making arrangements for all kettle trips this Section? Do we all come to you for permission now?"

He interrupted himself with occasional exclamations of "Answer me," then continued pouring more questions into the boiling interrogative cauldron.

He said finally, "If you ever get above yourself this way again, I'll have you on plumbing repair and for good. Do you understand me?"

Harlan, pale with his own gathering embarrassment, said, "I was never told that Cub Cooper was not to be taken on the kettle."

The explanation did not act as an emollient. "What kind of excuse is a double negative, boy? You were never told to get him drunk. You were never told not to shave him bald. You were never told not to skewer him with a fine-edged Tav curve. Father Time, boy, what *were* you told to do with him?"

"I was told to teach him Primitive history."

"Then do so. Do nothing more than that." Twissell dropped his cigarette and ground it savagely underfoot as though it were the face of a lifelong enemy.

"I'd like to point out, Computer," said Harlan, "that many Centuries under the current Reality somewhat resemble specific eras of Primitive history in one or more respects. It had been my intention to take him out of those Times, under careful spatiotemporal charting, of course, as a form of field trip."

"What? Listen, you chucklehead, don't you ever intend to ask my permission for *anything*? That's out. Just teach him Primitive history. No field trips. No laboratory experiments, either. Next you'll be changing Reality just to show him how."

Harlan licked his dry lips with a dry tongue, muttered a resentful acquiescence, and, eventually, was allowed to leave.

It took weeks for his hurt feelings to heal over somewhat.

CHAPTER FOUR

COMPUTER

HARLAN had been two years a Technician when he re-entered the 482nd for the first time since leaving with Twissell. He found it unrecognizable.

It had not changed. He had.

Two years of Technicianhood had meant a number of things. In one sense it had increased his feeling for stability. He had no longer to learn a new language, get used to new styles of clothing and new ways of life with every new Observation project. On the other hand, it had resulted in a withdrawal on his own part. He had almost forgotten now the cameraderie that united all the rest of the Specialists in Eternity.

Most of all, he had developed the feeling of the *power* of being a Technician. He held the fate of millions in his finger tips, and if one must walk lonely because of it, one could also walk proudly.

So he could stare coldly at the Communications man behind the entry desk of the 482nd and announce himself in clipped syllables: "Andrew Harlan, Technician, reporting to Computer Finge for temporary assignment to the 482nd," disregarding the quick glance from the middleaged man he faced.

It was what some people called the "Technician glance", a quick, involuntary sidelong peek at the rose-red shoulder emblem of the Technician, then an elaborate attempt not to look at it again.

Harlan stared at the other's shoulder emblem. It was not the yellow of the Computer, the green of the Life-Plotter, the blue of the Sociologist, or the white of the Observer. It was not the Specialist's solid colour at all. It was simply a blue bar on white. The man was Communications, a subbranch of Maintenance, not a Specialist at all.

And *he* gave the "Technician glance", too.

Harlan said a little sadly, "Well?"

Communications said quickly, "I'm ringing Computer Finge, sir."

Harlan remembered the 482nd as solid and massive, but now it seemed almost squalid.

Harlan had grown used to the glass and porcelain of the 575th, to its fetish of cleanliness. He had grown accustomed to a world of whiteness and clarity, broken by sparse patches of light pastel.

The heavy plaster swirls of the 482nd, its splashy pigments, its areas of painted metals, were almost repulsive.

Even Finge seemed different, less than life-size, somewhat. Two years earlier, to Observer Harlan, Finge's every gesture had seemed sinister and powerful.

Now, from the lofty and isolated heights of Technicianhood, the man semed pathetic and lost. Harlan watched him as he leafed through a sheaf of foils and got ready to look up, with the air of someone who is beginning to think he has made his visitor wait the duly required amount of time.

Finge was from an energy-centred Century in the 600's. Twissell had told him that and it explained a good deal. Finge's flashes of ill-temper could easily be the result of the natural insecurity of a heavy man used to the firmness of field-forces and unhappy to be dealing with nothing more than flimsy matter. His tiptoeing walk (Harlan remembered Finge's cat-like tread well; often he would look up from his desk, see Finge standing there staring at him, his approach having been unheard) was no longer something sly and sneaking, but rather the fearful and reluctant tread of one who lives in the constant, if unconscious, fear that the flooring would break under his weight.

Harlan thought, with a pleasant condescension: the man is poorly adjusted to the Section. Reassignment is probably the only thing that would help him.

Finge said, "Greetings, Technician Harlan."

"Greetings, Computer," said Harlan.

Finge said, "It seems that in the two years since –"

"Two physioyears," said Harlan.

Finge looked up in surprise. "Two physioyears, of course."

In Eternity there was no Time as on ordinarily thought of Time in the universe outside, but men's bodies grew older and that was the unavoidable measure of Time even in the absence of meaningful physical phenomena. Physiologically Time passed, and in a physioyear within Eternity a man grew as much older as he would have in an ordinary year in Time.

Yet even the most pedantic Eternal remembered the distinction only rarely. It was too convenient to say, "See you to-morrow," or "I missed you yesterday," or "I will see you next week," as though there were a tomorrow or a yesterday or a last week in any but a physiological sense. And the instincts of humanity were catered to by having the activities of Eternity tailored to an arbitrary twenty-four "physiohour" day, with a solemn assumption of day and night, today and tomorrow.

Finge said, "In the two *physioyears* since you left, a crisis has gradually gathered about the 482nd. A rather peculiar one. A delicate one. Almost unprecedented. We need accurate Observation now as we never have needed it before."

"And you want me to Observe?"

"Yes. In a way, it's a waste of talent to ask a Technician to do a job of Observation, but your previous Observations, for clarity and insight, were perfect. We need that again. Now I'll just sketch in a few details...."

What those details were Harlan was not to find out just then. Finge spoke, but the door opened, and Harlan did not hear him. He stared at the person who entered.

It was not that Harlan had never seen a girl in Eternity before. Never was too strong a word. Rarely, yes, but not never.

But a girl such as *this*! And in *Eternity*!

Harlan had seen many women in his passages through Time, but in Time they were only objects to him, like walls and balls, barrows and harrows, kittens and mittens. They were facts to be Observed.

In Eternity a girl was a different matter. And one like *this*!

She was dressed in the style of the upper classes of the 482nd, which meant transparent sheathing and not very much else above the waist, and flimsy, knee-length trousers below. The latter, while opaque enough, hinted delicately at gluteal curves.

Her hair was glossily dark and shoulder length, her lips redly penciled thin above and full below in an exaggerated pout. Her upper eyelids and her ear lobes were tinted a pale rose and the rest of her youthful (almost girlish) face was a startlingly milky white. Jewelled pendants descended forward from mid-shoulder to tinkle now this side, now that of the graceful breasts to which they drew attention.

She took her seat at a desk in the corner of Finge's office, lifting her eyelashes only once to sweep her dark glance across Harlan's face.

When Harlan heard Finge's voice again, the Computer was saying, "You'll get all this in an official report and meanwhile you can have your old office and sleeping quarters."

Harlan found himself outside Finge's office without quite remembering the details of his leaving. Presumably he had walked out.

The emotion within him that was easiest to recognize was anger. *By Time*, Finge ought not to be allowed to do this. It was bad for morale. It made a mockery –

He stopped himself, unclenched his fist, unclamped his jaw. Let's see, now! His footsteps sounded sharply in his own ear as he strode firmly towards the Communications man behind the desk.

Communications looked up, without quite meeting his eye, and said cautiously, "Yes, sir."

Harlan said, "There's a woman at a desk in Computer Finge's office. Is she new here?"

He had meant to ask it casually. He had meant to make it a bored, indifferent question. It rang out, instead, like a pair of cymbals clashing.

But it roused Communications. The look in his eye became something that made all men kin. It even embraced the Technician, drew him in as a fellow. Communications said, "You mean the babe? Wow! Isn't she built like a force-field latrine, though?"

Harlan stammered a bit. "Just answer my question."

Communications stared and some of his steam evaporated. He said, "She's new. She's a Timer."

"What's her job?"

A slow smile crept over Communications' face and grew into a leer. "She's supposed to be the boss's secretary. Her name is Noÿs Lambent."

"All right," Harlan turned on his heel and left.

Harlan's first Observation trip into the 482nd came the next day, but it lasted for thirty minutes only. It was obviously only an orientation trip, intended to get him into the feel of things. He entered it for an hour and a half the next day and not at all on the third.

He occupied his time in working his way through his original reports, relearning his own knowledge, brushing up on the language system of the time, accustoming himself to the local costumes again.

One Reality Change had hit the 482nd, but it was very minor. A political clique that had been In was now Out, but there seemed no change in the society otherwise.

Without quite realizing it he slipped into the habit of searching his old reports for information on the aristocracy. Surely he had made Observations.

He had, but they were impersonal, from a distance. His data concerned them as a class, not as individuals.

Of course his spatio-temporal charts had never demanded or even permitted him to observe the aristocracy from within. What the reasons for that might have been was beyond the purview of an Observer. He was impatient with himself at feeling curiosity concerning that now.

During those three days he had caught glimpses of the girl, Noÿs Lambent, four times. At first he had been aware only of her clothes and her ornaments. Now he noticed that she was five feet six in height, half a head shorter than himself, yet slim enough and with carriage erect and graceful enough to give an impression of height. She was older than she first seemed, approaching thirty perhaps, certainly over twenty-five.

She was quiet and reserved, smiled at him once when he passed her in the corridor, then lowered her eyes. Harlan drew aside to avoid touching her, then walked on feeling angry.

By the close of the third day Harlan was beginning to feel that his duty as an Eternal left him only one course of action. Doubtless her position was a comfortable one for herself. Doubtless Finge was within the letter of the law. Yet Finge's indiscretion in the matter, his carelessness, certainly went against the spirit of the law, and something should be done about it.

Harlan decided that, after all, there wasn't a man in Eternity he disliked quite as much as Finge. The excuses he had found for the man only a few days before vanished.

On the morning of the fourth day Harlan asked for and received permission to see Finge privately. He walked in with a determined step and, to his own surprise, made his point instantly. "Computer Finge, I suggest that Miss Lambent be returned to Time."

Finge's eyes narrowed. He nodded towards a chair, placed clasped hands under his soft, round chin, and showed some of his teeth. "Well, sit down. Sit down. You find Miss Lambent incompetent? Unsuitable?'

"As to her incompetence and unsuitability, Computer, I cannot say. It depends on the uses to which she is put, and I have put her to none. But you must realize that she is bad for the morale of this Section."

Finge stared at him distantly as though his Computer's mind were weighing abstractions beyond the reach of an ordinary Eternal. "In what way is she hurting morale, Technician?'

"There's no real necessity for you to ask," said Harlan, his anger deepening. "Her costume is exhibitionistic. Her –"

"Wait, wait. Now wait a while, Harlan. You've been an Observer in this era. You know her clothes are standard costume for the 482nd."

"In her own surroundings, in her own cultural milieu, I would have no fault to find, though I'll say right now that her costume is extreme even for the 482nd. You'll allow me to be the judge of that. Here in Eternity, a person such as she is certainly out of place."

Finge nodded his head slowly. He actually seemed to be enjoying himself. Harlan stiffened.

Finge said, "She is here for a deliberate purpose. She is performing an essential function. It is only temporary. Try to endure her meanwhile."

Harlan's jaw quivered. He had protested and was being fobbed off. To hell with caution. He would speak his mind. He said, "I can imagine what the woman's 'essential function' is. To keep her so openly will not be allowed to pass."

He turned stiffly, walked to the door. Finge's voice stopped him.

"Technician," Finge said, "your relationship with Twissell may have given you a distorted notion about your own importance. Correct that! And meanwhile tell me, Technician, have you ever had a" (he hesitated, seeming to pick among words) "girl friend?"

With painstaking and insulting accuracy, back still turned, Harlan quoted: "In the interest of avoiding emotional entanglements with Time, an Eternal may not marry. In the interest of avoiding emotional entanglements with family, an Eternal may not have children."

The Computer said gravely, "I didn't ask about marriage or children."

Harlan quoted further: "Temporary liaisons may be made with Timers only after application with the Central Charting Board of the Allwhen Council for an appropriate Life-Plot of the Timer concerned. Liaisons may be conducted thereafter only according to the requirements of specific spatio-temporal charting."

"Quite true. Have you ever applied for temporary liaison, Technician?"

"No, Computer."

"Do you intend to?"

"No, Computer."

"Perhaps you ought to. It would give you a greater breadth of view. You would become less concerned about the details of a woman's costume, less disturbed about her possible personal

43

relations with other Eternals."

Harlan left, speechless with rage.

He found it almost impossible to perform his near-daily trek into the 482nd (the longest continuous period remaining something under two hours.)

He was upset, and he knew why. Finge! Finge, and his coarse advice concerning liaisons with Timers.

Liaisons existed. Everyone knew that. Eternity had always been aware of the necessity for compromising with human appetites (to Harlan the phrase carried a quivery repulsion), but the restriction involved in choosing mistresses made the compromise anything but lax, anything but generous. And those who were lucky enough to qualify for such an arrangement were expected to be most discreet about it, out of common decency and consideration for the majority.

Among the lower classes of Eternals, particularly among Maintenance, there were always the rumours (half hopeful, half resentful) of women imported on a more or less permanent basis for the obvious reasons. Always rumour pointed to the Computers and Life-Plotters as the benefiting groups. They and only they could decide which women could be abstracted from Time with danger of significant Reality Change.

Less sensational (and therefore less tongue-worthy) were the stories concerning the Timer employees that every Section engaged temporarily (when spatio-temporal analysis permitted) to perform the tedious tasks of cooking, cleaning, and heavy labour.

But a Timer, and *such* a Timer, employed as "secretary," could only mean that Finge was thumbing a nose at the ideals that made Eternity what it was.

Regardless of the fact of life to which the practical men of Eternity made a perfunctory obeisance it remained true that the ideal Eternal was a dedicated man living for the mission he had to perform, for the betterment of Reality and the improvement of the sum of human happiness. Harlan liked to think that Eternity was like the monasteries of Primitive times.

He dreamed that night that he spoke to Twissell about the matter, and that Twissell, the ideal Eternal, shared his horror. He dreamed of a broken Finge, stripped of rank. He dreamed of himself with the yellow Computer's insigne, instituting a new regime in the 482nd, ordering Finge grandly to a new position in Maintenance. Twissell sat next to him, smiling with admiration, as he drew up a new organizational chart, neat, orderly, consistent, and asked Noÿs Lambent to distribute copies.

But Noÿs Lambent was nude, and Harlan woke up, trembling and ashamed.

He met the girl in a corridor one day and stood aside, eyes averted, to let her pass.

But she remained standing, looking at him, until he had to look up and meet her eyes. She was all colour and life and Harlan was conscious of a faint perfume about her.

She said, "You're Technician Harlan, aren't you?"

His impulse was to snub her, to force his way past, but, after all, he told himself, all this wasn't her fault. Besides, to move past her now would mean touching her.

So he nodded briefly. "Yes."

"I'm told you're quite an expert on our Time."

"I have been in it."

"I would love to talk to you about it someday."

"I am busy. I wouldn't have time."

"But Mr. Harlan, surely you could *find* time someday."

She smiled at him.

Harlan said in a desperate whisper, "Will you pass, please? Or will you stand aside to let me pass? Please!"

She moved by with a slow swing of her hips that brought blood tingling to his embarrassed cheeks.

He was angry at her for embarrassing him, angry at himself for being embarrassed, and angry, most of all, for some obscure reason, at Finge.

Finge called him in at the end of two weeks. On his desk was a sheet of perforated flimsy the length and intricacy of which told Harlan at once that this concerned no half-hour excursion into Time.

Finge said, "Would you sit down, Harlan, and scan this thing right now? No, not by eye. Use the machine."

Harlan lifted indifferent eyebrows, and inserted the sheet carefully between the lips of the scanner on Finge's desk. Slowly it passed into the intestines of the machine and, as it did so, the perforation pattern was translated into words that appeared on the cloudy-white rectangle that was the visual attachment.

Somewhere about midpoint, Harlan's hand shot out and disconnected the scanner. He yanked the flimsy out with a force that tore its tough cellulite structure.

Finge said calmly, "I have another copy."

But Harlan was holding the remnants between thumb and forefinger as though it might explode. "Computer Finge, there is some mistake. Surely I am not expected to use the home of this woman as base for a near-week stay in Time."

The Computer pursed his lips. "Why not, if the spatio-temporal requirements are such. If there is a personal problem involved between yourself and Miss Lam –"

"No personal problem at all," interposed Harlan hotly.

"Some kind of problem, certainly. In the circumstances, I will go as far as to explain certain aspects of the Observational problem. This is not to be taken as a precedent, of course."

Harlan sat motionless. He was thinking hard and fast. Ordinarily professional pride would have forced Harlan to disdain explanation. An Observer, or Technician, for that matter, did his job without question. And ordinarily a Computer would never dream of offering explanation.

Here, however, was something unusual. Harlan had complained concerning the girl, the so-called secretary. Finge was afraid the complaint might go further. ("The guilty fleeth when no man pursueth," thought Harlan with grim satisfaction and tried to remember where he had read that phrase.)

Finge's strategy was obvious, therefore. By stationing Harlan in the woman's dwelling-place he would be ready to make counter-accusations if matters went far enough. Harlan's value as a witness against him would be destroyed.

And, of course, he would have to have some precious explanation for placing Harlan in such a place, and this would be it. Harlan listened with barely hidden contempt.

Finge said, "As you know, the various Centuries are aware of the existence of Eternity. They know that we supervise inter-temporal trade. They consider that to be our chief function, which is good. They have a dim knowledge that we are also here to prevent a catastrophe from striking mankind. That is more a superstition than anything else, but it is more or less correct, and good, too. We supply the generations with a mass father image and a certain feeling of security. You see all that, don't you?"

Harlan thought: Does the man think I'm still a Cub?

But he nodded briefly.

Finge went on. "There are some things, however, they must not know. Prime among them, of course, is the manner in which

46

we alter Reality when necessary. The insecurity such knowledge would arouse would be most harmful. It is always necessary to breed out of Reality any factors that might lead to such knowledge and we have never been troubled with it.

"However, there are always other undesirable beliefs about Eternity which spring up from time to time in one Century or another. Usually, the dangerous beliefs are those which concentrate particularly in the ruling classes of an era; the classes that have most contact with us and, at the same time, carry the important weight of what is called public opinion."

Finge paused as though he expected Harlan to offer some comment or ask some question. Harlan did neither.

Finge continued. "Ever since the Reality Change 433-486, Serial Number F-2, which took place about a year – a physio-year ago, there has been evidence of the bringing into Reality of such an undesirable belief. I have come to certain conclusions about the nature of that belief and have presented them to the Allwhen Council. The Council is reluctant to accept them since they depend upon the realization of an alternate in the Computing Pattern of an extremely low probability.

"Before acting on my recommendation, they insist on confirmation by direct Observation. It's a most delicate job, which is why I recalled you, and why Computer Twissell allowed you to be recalled. Another thing I did was to locate a member of the current aristocracy, who thought it would be thrilling or exciting to work in Eternity. I placed her in this office and kept her under close observation to see if she were suitable for our purpose –"

Harlan thought: Close observation! Yes!

Again his anger focused itself on Finge rather than upon the woman.

Finge was still speaking. "By all standards, she is suitable. We will now return her to her Time. Using her dwelling as a base, you will be able to study the social life of her circle. You do understand now the reason I had the girl here and the reason I want you in her house?"

Harlan said with an almost open irony, "I understand quite well, I assure you."

"Then you will accept this mission."

Harlan left with fire of battle burning inside his chest. Finge was *not* going to outsmart him. He was *not* going to make a fool of him.

Surely it was that fire of battle, the determination to outwit Finge, that caused him to experience an eagerness, almost an exhilaration, at the thought of this next excursion into the 482nd.

Surely it was nothing else.

CHAPTER FIVE

TIMER

NOŸS LAMBENT'S estate was fairly isolated, yet within easy reach of one of the larger cities of the Century. Harlan knew that city well; he knew it better than any of its inhabitants could. In his exploratory Observations into this Reality he had visited every quarter of the city and every decade within the purview of the Section.

He knew the city both in Space and Time. He could piece it together, view it as an organism, living and growing, with its catastrophes and recoveries, its gaieties and troubles. Now he was in a given week of Time in that city, in a moment of suspended animation of its slow life of steel and concrete.

More than that, his preliminary explorations had centred themselves more and more closely about the "perioeci", the inhabitants who were the most important of the city, yet who lived outside the city, in roomy and relative isolation.

The 482nd was one of the many Centuries in which wealth was unevenly distributed. The Sociologists had an equation for the phenomenon (which Harlan had seen in print, but which he understood only vaguely). It worked itself out for any given Century to three relationships, and for the 482nd those relationships stood near the limits of what could be permitted. Sociologists shook their heads over it and Harlan had heard one say at one time that any further deterioration with new Reality Changes would require "the closest Observation."

Yet there was this to be said for unfavourable relationships in the wealth-distribution equation. It meant the existence of a leisure class and the development of an attractive way of life which, at its best, encouraged culture and grace. As long as the other end of the scale was not too badly off, as long as the leisure classes did not entirely forget their responsibilities while

48

enjoying their privileges, as long as their culture took no obviously unhealthy turn, there was always the tendency in Eternity to forgive the departure from the ideal, wealth-distribution pattern and to search for other, less attractive maladjustments.

Against his will Harlan began to understand this. Ordinarily his overnight stays in Time involved hotels in the poorer sections, where a man might easily stay anonymous, where strangers were ignored, where one presence more or less was nothing and therefore did not cause the fabric of Reality to do more than tremble. When even that was unsafe, when there was a good chance that the trembling might pass the critical point and bring down a significant part of the card house of Reality, and was not unusual to have to sleep under a particular hedge in the countryside.

And it was usual to survey various hedges to see which would be least disturbed by farmers, tramps, even stray dogs, during the night.

But now Harlan, at the other end of the scale, slept in a bed with a surface of field-permeated matter, a peculiar welding of matter and energy that entered only the highest economic levels of this society. Throughout Time it was less common than pure matter but more common than pure energy. In any case it moulded itself to his body as he lay down, firm when he lay still, yielding when he moved or turned.

Reluctantly he confessed the attraction of such things, and he accepted the wisdom which caused each Section of Eternity to live on the *median* scale of its Century rather than at its most comfortable level. In that way it could maintain contact with the problems and "feel" of the Century, without succumbing to too close an identification with a sociological extreme.

It is easy, thought Harlan, that first evening, to live with aristocrats.

And just before he fell asleep, he thought of Noÿs.

He dreamed he was on the Allwhen Council, fingers clasped austerely before him. He was looking down on a small, a very small, Finge, listening in terror to the sentence he was casting him out of Eternity to perpetual Observation of one of the unknown Centuries of the far, far upwhen. The sombre words of exile were coming from Harlan's own mouth, and immediately to his right sat Noÿs Lambent.

He hadn't noticed her at first, but his eyes kept sliding to his

49

right, and his words faltered.

Did no one else see her? The rest of the members of the Council looked steadily forward, except for Twissell. He turned to smile at Harlan, looking through the girl as though she weren't there.

Harlan wanted to order her away, but words were no longer coming out of his mouth. He tried to beat at the girl, but his arm moved sluggishly and she did not move. Her flesh was cold.

Finge was laughing – louder – louder –

– and it was Noÿs Lambent laughing.

Harlan opened his eyes to bright sunlight and stared at the girl in horror for a moment before he remembered where she was and where he was.

She said, "You were moaning and beating the pillow. Were you having a bad dream?"

Harlan did not answer.

She said, "Your bath is ready. So are your clothes. I've arranged to have you join the gathering tonight. It felt queer to step back into my ordinary life after being in Eternity so long."

Harlan felt acutely disturbed at her easy flow of words. He said, "You didn't tell them who I was, I hope."

"Of *course* not."

Of *course* not! Finge would have taken care of that little matter by having her lightly psyched under narcosis, if he felt that necessary. He might have thought it necessary, however. After all, he had given her "close observation".

The thought annoyed him. He said, "I'd prefer to be left to myself as much as possible."

She looked at him uncertainly a moment or two and left.

Harlan went through the morning ritual of washing and dressing glumly. He had no great hopes of an exciting evening. He would have to say as little as possible, do as little as possible, be part of the wall as much as possible. His true function was that of a pair of ears and a pair of eyes. Connecting those senses with the final report was his mind, which, ideally, had no other function.

Ordinarily it did not disturb him that, as an Observer, he did not know what he was looking for. An Observer, he had been taught as a Cub, must not have preconceived notions as to what data is desired or what conclusions are expected. The knowledge, it was said, would automatically distort his view, however conscientious he tried to be.

50

But under the circumstances ignorance was irritating. Harlan suspected strongly that there was nothing to look for, that he was playing Finge's game in some way. Between that and Noÿs . . .

He stared savagely at the image of himself cast in three-dimensional accuracy two feet in front of him by the Reflector. The clinging garments of the 482nd, seamless and bright in colouring, made him, he thought, look ridiculous.

Noÿs Lambent came running to him just after he had finished a solitary breakfast brought to him by a Mekkano.

She said breathlessly, "It's June, Technician Harlan."

He said harshly, "Do not use the title here. What if it is June?"

"But it was February when I joined" – she paused doubtfully – "*that* place, and that was only a month ago."

Harlan frowned. "What year is it now?"

"Oh, it's the right year."

"Are you sure?"

"I'm quite positive. Has there been a mistake?" She had a disturbing habit of standing quite close to him as they talked and her slight lisp (a trait of the Century rather than of herself personally) gave her the sound of a young and rather helpless child. Harlan was not fooled by that. He drew away.

"No mistake. You've been put here because it's more suitable. Actually, in Time, you have been here all along."

"But how could I?" She looked more frightened still. "I don't remember anything about it. Are there two me's?"

Harlan was far more irritated than the cause warranted. How could he explain to her the existence of micro-changes induced by every interference with Time which could alter individual lives without appreciable effect on the Century as a whole. Even Eternals sometimes forgot the difference between micro-changes (small "c") and Changes (large "c") which significantly altered Reality.

He said, "Eternity knows what it's doing. Don't ask questions." He said it proudly, as though he, himself, were a Senior Computer and had personally decided that June was the proper moment in time and that the micro-change induced by skipping three months could not develop into a Change.

She said, "But then I've lost three months of my life."

He sighed. "Your movements through Time have nothing to do with your physiological age."

51

"Well, have I or haven't I?"

"Have or haven't what?"

"Lost three months."

"By Time, woman, I'm telling you as plainly as I can. You haven't lost any time out of your life. You can't lose any."

She stepped backward at his shout and then, suddenly, giggled. She said, "You have the funniest accent. Especially when you get angry."

He frowned at her retreating back. What accent? He spoke fifty-millennial as well as anyone in the Section. Better probably.

Stupid girl!

He found himself back at the Reflector staring at his image, which stared back at him, vertical furrows deep between his eyes.

He smoothed them and thought: I'm not handsome. My eyes are too small and my ears stick out and my chin is too big.

He had never particularly thought about the matter before, but now it occurred to him, quite suddenly, that it would be pleasant to be handsome.

Late at night Harlan added his notes to the conversations he had gathered, while it was all fresh in his mind.

As always in such cases he made use of a molecular recorder of 55th Century manufacture. In shape it was a featureless thin cylinder about four inches long by half an inch in diameter. It was coloured a deep but noncommittal brown. It could be easily held in cuff, pocket, or lining, depending on the style of clothing, or, for that matter, suspended from belt, button, or wristband.

However held, wherever kept, it had the capacity or recording some twenty million words on each of three molecular energy levels. With one end of the cylinder connected to a transliterator, resonating efficiently with Harlan's earpiece, and the other end connected field-wise to the small mike at his lips, Harlan could listen and speak simultaneously.

Every sound made during the hours of the "gathering" repeated itself now in his ear, and as he listened, he spoke words that recorded themselves on a second level, co-ordinate with but different from the primary level on which the gathering had been recorded. On this second level he described his own impressions, he ascribed significance, pointed out correlations. Eventually, when he made use of the molecular recorder to write a report, he would have, not simply a sound-for-sound recording, but an annotated reconstruction.

Noÿs Lambent entered. She did *not* signal her entrance in any way.

Annoyed, Harlan removed lip-piece and earpiece, clipped them to the molecular recorder, placed the whole into its kit, and clasped that shut.

"Why do you act so angry with me?" asked Noÿs. Her arms and shoulders were bare and her long legs shimmered in faintly luminescent foamite.

He said, "I am not angry. I have no feeling for you at all." At the moment he felt the statement to be rigidly true.

She said, "Are you still working? Surely, you must be tired."

"I can't work if you're here," he replied peevishly.

"You *are* angry with me. You did not say a word to me all evening."

"I said as little as I could to anybody. I wasn't there to speak." He waited for her to leave.

But she said, "I brought you another drink. You seemed to enjoy one at the gathering and one isn't enough. Especially if you're going to be working."

He noticed the small Mekkano behind her, gliding in on a smooth force-field.

He had eaten sparingly that evening, picking lightly at dishes concerning which he had reported in full in past Observations but which (except for fact-searching nibbles) he had thus far refrained from eating. Against his will, he had liked them. Against his will, he had enjoyed the foaming, light green, peppermint-flavoured drink (not quite alcoholic, something else, rather) that was currently fashionable. It had not existed in the Century two physioyears earlier, prior to the latest Reality Change.

He took the second drink from the Mekkano with an austere nod of thanks to Noÿs.

Now why had a Reality Change which had had virtually no physical effect on the Century brought a new drink into existence? Well, he wasn't a Computer, so there was no use asking himself that question. Besides, even the most detailed possible Computations could never eliminate all uncertainty, all random effects. If that weren't so, there would be no need for Observers.

They were alone together in the house, Noÿs and himself. Mekkanos were at the height of their popularity these two decades past and would remain so for nearly a decade more in this Reality, so there were no human servants about.

Of course, with the female of the species as economically independent as the male, and able to attain motherhood, if she so wished, without the necessities of physical childbearing, there could be nothing "improper" in their being together alone in the eyes of the 482nd, at least.

Yet Harlan felt compromised.

The girl was stretched out on her elbow on a sofa opposite. Its patterned covering sank beneath her as though avid to embrace her. She had kicked off the transparent shoes she had been wearing and her toes curled and uncurled within the flexible foamite, like the soft paws of a luxuriant cat.

She shook her head and whatever it was that had kept her hair arranged upward away from her ears in intricate intertwinings was suddenly loosened. The hair tumbled about her neck and her bare shoulders became more creamily lovely at the contrast with the black of the hair.

She murmured, "How old are you?"

That he certainly should not have answered. It was a personal question and the answer was none of her business. What he should have said at that point with polite firmness was: May I be left to my work? Instead what he heard himself saying was, "Thirty-two years." He meant physioyears, of course.

She said, "I'm younger than you. I'm twenty-seven. But I suppose I won't always look younger than you. I suppose you'll be like this when I'm an old woman. What made you decide to be thirty-two? Can you change if you wish? Wouldn't you want to be younger?"

"What are you talking about?" Harlan rubbed his forehead to clear his mind.

She said softly, "You live forever. You're an Eternal."

Was it a question or a statement?

He said, "You're mad. We grow old and die like anyone else."

She said, "You can tell me." Her voice was low and cajoling. The fifty-millennial language, which he had always thought harsh and unpleasant, seemed euphonious after all. Or was it merely that a full stomach and the scented air had dulled his ears?

She said, "You can see all Times, visit all places. I so wanted to work in Eternity. I waited the longest time for them to let me. I thought maybe they'd make me an Eternal, and then I found there were only men there. Some of them wouldn't even

54

talk to me because I was a woman. *You* wouldn't talk to me."

"We're all busy," mumbled Harlan, fighting to keep off something that could only be described as a numb content. "I was very busy."

"But why aren't there more women Eternals?"

Harlan couldn't trust himself to speak. What could he say? That members of Eternity were chosen with infinite care since two conditions had to be met. First, they must be equipped for the job; second, their withdrawal from Time must have no deleterious effect upon Reality.

Reality! That was the word he must not mention under any circumstances. He felt the spinning sensation in his head grow stronger and he closed his eyes for a moment to stop it.

How many excellent prospects had been left untouched in Time because their removal into Eternity would have meant the non-birth of children, the non-death of women and men, non-marriage, non-happenings, non-circumstance that would have twisted Reality in directions the Allwhen Council could not permit.

Could he tell her any of this? Of course not. Could he tell her that women almost never qualified for Eternity because, for some reason he did not understand (Computers might, but he himself certainly did not), their abstraction from Time was from ten to a hundred times as likely to distort Reality as was the abstraction of a man.

(All the thoughts jumbled together in his head, lost and whirling, joined to one another in a free association that produced odd, almost grotesque, but not entirely unpleasant, results. Noÿs was closer to him now, smiling.)

He heard her voice like a drifting wind. "Oh, you Eternals. You are so secretive. You won't share at all. Make me an Eternal."

Her voice was a sound now that didn't coalesce into separate words, just a delicately modulated sound that insinuated itself into his mind.

He wanted, he longed to tell her: There's no fun in Eternity, lady. We work! We work to plot out all the details of everywhen from the beginning of Eternity to where Earth is empty, and we try to plot out all the infinite possibilities of all the might-have-beens and pick out a might-have-been that is better than what is and decide where in Time we can make a tiny little change to twist the is to the might-be and we have a new is and look for a new might-be, forever, and forever, and that is how it has been since Vikkor Mallansohn discovered the Temporal Field in the 24th, way back in the Primitive 24th, and then it was possible to start Eternity in the 27th, the mysterious Mallansohn whom no man knows and who started Eternity, really, and the new might-be, forever and forever and forever and ...

He shook his head, but the whirligig of thought went on and on in stranger and more jagged breaks and leaps until it jumped into a sudden flash of illumination that persisted for a brilliant second, then died.

That moment steadied him. He grasped for it, but it was gone.

The peppermint drink?

Noÿs was still closer, her face not quite clear in his gaze. He could feel her hair against his cheek, the warm light pressure of her breath. He ought to draw away, but – strangely, strangely – he found he did not want to.

"If I were made an Eternal ..." she breathed, almost in his ear, though the words were scarcely heard above the beating of his heart. Her lips were moist and parted. "Wouldn't you like to?"

He did not know what she meant, but suddenly he didn't care. He seemed in flames. He put out his arms clumsily, gropingly. She did not resist, but melted and coalesced with him.

It all happened dreamily, as though it were happening to someone else.

It wasn't nearly as repulsive as he had always imagined it must be. It came as a shock to him, a revelation, that it wasn't repulsive at all.

Even afterward, when she leaned against him with her eyes all soft and smiling a little, he found he had to reach out and stroke her damp hair with slow and trembling delight.

She was entirely different in his eyes now. She was not a woman, not an individual at all. She was suddenly an aspect of himself. She was, in a strange and unexpected way, a part of himself.

The spatio-temporal chart said nothing of this, yet Harlan felt no guilt. It was only the thought of Finge that aroused strong emotion in Harlan's breast. And that wasn't guilt. Not at all.

It was satisfaction, even triumph!

In bed Harlan could not sleep. The lightheadedness had worn off now, but there was still the unusual fact that for the first time in his adult life a grown woman had shared his bed.

He could hear her soft breathing and in the ultra dim glow to which the internal light of the walls and ceiling had been reduced he could see her body as the merest shadow next to his.

He had only to move his hand to feel that warmth and softness of her flesh, and he dared not do that, lest he wake her out of whatever dreaming she might have. It was as though she were dreaming for the two of them, dreaming herself and himself and all that had happened, and as though her waking would drive it all from existence.

It was a thought that seemed a piece of those other queer, unusual thoughts he had experienced just before . . .

Those had been strange thoughts, coming to him at a moment between sense and nonsense. He tried to recapture them and could not. Yet suddenly it was very important that he recapture them. For although he could not remember the details, he could remember that, for just an instant, he had understood something.

He was not certain what that something was, but there had been the unearthly clarity of the half-asleep, when more than mortal eye and mind seems suddenly to come to life.

His anxiety grew. Why couldn't he remember? So much had been in his grasp.

For the moment even the sleeping girl beside him receded into the hinterland of his thoughts.

He thought: If I follow the thread . . . I was thinking of Reality and Eternity . . . yes, and Mallansohn and the Cub!

He stopped there. Why the Cub? Why Cooper? He *hadn't* thought of him.

But if he hadn't, then why should he think of Brinsley Sheridan Cooper now?

He frowned! What was the truth that connected all this? What was it he was trying to find? What made him so sure there *was* something to find?

Harlan felt chilled, for with these questions a distant glow of that earlier illumination seemed to break from the horizons of his mind and he almost knew.

He held his breath, did not press for it. Let it come.

Let it come.

And in the quiet of that night, a night already so uniquely

significant in his life, an explanation and interpretation of events came to him that at any saner, more normal time he would not have entertained for a moment.

He let the thought bud and flower, let it grow until he could see it explain a hundred odd points that otherwise simply remained – odd.

He would have to investigate this, check this, back in Eternity, but in his heart he was already convinced that he knew a terrible secret he was not meant to know.

A secret that embraced all Eternity!

CHAPTER SIX

LIFE-PLOTTER

A MONTH of physiotime had passed since that night in the 482nd, when he grew acquainted with many things. Now, if one calculated by ordinary time, he was nearly 2000 Centuries in Noÿs Lambent's future, attempting by a mixture of bribery and cajolery to learn what lay in store for her in a new Reality.

It was worse than unethical, but he was past caring. In the physiomonth just gone he had, in his own eyes, become a criminal. There was no way of glossing over the fact. He would be no more a criminal by compounding his crime and he had a great deal to gain by doing so.

Now, as part of his felonious manoeuvring (he made no effort to choose a milder phrase) he stood at the barrier before the 2456th. Entry into Time was much more complicated than mere passage between Eternity and the kettle shafts. In order to enter Time the co-ordinates fixing the desired region on Earth's surface had painstakingly to be adjusted and the desired moment of Time pin-pointed within the Century. Yet despite inner tension Harlan handled the controls with the ease and quick confidence of a man with much experience and a great talent.

Harlan found himself in the engine room he had seen first on the viewing screen within Eternity. At his physiomoment Sociologist Voy would be sitting safely before that screen watching for the Technician's Touch that was to come.

Harlan felt no hurry. The room would remain empty for the next 156 minutes. To be sure, the spatio-temporal chart allowed him only 110 minutes, leaving the remaining 46 as the customary 40 per cent "margin". Margin was there in case of necessity, but a Technician was not expected to have to use it. A "margin-eater" did not remain a Specialist long.

Harlan, however, expected to use no more than 2 minutes of the 110. Wearing his wrist-borne field generator so that he was surrounded by an aura of physiotime (an effluvium, so to speak, of Eternity) and therefore protected from any of the effects of Reality Change, he took one step towards the wall, lifted a small container from its position on a shelf, and placed it in a carefully adjusted spot on the shelf below.

Having done that, he re-entered Eternity in a way that seemed as prosaic to himself as a passage through any door might be. Had there been a Timer watching, it would have seemed to him that Harlan had simply disappeared.

The small container stayed where he put it. It played no immediate role in world history. A man's hand, hours later, reached for it but did not find it. A search revealed it half an hour later still, but in the interim a force-field had blanked out and a man's temper had been lost. A decision which would have remained unmade in the previous Reality was now made in anger. A meeting did not take place; a man who would have died lived a year longer, under other circumstances; another who would have lived dies somewhat sooner.

The ripples spread wider, reaching their maximum in the 2481st, which was twenty-five Centuries upwhen from the Touch. The intensity of the Reality Change declined thereafter. Theorists pointed out that nowhere to the infinite upwhen could the Change ever become zero, but by fifty Centuries upwhen from the Touch the Change had become too small to detect by the finest Computing, and that was the practical limit.

Of course no human being in Time could ever possibly be aware of any Reality Change having taken place. Mind changed as well as matter and only Eternals could stand outside it all and see the change.

Sociologist Voy was staring at the bluish scene in the 2481st, where earlier there had been all the activity of a busy space-port. He barely looked up when Harlan entered. He barely mumbled something that might have been a greeting.

A change had indeed blasted the space-port. Its shininess had gone; what buildings there stood were not the grand creations

59

they had been. A space-ship rusted. There were no people. There was no motion.

Harlan allowed himself a small smile that flickered for a moment, then vanished. It was M.D.R. all right. Maximum Desired Response. And it happened at once. The Change did not necessarily take place at the precise moment of the Technician's Touch. If the calculations that went into the Touch were sloppy, hours or days might elapse before the Change actually took place (counting, of course, by physiotime). It was only when all degrees of freedom vanished that the Change took place. While there was even a mathematical chance for alternate actions, the Change did *not* take place.

It was Harlan's pride that when *he* calculated an M.N.C., when it was *his* hand that contrived the Touch, the degrees of freedom vanished at once, and the Change took place instantly.

Voy said softly, "It had been very beautiful."

The phrase grated Harlan's ears, seeming to detract from the beauty of his own performance. "I wouldn't regret" he said, "having space-travel bred out of Reality altogether."

"No?" said Voy.

"What good is it? It never lasts more than a millennium or two. People get tired. They come back home and the colonies die out. Then after another four or five millennia, or forty or fifty, they try again and it fails again. It is a waste of human ingenuity and effort."

Voy said dryly, "You're a philosopher."

Harlan flushed. He thought: What's the use in talking to any of them? He said, angrily, with a sharp change of subject, "What about the Life-Plotter?"

"What about him?"

"Would you check with the man? He ought to have made some progress by now."

The Sociologist let a look of disapproval drift across his face, as though to say: You're the impatient one, aren't you? Aloud, he said, "Come with me and let's see."

The name plate on the office door said Neron Feruque, which struck Harlan's eye and mind because of its faint similarity to a pair of rulers in the Mediterranean area during Primitive times. (His weekly discourses with Cooper had sharpened his own preoccupation with the Primitive almost feverishly.)

The man, however, resembled neither ruler, as Harlan recalled it. He was almost cadaverously lean, with skin stretched tightly over a high-bridged nose. His fingers were long and his wrists knobby. As he caressed his small Summator, he looked like Death weighing a soul in the balance.

Harlan found himself staring at the Summator hungrily. It was the heart and blood of Life-Plotting, the skin and bones, sinew, muscle and all else. Feed it into the required data of a personal history, and the equations of the Reality Change; do that and it would chuckle away in obscene merriment for any length of time from a minute to a day, and then spit out the possible companion lives for a person involved (under the new Reality), each neatly ticketed with a probability value.

Sociologist Voy introduced Harlan. Feruque, having stared in open annoyance at the Technician's insigne, nodded his head and let the matter go.

Harlan said, "Is the young lady's Life-Plot complete yet?"

"It is not. I'll let you know when it is." He was one of those who carried contempt for the Technician to the point of open rudeness.

Voy said, "Take it easy, Life-Plotter."

Feruque had eyebrows which were light almost to invisibility. It heightened the resemblance of his face to a skull. His eyes rolled in what should have been empty sockets as he said, "Killed the space-ships?"

Voy nodded. "Cut it down a Century."

Feruque's lips twisted softly and formed a word.

Harlan folded his arms and stared at the Life-Plotter, who looked away in eventual discomfiture.

Harlan thought: He *knows* it's his guilt, too.

Feruque said to Voy, "Listen, as long as you're here, what in Time am I going to do about the anti-cancer serum requests? We're not the only Century with anti-cancer. Why do we get all the applications?"

"All the other Centuries are just as crowded. You know that."

"Then they've got to stop sending in applications altogether."

"How do we go about making them?"

"Easy. Let the Allwhen Council stop receiving them."

"I have no pull with the Allwhen Council."

"You have pull with the old man."

Harlan listened to the conversation dully, without real interest. At least it served to keep his mind on inconsequentials and away from the chuckling Summator. The "old man", he knew, would

61

be the Computer in charge of the Section.

"I've talked to the old man," said the Sociologist, "and he's talked to the Council."

"Nuts. He's just sent through a routine tape-strip. He has to fight for this. It's a matter of basic policy."

"The Allwhen Council isn't in the mood these days to consider changes in basic policy. You know the rumours going round."

"Oh, sure. They're busy on a big deal. Whenever there's dodging to do, the word gets round that Council's busy on some big deal."

(If Harlan could have found the heart for it, he would have smiled at that point.)

Feruque brooded a few moments, and then burst out, "What most people don't understand is that anti-cancer serum isn't a matter of tree seedlings or field motors. I know that every sprig of spruce has to be watched for adverse effects on Reality, but anti-cancer always involves a human life, and that's a hundred times as complicated.

"Consider! Think how many people a year die of cancer in each Century that doesn't have anti-cancer serums of one sort or another. You can imagine how many of the patients want to die. So the Timer governments in every Century are forever forwarding applications to Eternity to 'please, pretty please ship them seventy-five thousand ampules of serum on behalf of the men critically stricken who are absolutely vital to the cultures', enclosed see biographical data."

Voy nodded rapidly, "I know. I know."

But Feruque was not to be denied his bitterness. "So you read the biographical data and it's every man a hero. Every man an insupportable loss to his world. So you work it through. You see what would happen to Reality if each man lived, and for Time's sake, if different *combinations* of men lived.

"In the last month, I've done 572 cancer requests. Seventeen, count them, seventeen Life-Plots came out to involve no undesirable Reality Changes. Mind you, there wasn't one case of a possible *desirable* Reality Change, but the Council says neutral cases get the serum. Humanity, you know. So exactly seventeen people in assorted countries get cured this month.

"And what happens? Are the Centuries happy? Not on your life. One man gets cured and a dozen, same country, same Time, don't. Everyone says, Why *that* one? Maybe the guys we didn't

62

treat are better characters, maybe they're rosy cheeked philan-thropists beloved by all, while the one man we cure kicks his aged mother all around the block whenever he can spare the time from beating his kids. They don't know about Reality Changes and we can't tell them.

"We're just making trouble for ourselves, Voy, unless the All-when Council decides to screen all applications and approve only those which result in a desirable Reality Change. That's all. Either curing them does some good for humanity, or else it's out. Never mind this business of saying: 'Well, it does no harm'."

The Sociologist had been listening with a look of mild pain on his face, and now he said, "If it were *you* with cancer ..."

"That's a stupid remark, Voy. Is that what we base de-cisions on? In that case there'd never be a Reality Change. Some poor sucker always gets it in the neck, doesn't he? Sup-pose you were that sucker, hey?

"And another thing. Just remember that every time we make a Reality Change it's harder to find a good next one. Every physioyear, the chances that a random Change is likely to be for the worse increases. That means that the proportion of guys we can cure gets smaller anyway. It's always going to get smaller. Someday, we'll be able to cure only one guy a physioyear, even counting the neutral cases. Remember that."

Harlan lost even the faintest interest. This was the type of griping that went with the business. The Psychologists and Sociologists, in their rare introvertive studies of Eternity, called it identification. Men identified themselves with the Century with which they were associated professionally. Its battles, all too often, became their own battles.

Eternity fought the devil of identification as best it could. No man could be asigned to any Section within two Centuries of his homewhen, to make identification harder. Preference was given to Centuries with cultures markedly different from that of their homewhen. (Harlan thought of Finge and the 482nd.) What was more, their assignments were shifted as often as their reactions grew suspect. (Harlan wouldn't give a 50th Century grafenpiece for Feruque's chances of retaining this assignment longer than another physioyear at the outside.)

And still men identified out of a silly yearning for a home in Time (the Time-wish; everyone knew about it). For some reason this was particularly true in Centuries with space-travel. It was

63

something that should be investigated and would be but for Eternity's chronic reluctance to turn its eyes inward.

A month earlier Harlan might have despised Feruque as a blustering sentimentalist, a petulant oaf who eased the pain of watching the electro-gravitics lose intensity in a new Reality by railing against those of other Centuries who wanted anti-cancer serum.

He might have reported him. It would have been his duty to do so. The man's reactions obviously could no longer be trusted.

He could not do so, now. He even found sympathy for the man. His own crime was so much greater.

How easy it was to slip back to thoughts of Noÿs.

Eventually he had fallen asleep that night, and he woke in daylight, with brightness shining through translucent walls all about until it was as though he had awakened on a cloud in a misty morning sky.

Noÿs was laughing down at him. "*Goodness*, it was hard to wake you."

Harlan's first reflexive action was a scrabble for bedclothes, that weren't there. Then memory arrived and he stared at her hollowly, his face burning red. How should he feel about this?

But then something else occurred to him and he shot to a sitting position. "It isn't past one, is it? Father Time!"

"It's only eleven. You've got breakfast waiting and lots of time."

"Thanks," he mumbled.

"The shower controls are all set and your clothes are all ready."

What could he say? "Thanks," he mumbled.

He avoided her eyes during the meal. She sat opposite him, not eating, her chin buried in the palm of one hand, her dark hair combed thickly to one side and her eyelashes preternaturally long.

She followed every gesture he made while he kept his eyes lowered and searched for the bitter shame he knew he ought to feel.

She said, "Where will you be going at one?"

"Aeroball game," he muttered, "I have the ticket."

"That's the rubber game. And I missed the whole season because of just skipping the time, you know. Who'll win the game, Andrew?"

He felt oddly weak at the sound of his first name. He shook so easy.

"But surely you know. You've inspected this whole period, haven't you?"

Properly speaking, he ought to maintain a flat and cold negative, but weakly he explained, "There was a lot of Space and Time to cover. I wouldn't know little precise things like game scores."

"Oh, you just don't want to tell me."

Harlan said nothing to that. He inserted the pene-prong into the small, juicy fruit and lifted it, whole, to his lips.

After a moment Noÿs said, "Did you see what happened in this neighbourhood before you came?"

"No details, N – noÿs." (He forced her name past his lips.)

The girl said softly, "Didn't you see us? Didn't you know all along that –"

Harlan stammered. "No, no, I couldn't see myself. I'm not in Rea – I'm not here till I come. I can't explain." He was doubly flustered. First, that she should speak of it, Second, that he had almost been trapped into saying "Reality," of all the words the most forbidden in conversation with Timers.

She lifted her eyebrows and her eyes grew round and a little amazed. "Are you ashamed?"

"What we did was not proper."

"Why not?" And in the 482nd her question was perfectly innocent. "Aren't Eternals allowed to?" There was almost a joking cast to that question as though she were asking if Eternals weren't allowed to eat.

"Don't use the word," said Harlan. "As a matter of fact, we're not, in a way."

"Well, then, don't tell them. I won't."

And she walked about the table and sat down on his lap, pushing the small table out of the way with a smooth and flowing motion of her hip.

Momentarily he stiffened, lifted his hands in a gesture that might have been intended to hold her off. It didn't succeed.

She bent and kissed him on his lips, and nothing seemed shameful any more. Nothing that involved Noÿs and himself.

He wasn't sure when first he began to do something that an Observer, ethically, had no right to do. That is, he began to speculate on the nature of the problem involving the current

Reality and of the Reality Change that would be planned.

It was not the loose morals of the Century, not ectogenesis, not matriarchy, that disturbed Eternity. All of that was as it was in the previous Reality and the Allwhen Council had viewed it with equanimity then. Finge had said it was something very subtle.

The Change then would have to be very subtle and it would have to involve the group he was Observing. So much seemed obvious.

It would involve the aristocracy, the well-to-do, the upper classes, the beneficiaries of the system.

What bothered him was that it would most certainly involve Noÿs.

He got through the remaining three days called for in his chart in a gathering cloud that dampened even his joy in Noÿs's company.

She said to him, "What happened? For a while, you seemed all different from the way you were in Eter – in that place. You weren't stiff at all. Now, you seem concerned. Is it because you have to go back?'

Harlan said, "Partly."

"Do you have to?"

"I have to."

"Well, who would care if you were late?"

Harlan almost smiled at that. "They wouldn't like me to be late," he said, yet thought longingly just the same of the two-day margin allowed for in his chart.

She adjusted the controls of a musical instrument that played soft and complicated strains out of its own creative bowels by striking notes and chords in a random manner; the randomness weighted in favour of pleasant combinations by intricate mathematical formulae. The music could not more repeat itself than could snowflakes, and could no more fail of beauty.

Through the hypnosis of sound Harlan gazed at Noÿs and his thoughts wound tightly about her. What would she be in the new dispensation? A fishwife, a factory girl, the mother of six, fat, ugly, diseased? Whatever she was, she would not remember Harlan. He would have been no part of her life in a new Reality. And whatever she would be then, she would not be Noÿs.

He did not simply love a *girl*. (Strangely, he used the word "love" in his own thoughts for the first time and did not even pause long enough to stare at the strange thing and wonder at it.) He loved a complex of factors; her choice of clothes, her walk, her manner of speech, her tricks of expression. A quarter century of life and experience in a given Reality had gone into the manufacture of all that. She had not been his Noÿs in the previous Reality of a physioyear earlier. She would not be his Noÿs in the next Reality.

The new Noÿs might, conceivably, be better in some ways, but he knew one thing very definitely. He wanted this Noÿs here, the one he saw at this moment, the one of his Reality. If she had faults, he wanted those faults, too.

What could he do?

Several things occurred to him, all illegal. One of them was to learn the nature of the Change and find out definitely how it would affect Noÿs. One could not, after all, be certain that . . .

A dead silence wrenched Harlan out of his reverie. He was in the Life-Plotter's office once more. Sociologist Voy was watching him out of the corner of his eye. Feruque's death's-head was lowering at him.

And the silence was piercing.

It took a moment for the significance to penetrate. Just a moment. The summator had ceased its inner clucking.

Harlan jumped up. "You have the answer, Life-Plotter."

Fereque looked down at the flimsies in his hand. "Yeah. Sure. Sort of funny."

"May I have it?" Harlan held out his hand. It was trembling visibly.

'There's nothing to see. That's what's funny."

"What do you mean — nothing?" Harlan stared at Feruque with eyes that suddenly smarted till there was only a tall, thin blur where Feruque stood.

The Life-Plotter's matter-of-fact voice sounded thin. "The dame doesn't exist in the new Reality. No personality shift. She's just out, that's all. Gone. I ran the alternatives down to Probablility 0.0001. She doesn't make it anywhere. In fact" — and he reached up to rub his cheek with long, spare fingers — "with the combination of factors you handed me I don't quite see how she fits in the old Reality."

Harlan hardly heard. "But — the Change was such a small one."

"I know. A funny combination of factors. Here, you want the flimsies?"

Harlan's hand closed over them, unfeeling. Noÿs gone? Noÿs nonexistent? How could that be?

He felt a hand on his shoulder and Voy's voice clashed on his ear. "Are you ill, Technician?" The hand drew away as though it already regretted its careless contact with the Technician's body.

Harland swallowed and with an effort composed his features. "I'm quite well. Would you take me to the kettle?"

He *must not* show his feelings. He must act as though this were what he represented it to be, a mere academic investigation. He must disguise the fact that with Noÿs's nonexistence in the new Reality he was almost physically overwhelmed by a flood of pure elation, unbearable joy.

CHAPTER SEVEN

PRELUDE TO CRIME

HARLAN stepped into the kettle at the 2456th and looked backward to make certain that the barrier that separated the shaft from Eternity was truly flawless; that Sociologist Voy was not watching. In these last weeks it had grown to be a habit with him, an automatic twitch; there was always the quick backward glance across the shoulder to make sure no one was behind him in the kettle shafts.

And then, though already in the 2456th, it was for *up*when that Harlan set the kettle controls. He watched the numbers on the temporometer rise. Though they moved with blurry quickness, there would be considerable time for thought.

How the Life-Plotter's findings changed matters! How the very nature of his crime had changed!

And it had all hinged on Finge. The phrase caught at him with its ridiculous rhyme and its heavy beat circled dizzyingly inside his skull. It hinged on Finge. It hinged on Finge....

Harland had avoided any personal contact with Finge on his return to Eternity after those days with Noÿs in the 482nd. As Eternity closed in about him, so did guilt. A broken oath of office, which seemed nothing in the 482nd, was enormous in Eternity.

He had sent in his report by impersonal air-chute and took himself off to personal quarters. He needed to think out this, gain time to consider and grow accustomed to the new orientation within himself.

Finge did not permit it. He was in communication with Harlan less than an hour after the report had been coded for proper direction and inserted into the chute.

The Computer's image stared out of the vision plate. His voice said, "I expected you to be in your office."

Harlan said, "I delivered the report, sir. It doesn't matter where I wait for a new assignment."

"Yes?" Finge scanned the roll of foil he held in his hands, holding it up, squint-eyed, and peering at its perforation pattern.

"It is scarcely complete," he went on. "May I visit your rooms?"

Harlan hesitated a moment. The man was his superior and to refuse the self-invitation at this moment would have a flavour of insubordination. It would advertise his guilt, it seemed, and his raw, painful conscience dared not permit that.

"You will be welcome, Computer," he said stiffly.

Finge's sleek softness introduced a jarring element of epicureanism into Harlan's angular quarters. The 95th, Harlan's homewhen, tended towards the Spartan in house furnishings and Harlan had never completely lost his taste for the style. The tubular metal chairs had been surfaced with a dull veneer that had been artificially grained into the appearance of wood (though not very successfully). In one corner of the room was a small piece of furniture that represented an even wider departure from the customs of the times.

It caught Finge's eye almost at once.

The Computer put a pudgy finger on it, as though to test its texture. "What is this material?"

"Wood, sir," said Harlan.

"The real thing? Actual wood? Amazing! You use wood in your homewhen, I believe?"

"We do."

"I see. There's nothing in the rules against this, Technician," – he dusted the finger with which he had touched the object against the side seam of his trouser leg – "but I don't know that it's advisable to allow the culture of the homewhen to affect one. The true Eternal adopts whatever culture he is surrounded by.

69

I doubt, for instance if I have eaten out of an energic utensil more than twice in five years." He sighed. "And yet to allow food to touch matter has always seemed unclean. But I don't give in. I don't give in."

His eyes returned to the wooden object, but now he held both hands behind his back, and said, "What is it? What is its purpose?"

"It's a bookcase," said Harlan. He had the impulse to ask Finge how he felt now that his hands rested firmly upon the small of his back. Would he not consider it cleaner to have his clothes and his own body constructed of pure and undefiled energy fields?

Finge's eyebrows lifted. "A bookcase. Then those objects resting upon the shelves are books. Is that right?"

"Yes, sir."

"Authentic specimens?"

"Entirely, Computer. I picked them up in the 24th. The few I have here date from the 20th. If – if you intend to look at them, I wish you'd be careful. The pages have been restored and impregnated, but they're not foil. They take careful handling."

"I won't touch them. I have no intention of touching them. Original 20th Century dust is on them, I imagine. Actual books!" He laughed. "Pages of cellulose, too? You implied that."

Harlan nodded. "Cellulose modified by the impregnation treatment for longer life. Yes." He opened his mouth for a deep breath, forcing himself to remain calm. It was ridiculous to identify himself with these books, to feel a slur upon them to be a slur upon himself.

"I dare say," said Finge, still on the subject, "that the whole content of those books can be placed on two meters of film and stored in a finger's end. What do the books contain?"

Harlan said, "They are bound volumes of a news magazine of the 20th."

"You read that?"

Harlan said proudly. "These are a few volumes of the complete collection I have. No library in Eternity can duplicate it."

"Yes, your hobby. I remember now you once told me about your interest in the Primitive. I'm amazed your Educator ever allowed you to grow interested in such a thing. A complete waste of energy."

Harlan's lips thinned. The man, he decided, was deliberately trying to irritate him out of possession of calm reasoning faculties. If so, he must not be allowed to succeed.

Harlan said flatly, "I think you've come to see me about my report."

"Yes, I have." The Computer looked about, selected a chair, and sat down gingerly. "It is not complete, as I said over the communicator."

"In what way, sir?" (Calm! Calm!)

Finge broke into a nervous twitch of a smile. "What happened that you didn't mention, Harlan?"

"Nothing, sir." And though he said it firmly, he stood there, hang-dog.

"Come, Technician. You spent several periods of time in the society of the young lady. Or you did if you followed the spatio-temporal chart. You did follow it, I suppose?"

Harlan's guilt riddled him to the point where he could not even rise to the bait of this open assault upon his professional competence.

He could only say, "I followed it."

"And what happened? You include nothing of the private interludes with the woman."

"Nothing of importance happened," said Harlan, dry-lipped.

"That is ridiculous. At your time of life and with your experience, I don't have to tell you that it is not for an Observer to judge what is important and what is not."

Finge's eyes were keenly upon Harlan. They were harder and more eager than quite befitted his soft line of questioning.

Harlan noted that well and was not fooled by Finge's gentle voice, yet the habit of duty tugged at him. An Observer must report *everything*. An Observer was merely a sense-perceptive pseudopod thrust out by Eternity into Time. It tested its surroundings and was drawn back. In the fulfillment of his function an Observer had no individuality of his own; he was not really a man.

Almost automatically Harlan began his narration of the events he had left out of his report. He did it with the trained memory of the Observer, reciting the conversations with word-for-word accuracy, reconstructing the tone of voice and cast of countenance. He did it lovingly, for in the telling he lived it again, and almost forgot in the process, that a combination of Finge's probing and his own healing sense of duty was driving

71

him into an admission of guilt.

It was only as he approached the end result of that first long conversation that he faltered and the shell of his Observer's objectivity showed cracks.

He was saved from further details by the hand that Finge suddenly raised and by the Computer's sharp, edgy voice. "Thank you. It is enough. You were about to say that you made love to the woman."

Harlan grew angry. What Finge said was the literal truth, but Finge's tone of voice made it sound lewd, coarse, and, worse than that, commonplace. Whatever else it was, or might be, it was not commonplace.

Harlan had an explanation for Finge's attitude, for his anxious cross-examination, for his breaking off the verbal report at the moment he did. Finge was jealous! That much Harlan would have sworn was obvious. Harlan had succeeded in taking away a girl that Finge meant to have.

Harlan felt the triumph in that and found it sweet. For the first time in his life, he knew an aim that meant more to him than the frigid fulfillment of Eternity. He was going to keep Finge jealous, because Noÿs Lambent was to be permanently his.

In this mood of sudden exaltation he plunged into the request that originally he had planned to present only after a wait of a discreet four or five days.

He said, "It is my intention to apply for permission to form a liaison with a Timed individual."

Finge seemed to snap out of a reverie. "With Noÿs Lambent, I presume."

"Yes, sir. As Computer in charge of the Section, it will have to go through you. . . ."

Harlan wanted it to go through Finge. Make him suffer. If he wanted the girl himself, let him say so and Harlan could insist on allowing Noÿs to make her choice. He almost smiled at that. He hoped it would come to that. It would be the final triumph.

Ordinarily, of course, a Technician could not hope to push through such a matter in the face of a Computer's desires, but Harlan was sure he could count on Twissell's backing, and Finge had a long way to go before he could buck Twissell.

Finge, however, seemed tranquil. "It would seem," he said, "that you have already taken illegal possession of the girl."

Harlan flushed and was moved to a feeble defence. "The spatio-temporal chart insisted on our remaining alone together. Since nothing of what happened was specifically forbidden, I feel no guilt."

Which was a lie, and from Finge's half-amused expression one could feel that he knew it to be a lie.

He said, "There will be a Reality Change."

Harlan said, "If so, I will amend my application to request liaison with Miss Lambent in the new Reality."

"I don't think that would be wise. How can you be sure in advance? In the new Reality, she may be married, she may be deformed. In fact I can tell you this, in the new Reality, she will not want you. She will *not* want you."

Harlan quivered. "You know nothing about it."

"Oh? You think this great love of yours is a matter of soul-to-soul contact? That it will survive all external changes? Have you been reading novels out of Time?"

Harlan was goaded into indiscretion. "For one thing, I don't believe you."

Finge said coldly, "I beg pardon."

"You're lying," Harlan didn't care what he said now. "You're jealous. It's all it amounts to. You're jealous. You had your own plans for Noÿs but she chose me."

Finge said, "Do you realize –"

"I realize a great deal. I'm no fool. I may not be a Computer, but neither am I an ignoramus. You say she won't want me in the new Reality. How do you know? You don't even know yet what the new Reality will be. You don't know if there must be a new Reality at all. You just received my report. It must be analyzed before a Reality Change can be computed, let alone submitted for approval. So when you affect to know the nature of the Change, you are lying."

There were a number of ways in which Finge might have made response. Harlan's heated mind was aware of many. He did not try to choose among them. Finge might stalk out in affected dudgeon; he might call in a member of Security and have Harlan taken into custody for insubordination; he might shout back, yelling as angrily as Harlan; he might put in an immediate call to Twissell, lodging a formal complaint; he might – he might. . . .

Finge did none of this.

He said gently, "Sit down, Harlan. Let's talk about this."

And because that response was completely unexpected, Harlan's jaw sagged and he sat down in confusion. His resolution faltered. What was this?

"You remember, of course," said Finge, "that I told you that our problem with the 482nd involved an undesirable attitude on the part of the Timers of the current Reality towards Eternity. You do remember that, don't you?" He spoke with the mild urging of a schoolmaster towards a somewhat backward student, yet Harlan thought he could detect a kind of hard glitter in his eye.

Harlan said, "Of course."

"You remember, too, that I told you that the Allwhen Council was reluctant to accept my analysis of the situation without specific confirming Observations. Doesn't that imply to you that I had already Computed the necessary Reality Change?"

"But my own observations represent the confirmation, don't they?"

"They do."

"And it would take time to analyze them properly."

"Nonsense. Your report means nothing. The confirmation lay in what you told me orally moments ago."

"I don't understand you."

"Look, Harlan, let me tell you what is wrong with the 482nd. Among the upper classes of this Century, particularly among the women, there has grown up the notion that Eternals are really Eternal, literally so; that they live forever ... Great Time, man, Noÿs Lambent told you so much. You repeated her statements to me not twenty minutes ago."

Harlan stared blankly at Finge. He was remembering Noÿs's soft, caressing voice as she leaned towards him and caught at his eyes with her own lovely, dark glance. *You live forever. You're an Eternal.*

Finge went on. "Now a belief like that is bad, but, in itself, not too bad. It can lead to inconveniences, increase difficulties for the Section, but Computation would show that only in a minority of cases would Change be necessary. Still, if a Change *is* desirable, isn't it obvious to you that the inhabitants of the Century, who must, above all, change maximally with the Change, be those who are subject to the superstition. In other words, the female aristocracy. Noÿs."

"It may be, but I'll take my chance," said Harlan.

"You have no chance at all. Do you think your fascinations and charm persuaded the soft aristocrat to fall into the arms of an unimportant Technician? Come, Harlan, be realistic about this."

Harlan's lips grew stubborn. He said nothing.

Finge said, "Can't you guess the additional superstition which these people have added to their belief in the actual eternal life of the Eternals? Great Time, Harlan! Most of the women believe that intimacy with an Eternal will enable a mortal woman (as they think of themselves) to live forever!"

Harlan swayed. He could hear Noÿs's voice again so clearly: *If I were made an Eternal . . .*

And then her kisses.

Finge went on. "The existence of such a superstition was hard to believe, Harlan. It was unprecedented. It lay within the region of random error so that a search through the Computations for the previous Change yielded no information respecting it one way or the other. The Allwhen Council wanted firm evidence, direct substantiation. I chose Miss Lambent as a good example of her class. I chose you as the other subject –"

Harlan struggled to his feet. "You chose *me*? As a *subject*?"

"I'm sorry," said Finge stiffly, "but it was necessary. You made a very good subject."

Harlan stared at him.

Finge had the grace to squirm a bit under that wordless stare. He said, "Don't you see? No, you still don't. Look, Harlan, you're a coldfish product of Eternity. You won't look at a woman. You consider women and all that concerns them unethical. No, there's a better word. You consider them *sinful*. That attitude shows all over you, and to any woman you'd have all the sex appeal of a month-dead mackerel. Yet here we have a woman, a beautiful pampered product of a hedonistic culture, who ardently seduces you on your first evening together, virtually begging for your embrace. Don't you understand that that is ridiculous, impossible, unless – well, unless it is the confirmation we were looking for."

Harlan struggled for words. "You say she sold herself –"

"Why that expression? There is no shame attached to sex in this Century. The only strange thing is that she chose you as partner, and *that* she did for the sake of eternal life. It's plain."

And Harlan, arms raised, hands claw-bent, with no rational thought in his mind, or any irrational one other than to choke

75

and throttle Finge, sprang forward.

Finge stepped back hastily. He brought out a blaster with a quick, trembling gesture. "Don't touch me! Back!"

Harlan had just enough sanity to halt his rush. His hair was matted. His shirt was stained with perspiration. His breath whistled through pinched nostrils.

Finge said shakily, "I know you very well, you see, and I thought your reaction might be violent. Now I'll shoot if I have to."

Harlan said, "Get out."

"I will. But first you listen. For attacking a Computer, you can be declassified, but we'll let that go. You will understand, however, that I did not lie. The Noÿs Lambent of the new Reality, whatever else may be or not be, will lack this superstition. The whole purpose of the Change will be to wipe out the superstition. And without it, Harlan" – his voice was almost a snarl – "how could a woman like Noÿs want a man like you?"

The pudgy Computer backed towards the door of Harlan's personal quarters, blaster still levelled.

He paused to say, with a sort of grim gaiety, "Of course, if you had her now, Harlan, if you had her now, you could enjoy her. You could keep your liaison and make it formal. That is, if you had her now. But the Change will come soon, Harlan, and after that, you will not have her. What a pity, the now does not last, even in Eternity, eh, Harlan?"

Harlan no longer looked at him. Finge had won after all and was leaving in clear and leering possession of the field. Harlan stared unseeingly at his own toes, and when he looked up Finge was gone – whether five seconds earlier or fifteen minutes Harlan could not have said.

Hours had passed nightmarishly and Harlan felt trapped in the prison of his mind. All that Finge had said was so true, so transparently true. Harlan's Observer mind could look back upon the relationship of himself and Noÿs, that short, unusual relationship, and it took on a different texture.

It wasn't a case of instant infatuation. How could he have believed it was? Infatuation for a man like himself?

Of course not. Tears stung his eyes and he felt ashamed. How obvious it was that the affair was a case of cool calculation. The girl had certain undeniable physical assets and no ethical principles to keep her from using them. So she used them and that had nothing to do with Andrew Harlan as a person. He simply represented her distorted view of Eternity and what it meant.

Automatically Harlan's long fingers caressed the volumes in his small bookshelf. He took one out and, unseeingly, opened it.

The print blurred. The faded colours of the illustrations were ugly, meaningless blotches.

Why had Finge troubled to tell him all this? In the strictest sense he ought not to have. An Observer, or anyone acting as Observer, ought never to know the ends attained by his Observation. It removed him by so much from the ideal position of the objective non-human tool.

It was to crush him, of course; to take a mean and jealous revenge!

Harlan fingered the open page of the magazine. He found himself staring at a duplication, in startling red, of a ground vehicle, similar to vehicles characteristic of the 45th, 182nd, 590th, and 984th Centuries, as well as of late Primitive times. It was a very common sort of affair with an internal-combustion motor. In the Primitive era natural petroleum fractions were the source of power and natural rubber cushioned the wheels. That was true of none of the later centuries, of course.

Harlan had pointed that out to Cooper. He had made quite a point of it, and now his mind, as though longing to turn away from the unhappy present, drifted back to that moment. Sharp, irrelevant images filled the ache within Harlan.

"These advertizements," he had said, "tell us more of Primitive times than the so-called news articles in the same magazine. The news articles assume the basic knowledge of the world it deals with. It uses terms it feels no necessity of explaining. What is a 'golf ball', for instance?"

Cooper had professed his ignorance readily.

Harlan went on in the didactic tone he could scarcely avoid on occasions such as this. "We could deduce that it was a small pellet of some sort from the nature of the casual mentions it receives. We know that it is used in a game, if only because it is mentioned in an item under the heading 'Sport'. We can even make further deductions that it is hit by a long rod of some sort and that the object of the game is to drive the ball into a hole in the ground. But why bother with deduction and reasoning? Observe this advertizement! The object of it is only to induce readers to buy the ball, but in so doing we are presented with an excellent close-range portrait of one, with a

77

section cut into it to show its construction."

Cooper, coming from an era in which advertizement was not as wildly proliferative as it was in the later Centuries of Primitive times, found all this difficult to appreciate. He said, "Isn't it rather disgusting the way these people blow their own horn? Who would be fool enough to believe a person's boastings about his own products? Would he admit defects? Is he likely to stop at any exaggeration?"

Harlan, whose homewhen was middling fruitful in advertizement, raised tolerant eyebrows and merely said, "You'll have to accept that. It's their way and we never quarrel with the ways of any culture as long as it does not seriously harm mankind as a whole."

But now Harlan's mind snapped back to his present situation and he was back in the present, staring at the loudmouthed brassy advertizements in the news magazine. He asked himself in sudden excitement: Were the thoughts he had just experienced really irrelevant? Or was he tortuously finding a way out of the blackness and back to Noÿs?

Advertizement! A device for forcing the unwilling into line. Did it matter to a ground-vehicle manufacturer whether a given individual felt an original or spontaneous desire for his product? If the prospect (that was the word) could be artificially persuaded or cajoled into feeling that desire and acting upon it, would that not be just as well.

Then what did it matter if Noÿs loved him out of passion or out of calculation? Let them but be together long enough and she would grow to love him. He would *make* her love him and, in the end, love and not its motivation was what counted. He wished now he had read some of the novels out of Time that Finge had mentioned scornfully.

Harlan's fists clenched at a sudden thought. If Noÿs had come to *him*, to *Harlan*, for immortality, it could only mean that she had not yet fulfilled the requirement for that gift. She could have made love to no Eternal previously. That meant that her relationship to Finge had been nothing more than that of secretary and employer. Otherwise what need would she have had for Harlan?

Yet Finge surely must have tried – must have attempted ... (Harlan could not complete that thought even in the secrecy of his own mind.) Finge could have proved the superstition's existence on his own person. Surely he could not have missed the thought with Noÿs an ever-present temptation. Then she must have refused him.

He had had to use Harlan and Harlan had succeeded. It was for that reason that Finge had been driven into the jealous revenge of torturing Harlan with the knowledge that Noÿs's motivation had been a practical one, and that he could never have her.

Yet Noÿs had refused Finge even with eternal life at stake and *had* accepted Harlan. She had that much of a choice and she had made it in Harlan's favour. So it wasn't calculation entirely. Emotion played a part.

Harlan's thoughts were wild and jumbled, and grew more heated with every moment.

He *must* have her, and *now*. Before any Reality Change. What was it Finge had said to him, jeering: *The now does not last, even in Eternity.*

Doesn't it, though? Doesn't it?

Harlan had known exactly what he must do. Finge's angry taunting had goaded him into a frame of mind where he was ready for crime and Finge's final sneer had, at least, inspired him with the nature of the deed he must commit.

He had not wasted a moment after that. It was with excitement and even joy that he left his quarters, at all but a run, to commit a major crime against Eternity.

CHAPTER EIGHT

CRIME

No one had questioned him. No one had stopped him. There was that advantage, anyway, in the social isolation of a Technician. He went via the kettle channels to a door in Time and set its controls. There was the chance, of course, that someone would happen along on a legitimate errand and wonder why the door was in use. He hesitated, and then decided to stamp his seal on the marker. A sealed door would draw little attention. An unsealed door in active use would be a nine-day wonder.

Of course, it might be Finge who stumbled upon the door. He would have to chance that.

Noÿs was still standing as he had left her. Wretched hours (physiohours) had passed since Harlan had left the 482nd for a lonely Eternity but he returned now to the same Time, within a matter of seconds, that he had left. Not a hair on Noÿs's head had stirred.

She looked startled. "Did you forget something, Andrew?"

Harlan stared at her hungrily, but made no move to touch her. He remembered Finge's words, and he dared not risk a repulse. He said stiffly, "You've got to do as I say."

She said, "But is something wrong, then? You just left. You just this minute left."

"Don't worry," said Harlan. It was all he could do to keep from taking her hand, from trying to sooth her. Instead he spoke harshly. It was as though some demon were forcing him to do all the wrong things. Why had he come back at the first available moment? He was only disturbing her by his almost instantaneous return after leaving.

(He knew the answer to that, really. He had a two-day margin of grace allowed by the spatio-temporal chart. The earlier portions of that period of grace were safer and yielded least chance of discovery. It was a natural tendency to crowd it as far down-when as he could. A foolish risk, too, though. He might easily have miscalculated and entered Time before he had left it physiohours earlier. What then? It was one of the first rules he had learned as an Observer: One person occupying two points in the same Time of the same Reality runs a risk of meeting himself.

Somehow that was something to be avoided. Why? Harlan knew he didn't want to meet himself. He didn't want to be staring into the eyes of another and earlier (or later) Harlan. Beyond that it would be a paradox, and what was it Twissell was fond of saying? "There are no paradoxes in Time, but only because Time deliberately avoids paradoxes.")

All the time Harlan thought dizzily of all this Noÿs stared at him with large, luminous eyes.

Then she came to him and put cool hands on either burning cheek and said softly, "You're in trouble."

To Harlan her glance seemed kindly, loving. Yet how could that be? She had what she wanted. What else was there? He seized her wrists and said huskily, "Will you come with me? Now? Without asking any questions? Doing exactly as I say?"

"Must I?" she asked.

"You must, Noÿs. It's very important."

"Then I'll come." She said it matter-of-factly, as though such a request came to her each day and was always accepted.

At the lip of the kettle Noÿs hesitated a moment, then stepped in.

Harlan said, "We're going upwhen, Noÿs."

"That means the future, doesn't it?"

The kettle was already faintly humming as she entered it and she was scarcely seated when Harlan unobtrusively moved the contact at his elbow.

She showed no signs of nausea at the beginnings of that indescribable sensation of "motion" through Time. He was afraid she might.

She sat there quietly, so beautiful and so at ease that he ached, looking at her, and gave not the particle of a damn that, by bringing a Timer, unauthorized, into Eternity, he had committed a felony.

She said, "Does that dial show the numbers of the years, Andrew?"

"The Centuries."

"You mean we're a thousand years in the future? Already?"

"That's right."

"It doesn't feel like it."

"I know."

She looked about. "But how are we moving?"

"I don't know, Noÿs."

"You *don't*?"

"There are many things about Eternity that are hard to understand."

The numbers on the temporometer *marched*. Faster and faster they moved till they were a blur. With his elbow Harlan had nudged the speed stick to high. The power drain might cause some surprise in the power plants, but he doubted it. No one had been waiting for him in Eternity when he returned with Noÿs, and that was nine tenths the battle. Now it was only necessary to get her to a safe place.

Again Harlan looked at her. "Eternals don't know everything."

"And I'm not an Eternal," she murmured. "I know so little."

Harlan's pulse quickened. *Still* not an Eternal? But Finge said . . .

Leave it at that, he pleaded with himself. Leave it at that. She's coming with you. She smiles at you. What more do you want?

But he spoke anyway. He said, "You think an Eternal lives forever, don't you?"

"Well, they call them Eternals, you know, and everyone says they do." She smiled at him brightly. "But they don't, do they?"

"You don't think so, then?"

"After I was in Eternity a while, I didn't. People didn't talk as though they lived forever, and there were old men there."

"Yet you told me I lived forever – that night."

She moved closer to him along the seat, still smiling, "I thought: who knows?"

He said, without being quite able to keep the strain out of his voice, "How does a Timer go about becoming an Eternal?"

Her smile vanished and was it his imagination or was there a trace of heightened colour in her cheek. She said, "Why do you ask that?"

"To find out."

"It's silly," she said. "I'd rather not talk about it." She stared down at her graceful fingers, edged with nails that glittered colourlessly in the muted light of the kettle shaft. Harlan thought abstractedly and quite apropos of nothing that at an evening gathering, with a touch of mild ultraviolet in the wall illumination, those nails would glow a soft apple-green or a brooding crimson, depending on the angle she held her hands. A clever girl, one like Noÿs, could produce half a dozen shades out of them, and make it seem as though the colours were reflecting her moods. Blue for innocence, bright yellow for laughter, violet for sorrow, and scarlet for passion.

He said, "Why did you make love to me?"

She shook her head back and looked at him out of a pale, grave face. She said, "If you must know, part of the reason was the theory that a girl can become an Eternal that way. I wouldn't mind living forever."

"I thought you said you didn't believe that."

"I didn't, but it couldn't hurt a girl to take the chance. Especially –"

He was staring at her sternly, finding refuge from hurt and disappointment in a frozen look of disapproval from the heights of the morality of his homewhen. "Well?"

"Especially since I wanted to, anyway."

"Wanted to make love to me?"

"Yes."

"Why me?"

"Because I liked you. Because I thought you were funny."

82

"Funny!"

"Well, odd, if you like that better. You always worked so hard not to look at me, but you always looked at me anyway. You tried to hate me and I could see you wanted me. I was sorry for you a little, I think."

"What were you sorry about?" He felt his cheeks burning.

"That you should have such trouble about wanting me. It's such a simple thing. You just ask a girl. It's so easy to be friendly. Why suffer?"

Harlan nodded. The morality of the 482nd! "Just ask a girl," he muttered. "So simple. Nothing more necessary."

"The girl has to be willing, of course. Mostly she is, if she's not otherwise engaged. Why not? It's simple enough."

It was Harlan's turn to drop his eyes. Of course, it was simple enough. And nothing wrong with it, either. Not in the 482nd. Who in Eternity should know this better? He would be a fool, an utter and unspeakable fool, to ask her now about earlier affairs. He might as well ask a girl of his own homewhen if she had ever eaten in the presence of a man and how dared she?

Instead he said humbly, "And what do you think of me now?"

"That you are very nice," she said softly, "and that if you ever relaxed – Won't you smile?"

"There's nothing to smile about, Noÿs."

"*Please*. I want to see if your cheeks can crease right. Let's see." She put her fingers to the corners of his mouth and pressed them backward. He jerked his head back in surprise and couldn't avoid smiling.

"See. Your cheeks didn't even crack. You're almost handsome. With enough practice – standing in front of a mirror and smiling and getting a twinkle in your eye – I'll bet you could be really handsome."

But the smile, fragile enough to begin with, vanished.

Noÿs said, "We *are* in trouble, aren't we?"

"Yes, we are, Noÿs. Great trouble."

"Because of what we did? You and I? That evening?"

"Not really."

"That was my fault, you know. I'll tell them so, if you wish."

"Never," said Harlan with energy. "Don't take on any fault in this. You've done nothing, *nothing*, to be guilty for. It's something else."

Noÿs looked uneasily at the temperometer. "Where are we?

I can't even see the numbers."

"*When* are we?" Harlan corrected her automatically. He slowed the velocity and the Centuries came into view.

Her beautiful eyes widened and the lashes stood out against the whiteness of her skin. "Is that *right*?"

Harlan looked at the indicator casually. It was in the 72,000's. "I'm sure it is."

"But where are we going?"

"To *when* are we going. To the far upwhen," he said, grimly. "Good and far. Where they won't find you."

And in silence they watched the numbers mount. In silence Harlan told himself over and over that the girl was innocent of Finge's charges. She had owned up frankly to its partial truth and she had admitted, just as frankly, the presence of a more personal attraction.

He looked up, then, as Noÿs shifted position. She had moved to his side of the kettle and, with a resolute gesture, brought the kettle to a halt at a most uncomfortable temporal deceleration.

Harlan gulped and closed his eyes to let the nausea pass. He said, "What's the matter?"

She looked ashen and for a moment made no reply. Then she said, "I don't want to go any further. The numbers are so high."

The temperometer read: 111,394.

He said, "Far enough."

Then he held out his hand gravely, "Come, Noÿs. This will be your home for a while."

They wandered through the corridors like children, hand in hand. The lights along the mainways were on, and the darkened rooms blazed at the touch of a contact. The air was fresh and had a liveliness about it which, without sensible draft, yet indicated the presence of ventilation.

Noÿs whispered, "Is there no one here?"

"No one," said Harlan. He tried to say it firmly and loudly. He wanted to break the spell of being in a "Hidden Century", but he said it in only a whisper after all.

He did not even know how to refer to anything so far upwhen. To call it the one-one-one-three-ninety-fourth was ridiculous. One would have to say simply and indefinitely, "The hundred thousands."

It was a foolish problem to be concerned with, but now that

the exaltation of actual flight was done with, he found himself alone in a region of Eternity where no human footsteps had wandered and he did not like it. He was ashamed, doubly ashamed since Noÿs was witness, at the fact that the faint chill within him was the faint chill of a faint fear.

Noÿs said, "It's so clean. There's no dust."

"Self-cleaning," said Harlan. With an effort that seemed to tear at his vocal cords he raised his voice to near-normal level. "But no one's here, upwhen or downwhen for thousands and thousands of Centuries."

Noÿs seemed to accept that. "And everything is fixed up so? We passed food stores and a viewing-film library. Did you see that?"

"I saw that. Oh, it's fully equipped. They're all fully equipped. Every Section."

"But why, if no one ever comes here?"

"It's logical," said Harlan. Talking about it took away some of the eeriness. Saying out loud what he already knew in the abstract would pin-point the matter, bring it down to the level of the prosaic. He said, "Early in the history of Eternity, one of the Centuries in the 300's came up with a mass duplicator. Do you know what I mean? By setting up a resonating field, energy could be converted to matter with subatomic particles taking up precisely the same pattern of positions, within the uncertainty requirements, as those in the model being used. The result is an exact copy.

"We in Eternity commandeered the instrument for our own purposes. At that time, there were only about six or seven hundred Sections built up. We had plans for expansion, of course. 'Ten new Seconds a physioyear' was one of the slogans of the time. The mass duplicator made that all unnecessary. We built one new Section complete with food, power supply, water supply, all the best automatic features; set up the machine and duplicated the Section once each Century all along Eternity. I don't know how long they kept it going – millions of Centuries, probably."

"All like this, Andrew?"

"All exactly like this. And as Eternity expands, we just fill in, adapting the construction whatever fashion turns out to be current in the Century. The only troubles come when we hit an energy-centred Century. We – we haven't reached this Section yet." (No use telling her that the Eternals couldn't penetrate

85

into Time here in the Hidden Centuries. What difference did that make?)

He glanced at her and she seemed troubled. He said hastily, "There's no waste involved in building the Sections. It took energy, nothing more, and with the nova to draw on –"

She interrupted. "No. I just don't remember."

"Remember what?"

"You said the duplicator was invented in the 300's. We don't have it in the 492nd. I don't remember viewing anything about it in history."

Harlan grew thoughtful. Although she was within two inches of being as tall as himself, he suddenly felt giant-size by comparison. She was a child, an infant, and he was a demigod of Eternity who must teach her and lead her carefully to the truth.

He said, "Noÿs, dear, let's find a place to sit down and – and I'll have to explain something."

The concept of a variable Reality, a Reality that was not fixed and eternal and immutable, was not one that could be faced casually by anyone.

In the dead of the sleep period, sometimes, Harlan would remember the early days of his Cubhood and recall the wrenching attempts to divorce himself from his Century and from Time.

It took six months for the average Cub to learn all the truth, to discover that he could never go home again in a very literal way. It wasn't Eternity's law, alone, that stopped him, but the frigid fact that home as he knew it might very well no longer exist, might, in a sense, never have existed.

It affected Cubs differently. Harlan remembered Bonky Latourette's face turning white and gaunt the day Instructor Yarrow had finally made it unmistakably clear about Reality.

None of the Cubs ate that night. They huddled together in search of a kind of psychic warmth, all except Latourette, who had disappeared. There was a lot of false laughter and miserably poor joking.

Someone said with a voice that was tremulous and uncertain, "I suppose I never had a mother. If I go back into the 95th, they'd say: 'Who are you? We don't know you. We don't have any records of you. You don't exist'."

They smiled weakly and nodded their heads, lonely boys with nothing left but Eternity.

They found Latourette at bedtime, sleeping deeply and breathing shallowly. There was the slight reddening of a spray injection in the hollow of his left elbow and fortunately that was noted, too.

Yarrow was called and for a while it looked as though one Cub would be out of the course, but he was brought around eventually. A week later he was back in his seat. Yet the mark of that evil night was on his personality for as long as Harlan knew him thereafter.

And now Harlan had to explain Reality to Noÿs Lambent, a girl not much older than those Cubs, and explain it at once and in full. He had to. There was no choice about that. She must learn exactly what faced them and exactly what she would have to do.

He told her. They ate canned meats, chilled fruits, and milk at a long conference table designed to hold twelve, and there he told her.

He did it as gently as possible, but he scarcely found need for gentleness. She snapped quickly at every concept and before he was half through it was borne in upon him, to his great amazement, that she wasn't reacting badly. She wasn't afraid. She showed no sense of loss. She only seemed angry.

The anger reached her face and turned it a glowing pink while her dark eyes seemed somehow the darker for it.

"But that's criminal," she said. "Who are the Eternals to do this?"

"It's done for humanity's good," said Harlan. Of course, she couldn't really understand that. He felt sorry for the Time-bound thinking of a Timer.

"Is it? I suppose that's how the mass duplicator was wiped out."

"We have copies still. Don't worry about that. We've preserved it."

"*You've* preserved it. But what about us? We of the 482nd might have had it." She gestured with little movements of two clenched fists.

"It wouldn't have done you good. Look, don't be excited, dear, and listen." With an almost convulsive gesture (he would have to learn how to touch her naturally, without making the movement seem a sheepish invitation to a repulse) he took her hands in his and held them tightly.

For a moment she tried to free them, and then she relaxed.

87

She even laughed a bit. "Oh, go ahead, silly, and don't look so solemn. I'm not blaming you."

"You mustn't blame anyone. There is no blame necessary. We do what must be done. That mass duplicator is a classic case. I studied it in school. When you duplicate mass, you can duplicate persons, too. The problems that arise are very complicated."

"Isn't it up to the society to solve its own problems?"

"It is, but we studied that society throughout Time and it doesn't solve the problem satisfactorily. Remember that its failure to do so affects not only itself but all its descendant societies. In fact, there is no satisfactory solution to the mass-duplicator problem. It's one of those things like atomic wars and dreamies that just can't be allowed. Developments are never satisfactory."

"What makes you so sure?"

"We have our Computing machines, Noÿs; Computaplexes far more accurate than any ever developed in any single Reality. They Compute the possible Realities and grade the desirabilities of each over a summation of thousands and thousands of variables."

"Machines!" She said it with scorn.

Harlan frowned, then relented hastily. "Now don't be like that. Naturally, you resent learning that life is not as solid as you thought. You and the world you lived in might have been only a probability shadow a year ago, but what's the difference? You have all your memories, whether they're of probability shadows or not, haven't you? You remember your childhood and your parents, don't you?"

"Of course."

"Then it's just as if you lived it, isn't it? Isn't it? I mean, whether you did or not?"

"I don't know. I'll have to think about it. What if tomorrow it's a dream world again, or a shadow, or whatever you call it?"

"Then there will be a new Reality and a new you with new memories. It would be just as though nothing had happened, except that the sum of human happiness would have been increased again."

"I don't find that satisfying, somehow."

"Besides,' 'said Harlan hastily, "nothing will happen to you now. There *will* be a new Reality but you're in Eternity. You won't be changed."

"But you say it makes no difference," said Noÿs gloomily. "Why go to all the trouble?"

With sudden ardour Harlan said, "Because I want you as you are. Exactly as you are. I don't want you changed. Not in any way."

He came within a hair of blurting out the truth, that without the advantage of the superstition about Eternals and eternal life she would never have inclined towards him.

She said, looking about with a slight frown, "Will I have to stay here forever, then? It would be – lonely."

"No, no. Don't think it," he said wildly, gripping her hands so tight that she winced. "I'll find out what you will be in the new Reality of the 482nd, and you'll go back in disguise, so to speak. I'll take care of you. I'll apply for permission for formal liaison and see to it that you remain safely through future Changes. I'm a Technician and a good one and I know about Changes." He added grimly, "And I know a few other things as well," and stopped there.

Noÿs said, "Is all this allowed? I mean, can you take people into Eternity and keep them from changing? It doesn't sound right, somehow, from the things you've told me."

For a moment Harlan felt shrunken and cold in the large emptiness of the thousands of Centuries that surrounded him upwhen and down. For a moment he felt cut off even from the Eternity that was his only home and only faith, doubly cast out from Time and Eternity; and only the woman for whom he had forsaken it all left at his side.

He said, and he meant it deeply, "No, it is a crime. It is a very great crime, and I am bitterly ashamed. But I would do it again, if I had to, and any number of times, if I had to."

"For me, Andrew? For me?"

He did not raise his eyes to her. "No, Noÿs, for myself. I could not bear to lose you."

She said, "And if we are caught . . .?"

Harlan knew the answer to that. He knew the answer since that moment of insight in bed in the 492nd, with Noÿs sleeping at his side. But, even yet, he dared not think of the wild truth.

He said, "I am not afraid of anyone. I have ways of protecting myself. They don't imagine how much I know."

CHAPTER NINE

INTERLUDE

It was, looking back at it, an idyllic period that followed. A hundred things took place in those physioweeks, and all confused itself inextricably in Harlan's memory, later, making the period seem to have lasted much longer than it did. The one idyllic thing about it was, of course, the hours he could spend with Noÿs, and that cast a glow over everything else.

Item One: At the 482nd he slowly packed his personal effects; his clothing and films, most of all his beloved and tenderly handled news-magazine volumes out of the Primitive. Anxiously he supervised their return to his permanent station in the 575th.

Finge was at his elbow as the last of it was lifted into the freight kettle by Maintenance men.

Finge said, choosing his words with unerring triteness, "Leaving us, I see." His smile was broad, but his lips were carefully held together so that only the barest trace of teeth showed. He kept his hands clasped behind his back and his pudgy body teetered forward on the balls of his feet.

Harlan did not look at his superior. He muttered a monotoned "Yes, sir."

Finge said, "I will report to Senior Computer Twissell concerning the entirely satisfactory manner in which you performed your Observational duties in the 482nd."

Harlan could not bring himself to utter even a sullen word of thanks. He remained silent.

Finge went on, in a suddenly much lower voice, "I will not report, for the present, your recent attempt at violence against me." And although his smile remained and his glance remained mild, there was a relish of cruel satisfaction about him.

Harlan looked up sharply and said, "As you wish, Computer."

Item Two: He re-established himself at the 575th.

He met Twissell almost at once. He found himself happy to see that little body, topped by that lined and gnomelike face. He was even happy to see the white cylinder nestling smokily between two stained fingers and being lifted rapidly towards Twissell's lips.

Harlan said, "Computer."

Twissell, emerging from his office, looked for a moment unseeingly and unrecognizably at Harlan. His face was haggard and his eyes squinted with weariness.

He said, "Ah, Technician Harlan. You are done with your work in the 482nd?"

"Yes, sir."

Twissell's comment was strange. He looked at his watch, which, like any watch in Eternity, was geared to physiotime, giving the day number as well as the time of day, and said, "On the nose, my boy, on the nose. Wonderful. Wonderful."

Harlan felt his heart give a small bound. When he had last seen Twissell he would not have been able to make sense of that remark. Now he thought he did. Twissell was tired, or he would not have spoken so close to the core of things, perhaps. Or the Computer might have felt the remark to be so cryptic as to feel safe despite its closeness to the core.

Harlan said, speaking as casually as he could to avoid letting it seem that his remark had any connection at all with what Twissell had just said, "How's my Cub?"

"Fine, fine," said Twissell, with only half his mind, apparently, on his words. He took a quick puff at the shortening tube of tobacco, indulged in a quick nod of dismissal, and hurried off.

Item Three: the Cub.

He seemed older. There seemed to be a greater feeling of maturity to him as he held out his hand and said, "Glad to see you back, Harlan."

Or was it merely that, where earlier Harlan had been conscious of Cooper only as a pupil, he now seemed more than a Cub. He now seemed a gigantic instrument in the hands of the Eternals. Naturally he could not help but attain a new stature in Harlan's eyes.

Harlan tried not to show that. They were in Harlan's own quarters, and the Technician basked in the creamy porcelain surfaces about him, glad to be out of the ornate splash of the 482nd. Try as he might to associate the wild baroque of the 482nd with Noÿs, he only succeeded in associating it with Finge. With Noÿs he associated a pink, satiny twilight and, strangely,

91

the bare austerity of the Sections of the Hidden Centuries.

He spoke hastily, almost as though he were anxious to hide his dangerous thoughts. "Well, Cooper, what have they been doing with you while I was away?"

Cooper laughed, brushed his drooping moustache self-consciously with one finger and said, "More math. Always math."

"Yes? Pretty advanced stuff by now, I guess."

"Pretty advanced."

"How's it coming?"

"So far it's bearable. It comes pretty easy, you know. I like it. But now they're really loading it on."

Harlan nodded and felt a certain satisfaction. He said, "Temporal Field matrices and all that?"

But Cooper, his colour a little high, turned towards the stacked volumes in the bookshelves, and said, "Let's get back to the Primitives. I've got some questions."

"About what?"

"City life in the 23rd. Los Angeles, especially."

"It's an interesting city. Don't you think so?"

"It is, but let's hit it in the 21st, then. It was at its peak in the 21st."

"Oh, let's try the 23rd."

Harlan said, "Well, why not?"

His face was impassive, but if the impassiveness could have been peeled off, there would have been a grimness about him. His grand, intuitional guess was more than a guess. Everything was checking neatly.

Item Four: research. Twofold research.

For himself, first. Each day, with ferreting eyes, he went through the reports on Twissell's desk. The reports concerned the various Reality Changes being scheduled or suggested. Copies went to Twissell routinely since he was a member of the Allwhen Council, and Harlan knew he would not miss one. He looked first for the coming Change in the 482nd. Secondly he looked for other Changes, any other Changes, that might have a flaw, an imperfection, some deviation from maximum excellence that might be visible to his own trained and talented Technician's eyes.

In the strictest sense of the word the reports were not for his study, but Twissell was rarely in his office these days, and no one else saw fit to interfere with Twissell's personal Technician.

That was one part of his research. The other took place in the 575th Section branch of the library.

For the first time he ventured out of those portions of the library which, ordinarily, monopolized his attention. In the past he had haunted the section on Primitive history (very poor indeed, so that most of his references and source materials had to be derived from the far downwhen of the 3rd millennium, as was only natural, of course). To an even greater extent he had ransacked the shelves devoted to Reality Change, its theory, technique, and history; an excellent collection (best in Eternity outside the Central branch itself, thanks to Twissell) of which he had made himself full master.

Now he wandered curiously among the other film-racks. For the first time he Observed (in the capital-O sense) the racks devoted to the 575th itself; its geographies, which varied little from Reality to Reality, its histories, which varied more, and its sociologies, which varied still more. These were not the books or reports written about the Century by Observing and Computing Eternals (with those he was familiar), but by the Timers themselves.

There were the works of literature of the 575th and these stirred memories of tremendous arguments he had heard of concerning the values of alternate Changes. Would this master-piece be altered or not? If so, how? How did past Changes affect works of art?

For that matter, could there ever be general agreement about art? Could it ever be reduced to quantitative terms amenable to mechanical evaluation by the Computing machines?

A Computer named August Sennor was Twissell's chief opponent in these matters. Harlan, stirred by Twissell's feverish denunciations of the man and his views, had read some of Sennor's papers and found them startling.

Sennor asked publicly and, to Harlan, disconcertingly, whether a new Reality might not contain a personality within itself analogous to that of a man who had been withdrawn into Eternity in a previous Reality. He analyzed then the possibility of an Eternal meeting his analogue in Time, either with or without knowing it, and speculated on the results in each case. (That came fairly close to one of Eternity's most potent fears, and Harlan shivered and hastened uneasily through the discussion.) And, of course, he discussed at length the fate of literature and art in various types and classifications of Reality Changes.

But Twissell would have none of the last. "If the values of art can't be computed," he would shout at Sennor, "then what's the use of arguing about it?"

And Twissell's views, Harlan knew, were shared by the large majority of the Allwhen Council.

Yet now Harlan stood at the shelves devoted to the novels of Eric Linkollew, usually described as the outstanding writer of the 575th, and wondered. He counted fifteen different "Complete Works" collections, each, undoubtedly, taken out of a different Reality. Each was somewhat different, he was sure. One set was noticeably smaller than all the others, for instance. A hundred Sociologists, he imagined, must have written analyses of the differences between the sets in terms of the sociological background of each Reality, and earned status thereby.

Harlan passed on to the wing of the library which was devoted to the devices and instrumentation of the various 575th's. Many of these last, Harlan knew, had been eliminated in Time and remained intact, as a product of human ingenuity, only in Eternity. Man had to be protected from his own too flourishing technical mind. That more than anything else. Not a physioyear passed but that somewhere in Time nuclear technology veered too close to the dangerous and had to be steered away.

He returned to the library proper and to the shelves on mathematics and mathematical histories. His fingers skimmed across individual titles, and after some thought he took half a dozen from the shelves and signed them out.

Item Five: Noÿs.

That was the really important part of the interlude, and all the idyllic part.

In his off-hours, when Cooper was gone, when he might ordinarily have been eating in solitude, reading in solitude, sleeping in solitude, waiting in solitude for the next day – he took to the kettles.

With all his heart he was grateful for the Technician's position in society. He was thankful, as he had never dreamed he could be, for the manner in which he was avoided.

No one questioned his right to be in a kettle, nor cared whether he aimed it upwhen or down. No curious eyes followed him, no willing hands offered to help him, no chattering mouths discussed it with him.

He could go where and when he pleased.

Noÿs said, "You've changed, Andrew. Heavens, you've changed."

He looked at her and smiled. "In what way, Noÿs?"

"You're smiling, aren't you? That's one of the ways. Don't you ever look in a mirror and see yourself smiling?"

"I'm afraid to. I'd say: 'I can't be that happy. I'm sick. I'm delirious. I'm confined in an asylum, living in daydreams, and unaware of it.'"

Noÿs leaned close to pinch him. "Feel anything?"

He drew her head towards him, felt bathed in her soft, black hair.

When they separated, she said breathlessly, "You've changed there, too. You've become very good at it."

"I've got a good teacher," began Harlan, and stopped abruptly, fearing that would imply displeasure at the thought of the many who might have had the making of such a good teacher.

But her laugh seemed untroubled by such a thought. They had eaten and she looked silky-smooth and warmly soft in the clothing he had brought her.

She followed his eyes and fingered the skirt gently, lifting it loose from the soft embrace of her thigh. She said, "I wish you wouldn't, Andrew. I really wish you wouldn't."

"There's no danger," he said carelessly.

"There *is* danger. Now don't be foolish. I can get along with what's here, until – until you make arrangements."

"Why shouldn't you have your own clothes and doodads?"

"Because they're not worth your going to my house in Time and being caught. And what if they make the Change while you're there?"

He evaded that uneasily. "It won't catch me." Then, brightening, "Besides my wrist generator keeps me in physiotime so that a Change can't affect me, you see."

Noÿs sighed. "I don't see. I don't think I'll ever understand it all."

"There's nothing to it." And Harlan explained and explained with great animation and Noÿs listened with sparkling eyes that never quite revealed whether she was entirely interested, or amused, or perhaps, a little of both.

It was a great addition to Harlan's life. There was someone to talk to, someone with whom to discuss his life, his deeds, and thoughts. It was as though she were a portion of himself, but a portion sufficiently separate to require speech in communication rather than thought. She was a portion sufficiently separate to be able to answer unpredictably out of independent thought processes. Strange, Harlan thought, how one might Observe a social phenomenon such as matrimony and yet miss so vital a truth about it. Could he have predicted in advance, for instance, that it would be the passionate interludes that he would later least often associate with the idyll?

She snuggled into the crook of his arm and said, "How is your mathematics coming along?"

Harlan said, "Want to look at a piece of it?"

"Don't tell me you carry it around with you?"

"Why not? The kettle trip takes time. No use wasting it, you know."

He disengaged himself, took a small viewer from his pocket, inserted the film, and smiled fondly as she put it to her eyes.

She returned the viewer to him with a shake of her head. "I never saw so many squiggles. I wish I could read your Standard Intertemporal."

"Actually," said Harlan, "most of the squiggles you mention aren't Intertemporal really, just mathematical notation."

"You understand it, though, don't you?"

Harlan hated to do anything to disillusion the frank admiration in her eyes, but he was forced to say, "Not as much as I'd like to. Still, I have been picking up enough math to get what I want. I don't have to understand everything to be able to see a hole in a wall big enough to push a freight kettle through."

He tossed the viewer into the air, caught it with a flick of his hand, and put it on a small end-table.

Noÿs's eyes followed it hungrily and sudden insight flashed on Harlan.

He said, "Father Time! You can't read Intertemporal, at that."

"No. Of course not."

"Then the Section library here is useless to you. I never thought of that. You ought to have your own films from the 482nd."

She said quickly, "No. I don't want any."

He said, "You'll have them."

"Honestly, I don't want them. It's silly to risk –"

"You'll have them!" he said.

96

For the last time he stood at the immaterial boundary separating Eternity from Noÿs's house in the 482nd. He had intended the time before to be the last time. The Change was nearly upon them now, a fact he had not told Noÿs out of the decent respect he would have had for anyone's feelings, let alone those of his love.

Yet it wasn't a difficult decision to make, this one additional trip. Partly it was bravado, to shine before Noÿs, bring her the book-films from out of the lion's mouth; partly it was a hot desire (what was the Primitive phrase?) "to singe the beard of the King of Spain," if he might refer to the smooth-cheeked Finge so.

Then, too, he would have the chance once again of savouring the weirdly attractive atmosphere about a doomed house.

He had felt it before, when entering it carefully during the period of grace allowed by the spatio-temporal charts. He had felt it as he wandered through its rooms, collecting clothing, small *objets d'art*, strange containers, and instruments from Noÿs's vanity table.

There was the sombre silence of a doomed Reality that was past merely the physical absence of noise. There was no way for Harlan to predict its analogue in a new Reality. It might be a small suburban cottage or a tenement in a city street. It might be zero with untamed scrubland replacing the parklike terrain on which it now stood. It might, conceivably, be almost unchanged. And (Harlan touched on this thought gingerly) it might be inhabited by the analogue of Noÿs or, of course, it might not.

To Harlan the house was already a ghost, a premature spectre that had begun its hauntings before it had actually died. And because the house, as it was, meant a great deal to him, he found he resented its passing and mourned it.

Once, only in five trips had there been any sound to break the stillness during his prowlings. He was in the pantry, then, thankful that the technology of that Reality and Century had made servants unfashionable and removed a problem. He had, he recalled, chosen among the cans of prepared foods, and was just deciding that he had enough for one trip, and that Noÿs would be pleased indeed to intersperse the hearty but uncolourful basic diet provided in the empty Section with some of her own dietary. He even laughed aloud to think that not long before he had thought her diet decadent.

It was in the middle of the laugh that he heard a distinct clapping noise. He froze!

The sound had come from somewhere behind him, and in the startled moment during which he had not moved the lesser danger that it was a housebreaker occurred to him first and the greatest danger of its being an investigating Eternal occurred second.

It *couldn't* be a housebreaker. The entire period of the spatio-temporal chart, grace period and all, had been painstakingly cleared and chosen out of other similar periods of Time because of the lack of complicating factors. On the other hand, he had introduced a micro-Change (perhaps not so micro at that) by abstracting Noÿs.

Heart pounding, he forced himself to turn. It seemed to him that the door behind had just closed, moving the last milli-meter required to bring it flush with the wall.

He repressed the impulse to open that door, to search the house. With Noÿs's delicacies in tow he returned to Eternity and waited two full days for repercussions before venturing into the far upwhen. There were none and eventually he forgot the incident.

But now, as he adjusted the controls to enter Time this one last time, he thought of it again. Or perhaps it was the thought of the Change, nearly upon him now, that preyed on him. Looking back on the moment later on, he felt that it was one or the other that caused him to misadjust the controls. He could think of no other excuse.

The misadjustment was not immediately apparent. It pin-pointed the proper room and Harlan stepped directly into Noÿs's library.

He had become enough of a decadent himself, now, to be not altogether repelled by the workmanship that went into the design of the film-cases. The lettering of the titles blended in with the intricate filigree until they were attractive but nearly unreadable. It was a triumph of aesthetics over utility.

Harlan took a few from the shelves at random and was sur-prised. The title of one was *Social and Economic History of Our Times*.

Somehow it was a side of Noÿs to which he had given little thought. She was certainly not stupid and yet it never occurred to him that she might be interested in weighty things. He had the impulse to scan a bit of the *Social and Economic History*, but fought it down. He would find it in the Section library of the 482nd, if he ever wanted it. Finge had undoubtedly rifled the libraries of this Reality for Eternity's records months earlier.

He put that film to one side, ran through the rest, selected the fiction and some of what seemed light non-fiction. Those and two pocket viewers. He stowed them carefully into a knapsack.

It was at that point that, once more, he heard a sound in the house. There was no mistake this time. It was not a short sound of indeterminate origin. It was a laugh, a man's laugh. He was *not* alone in the house.

He was unaware that he had dropped the knapsack. For one dizzy second he could think only that he was trapped!

CHAPTER TEN

TRAPPED!

ALL at once it had seemed inevitable. It was the rawest dramatic irony. He had entered Time one last time, tweaked Finge's nose one last time, brought the pitcher to the well one last time. It had to be then that he was caught.

Was it Finge who laughed?

Who else would track him down, lie in wait, stay a room away, and burst into mirth?

Well, then, all was lost? And because in that sickening moment he was sure all was lost it did not occur to him to run again or to attempt flight into Eternity once more. He would face Finge.

He would kill him, if necessary.

Harlan stepped to the door from behind which the laugh had sounded, stepped to it with the soft, firm step of the pre-meditated murderer. He flicked loose the automatic doorsignal and opened it by hand. Two inches. Three. It moved without sound.

The man in the next room had his back turned. The figure seemed too tall to be Finge and that fact penetrated Harlan's simmering mind and kept him from advancing further.

Then, as though the paralysis that seemed to hold both men in rigour was slowly lifting, the other turned, inch by inch.

Harlan never witnessed the completion of that turn. The other's profile had not yet come into view when Harlan, holding back a sudden gust of terror with a last fragment of moral strength, flung himself back out the door. Its mechanism, not Harlan, closed it soundlessly.

Harlan fell back blindly. He could breathe only by struggling violently with the atmosphere, fighting air in and pushing it out, while his heart beat madly as though in an effort to escape his body.

Finge, Twissell, all the Council together could not have disconcerted him so much. It was the fear of nothing physical that had unmanned him. Rather it was an almost instinctive loathing for the nature of the accident that had befallen him.

He gathered the stack of book-films to himself in a formless lump and managed, after two futile tries, to re-establish the door to Eternity. He stepped through, his legs operating mechanically. Somehow he made his way to the 575th, and then to personal quarters. His Technicianhood, newly valued, newly appreciated, saved him once again. The few Eternals he met turned automatically to one side and looked steadfastly over his head as they did so.

That was fortunate, for he lacked any ability to smooth his face out of the death's-head grimace he felt he was wearing, or any power to put the blood back into it. But they didn't look, and he thanked Time and Eternity and whatever blind thing wove Destiny for that.

He had not truly recognized the other man in Noÿs's house by his appearance, yet he knew his identity with a dreadful certainty.

The first time Harlan had heard a noise in the house he, Harlan, had been laughing and the sound that interrupted his laugh was of something weighty dropping in the next room. The second time someone had laughed in the next room and he, Harlan, had dropped a knapsack of book-films. The first time he, Harlan, had turned and caught sight of a door closing. The second time he, Harlan, closed a door as a stranger turned.

He had met himself!

In the same Time and nearly in the same place he and his earlier self by several physiodays had nearly stood face to face. He had misadjusted the controls, set it for an instant in Time which he had already used and he, Harlan, had seen him, Harlan.

He had gone about his work with the shadow of horror upon him for days thereafter. He cursed himself for a coward, but that did not help.

Indeed from that moment matters took a downward trend. He could put his anger on the Great Divide. The key moment was the instant in which he had adjusted the door controls for his entry into the 482nd for one last time and somehow had adjusted it wrongly. Since then things went badly, badly.

The Reality Change in the 482nd went through during that period of despondency and accentuated it. In the past two weeks he had picked up three proposed Reality Changes which contained minor flaws, and now he chose among them, yet could do nothing to move himself to action.

He chose Reality Change 2456-2781, V-5 for a number of reasons. Of the three, it was farthest upwhen, the most distant. The error was minute, but was significant in terms of human life. It needed, then, only a quick trip to the 2456th to find out the nature of Noÿs's analogue in the new Reality, by use of a little blackmailing pressure.

But the unmanning of his recent experience betrayed him. It seemed to him no longer a simple thing, this gentle application of threatened exposure. And once he found the nature of Noÿs's analogue, what then? Put Noÿs in her place as charwoman, seamstress, labourer, or whatever. Certainly. But what, then, was to be done with the analogue herself? With any husband the analogue might have? Family? Children?

He had thought of none of this earlier. He had avoided the thought. "Sufficiently unto the day . . ."

But now he could think of nothing else.

So he lay skulking in his room, hating himself, when Twissell called him, his tired voice questioning and a little puzzled.

"Harlan, are you ill? Cooper tells me you've skipped several discussion periods."

Harlan tried to smooth the trouble out of his face. "No, Computer Twissell. I'm a little tired."

"Well, that's forgivable, at any rate, boy." And then the smile on his face came about as close as it ever did to vanishing entirely. "Have you heard that the 482nd had been Changed?"

"Yes," said Harlan shortly.

"Finge called me," said Twissell, "and asked that you be told that the Change was entirely successful."

Harlan shrugged, then grew aware of Twissell's eyes staring

out of the Communiplate and hard upon him. He grew uneasy and said, "Yes, Computer?"

"Nothing," said Twissell, and perhaps it was the cloak of age weighing down upon his shoulders, but his voice was unaccountably sad. "I thought you were about to speak."

"No," said Harlan. "I had nothing to say."

"Well, then, I'll see you tomorrow at opening in the Computing Room, boy. I have a great deal to say."

"Yes, sir," said Harlan. He stared for long minutes at the plate after it went dark.

That had almost sounded like a threat. Finge had called Twissell, had he? What had he said that Twissell did not report?

But an outside threat was what he needed. Battling a sickness of the spirit was like standing in a quicksand and beating it with a stick. Battling Finge was another thing altogether. Harlan had remembered the weapon at his disposal and for the first time in days felt a fraction of self-confidence return.

It was as though a door had closed and another had opened. Harlan grew as feverishly active as previously he had been catatonic. He travelled to the 2456th and bludgeoned Sociologist Voy to his own exact will.

He did it perfectly. He got the information he sought.

And more than he sought. Much more.

Confidence is rewarded, apparently. There was a homewhen proverb that went: "Grip the nettle firmly and it will become a stick with which to beat your enemy."

In short, Noÿs had no analogue in the new Reality. No analogue at all. She could take her position in the new society in the most inconspicuous and convenient manner possible, or she could stay in Eternity. There could be no reason to deny him liaison except for the highly theoretical fact that he had broken the law – and he knew very well how to counter that argument.

So he went racing upwhen to tell Noÿs the great news, to bathe in undreamed-of success after a few days horrible with apparent failure.

And at this moment the kettle came to a halt.

It did not slow; it simply halted. If the motion had been one along any of the three dimensions of space, a halt that sudden would have smashed the kettle, brought its metal to a dull red heat, turned Harlan into a thing of broken bone and wet, crushed flesh.

As it was, it merely doubled him with nausea and cracked him with inner pain.

When he could see, he fumbled to the temporometer and stared at it with fuzzy vision. It read 100,000.

Somehow that frightened him. It was too round a number.

He turned feverishly to the controls. What had gone wrong?

That frightened him, too, for he could see nothing wrong. Nothing had tripped the drive-lever. It remained firmly geared into the upwhen drive. There was no short circuit. All the indicator dials were in the black safety range. There was no power failure. The tiny needle that marked the steady consumption of meg-megcoulombs of power calmly insisted that power was being consumed at the usual rate.

What, then, had stopped the kettle?

Slowly, and with considerable reluctance, Harlan touched the drive-lever, curled his hand about it. He pushed it to neutral, and the needle on the power gauge declined to zero.

He twisted the drive-lever back in the other direction. Up went the power gauge again, and this time the temporometer flicked downwhen along the line of Centuries.

Downwhen – downwhen – 99,983 – 99,972, – 99,959 –

Again Harlan shifted the lever. Upwhen again. Slowly. Very slowly.

Then 99,985 – 99,993 – 99,997 – 99,998 – 99,999 – 100,000 –

Smash! Nothing past 100,000. The power of Nova Sol was silently being consumed, at an incredible rate, to no purpose.

He went downwhen again, farther. He roared upwhen. Smash!

His teeth were clenched, his lips drawn back, his breath rasping. He felt like a prisoner hurling himself bloodily against the bars of a prison.

When he stopped, a dozen smashes later, the kettle rested firmly at 100,000. Thus far, and no farther.

He would change kettles! (But there was not much hope in that thought.)

In the empty silence of the 100,000th Century, Andrew Harlan stepped out of one kettle and chose another kettle shaft at random.

A minute later, with the drive-lever in his hand, he stared at the marking of 100,000 and knew that here, too, he could not pass.

He raged! Now! At this time! When things so unexpectedly had broken in his favour, to come to so sudden a disaster. The

103

curse of that moment of misjudgement in entering the 482nd was still on him.

Savagely he spun the lever downwhen, pressing it hard at maximum and keeping it there. At least in one way he was free now, free to do anything he wanted. With Noÿs cut off behind a barrier and out of his reach, what more could they do to him? What more had he to fear?

He carried himself to the 575th and sprang from the kettle with a reckless disregard for his surroundings that he had never felt before. He made his way to the Section Library, speaking to no one, regarding no one. He took what he wanted without glancing about to see if he were observed. What did he care?

Back to the kettle and downwhen again. He knew exactly what he would do. He looked at the large clock as he passed, measuring off Standard Physiotime, numbering the days and marking off the three coequal work shifts of the physioday. Finge would be at his private quarters now, and that was so much the better.

Harlan felt as though he were running a temperature when he arrived at the 482nd. His mouth was dry and cottony. His chest hurt. But he felt the hard shape of the weapon under his shirt as he held it firmly against his side with one elbow and that was the only sensation that counted.

Assistant Computer Hobbe Finge looked up at Harlan, and the surprise in his eyes slowly gave way to concern.

Harlan watched him silently for a while, letting the concern grow and waiting for it to change to fear. He circled slowly, getting between Finge and the Communiplate.

Finge was partly undressed, bare to the waist. His chest was sparsely haired, his breasts puffy and almost womanish. His tubby abdomen lapped over his waistband.

He looked undignified, thought Harlan with satisfaction, undignified and unsavoury. So much the better.

He put his right hand inside his shirt and closed it firmly on the grip of his weapon.

Harlan said, "No one saw me, Finge, so don't look towards the door. No one's coming here. You've got to realize, Finge, that you're dealing with a Technician. Do you know what that means?"

His voice was hollow. He felt angry that fear wasn't entering

Finge's eyes, only concern. Finge even reached for his shirt and, without a word, began to put it on.

Harlan went on, "Do you know the privilege of being a Technician, Finge? You've never been one, so you can't appreciate it. It means no one watches where you go or what you do. They all look the other way and work so hard at not seeing you that they really succeed at it. I could, for instance, go to the Section library, Finge, and help myself to any curious thing while the librarian busily concerns himself with his records and sees nothing. I can walk down the residential corridors of the 482nd and anyone passing turns out of my way and will swear later on he saw no one. It's that automatic. So you see, I can do what I want to do, go where I want to go. I can walk into the private apartments of the Assistant Computer of a Section and force him to tell the truth at weapon point and there'll be no one to stop me."

Finge spoke for the first time. "What are you holding?"

"A weapon," said Harlan, and brought it out. "Do you recognize it?" Its muzzle flared slightly and ended in a smooth metallic bulge.

"If you kill me ..." began Finge.

"I won't kill you," said Harlan. "At a recent meeting you had a blaster. This is not a blaster. It is an invention of one of the past Realities of the 575th. Perhaps you are not acquainted with it. It was bred out of Reality. Too nasty. It can kill, but at low power it activates the pain centres of the nerve system and paralyzes as well. It is called, or was called, a neuronic whip. It works. This one is fully charged. I tested it on a finger." He held up his left hand with its stiffened little finger. "It was very unpleasant."

Finge stirred restlessly. "What is all this about, for Time's sake?"

"There is some sort of a block across the kettle shafts at the 100,000th. I want it removed."

"A block across the shafts?"

"Let's not work away at being surprised. Yesterday you spoke to Twissell. Today there is the block. I want to know what you said to Twissell. I want to know what's been done and what will be done. By Time, Computer, if you don't tell me, I'll use the whip. Try me, if you doubt my word."

"Now listen" – Finge's words slurred a bit and the first edge of fear made its appearance, and also a kind of desperate anger – "if you want the truth, it's this. We know about you and Noÿs."

Harlan's eyes flickered. "What about myself and Noÿs?"

Finge said, "Did you think you were getting away with anything?" The Computer kept his eyes fixed on the neuronic whip and his forehead was beginning to glisten. "By Time, with the emotion you showed after your period of Observation, with what you did during the period of Observation, did you think we wouldn't observe *you*? I would deserve to be broken as Computer if I had missed that. We know you brought Noÿs into Eternity. We knew it from the first. You wanted the truth. There it is."

At that moment Harlan despised his own stupidity. "You knew?"

"Yes. We knew you had brought her to the Hidden Centuries. We knew every time you entered the 482nd to supply her with appropriate luxuries; playing the fool, with your Eternal's Oath completely forgotten."

"Then why didn't you stop me?" Harlan was tasting the very dregs of his own humiliation.

"Do you still want the truth?" Finge flashed back, and seemed to gain courage in proportion as Harlan sank into frustration.

"Go on."

"Then let me tell you that I didn't consider you a proper Eternal from the start. A flashy Observer, perhaps, and a Technician who went through the motions. But no Eternal. When I brought you here on this last job, it was to prove as much to Twissell, who values you for some obscure reason. I wasn't just testing the society in the person of the girl, Noÿs. I was testing you, too, and you failed as I thought you would fail. Now put away that weapon, that whip, whatever it is, and get out of here."

"And you came to my personal quarters once," said Harlan breathlessly, working hard to keep his dignity and feeling it slip from him as though his mind and spirit were as stiff and unfeeling as the whip-lashed little finger on his left hand. "to goad me into doing what I did."

"Yes, of course. If you want the phrase exactly, I tempted you. I told you the exact truth, that you could keep Noÿs only in the then-present Reality. You chose to act, not as an Eternal, but as a sniveller. I expected you to."

"I would do it again now," said Harlan gruffly, "and since it's all known, you can see I have nothing to lose." He thrust his whip outward towards Finge's plump waistline and spoke through pale lips and clenched teeth. "What has happened to Noÿs?"

"I have no idea."

"Don't tell me that. What has happen to Noÿs?"

"I tell you I don't know."

Harlan's fist tightened on the whip; his voice was low. "Your leg first. This will hurt."

"For Time's sake, listen. Wait!"

"All right. What has happened to her?"

"No, listen. So far its just a breach of discipline. Reality wasn't affected. I made checks on that. Loss of rating is all you'll get. If you kill me, though, or hurt me with intent to kill, you've attacked a superior. There's the death penalty for that."

Harlan smiled at the futility of the threat. In the face of what had already happened death would offer a way out that in finality and simplicity had no equal.

Finge obviously misunderstood the reasons for the smile. He said hurriedly, "Don't think there's no death penalty in Eternity because you've never come across one. We know of them; we Computers. What's more, executions have taken place, too. It's simple. In any Reality, there are numbers of fatal accidents in which bodies are not recovered. Rockets explode in mid-air, aeroliners sink in mid-ocean or crash to powder in mountains. A murderer can be put on one of those vessels minutes, or seconds, before the fatal results. Is this worth that to you?"

Harlan stirred and said, "If you're stalling for rescue, it won't work. Let me tell you this: I'm not afraid of punishment. Furthermore, I intend to have Noÿs. I want her now. She does not exist in the current Reality. She had no analogue. There is no reason why we cannot establish formal liaison."

"It is against regulations for a Technician –"

"We will let the Allwhen Council decide," said Harlan, and his pride broke through at last. "I am not afraid of an adverse decision, either, any more than I am afraid of killing you. I am no ordinary Technician."

"Because you are Twissell's Technician?" and there was a strange look on Finge's round, sweating face that might have been hatred or triumph or part of each.

Harlan said, "For reasons much more important than that. And now . . ."

With grim determination he touched finger to the weapon's activator.

Finge screamed, "Then go to the Council. The Allwhen Council; *they* know. If you are that important –" He ended, gasping.

For a moment Harlan's finger hovered irresolutely. "What?"

"Do you think I would take unilateral action in a case like this? I reported this whole incident to the Council, timing it with the Reality Change. Here! Here are the duplicates."

"Hold on, don't move."

But Finge disregarded that order. With a speed as from the spur of a possessing fiend Finge was at his files. The fingers of one hand located the code combination of the record he wanted, the fingers of the other punched it into the file. A silvery tongue of tape slithered out of the desk, its pattern of dots just visible to the naked eye.

"Do you want it sounded?" asked Finge, and without waiting threaded it into the sounder.

Harlan listened, frozen. It was clear enough. Finge had reported in full. He had detailed every motion of Harlan's in the kettle shafts. He hadn't missed one that Harlan could remember up to the point of making the report.

Finge shouted when the report was done, "Now, then, go to the Council. I've put no block in Time. I wouldn't know how. And don't think they're unconcerned about the matter. You said I spoke to Twissell yesterday. You're right. But I didn't call him; he called me. So go; ask Twissell. Tell them what an important Technician you are. And if you want to shoot me first; shoot and to Time with you."

Harlan could not miss the actual exultation in the Computer's voice. At that moment he obviously felt enough the victor to believe that even a neuronic whipping would leave him on the profit side of the ledger.

Why? Was the breaking of Harlan so dear to his heart? Was his jealousy over Noÿs so all-consuming a passion?

Harlan did scarcely more than formulate the questions in his mind, and then the whole matter, Finge and all, seemed suddenly meaningless to him.

He pocketed his weapon, whirled out the door, and towards the nearest kettle shaft.

It was the Council, then, or Twissell, at the very least. He was afraid of none of them, nor of all put together.

With each passing day of the last unbelievable month he had grown more convinced of his own indispensability. The Council, even the Allwhen Council itself, would have no choice but to come to terms when it was a choice of bartering one girl for the existence of all of Eternity.

CHAPTER ELEVEN

FULL CIRCLE

IT was with a dull surprise that Technician Andrew Harlan, on bursting into the 575th, found himself in the night shift. The passing of the physiohours had gone unnoticed during his wild streaks along the kettle shafts. He stared hollowly at the dimmed corridors, the occasional evidence of the thinned-out night force at work.

But in the continued grip of his rage Harlan did not pause long to watch uselessly. He turned towards personal quarters. He would find Twissell's room on Computer Level as he had found Finge's and he had as little fear of being noticed or stopped.

The neuronic whip was still hard against his elbow as he stopped before Twissell's door (the name plate upon it advertising the fact in clear, inlaid lettering).

Harlan activated the door signal brashly on the buzzer level. He shorted the contact with a damp palm and let the sound become continuous. He could hear it dimly.

A step sounded lightly behind him and he ignored it in the sure knowledge that the man, whoever he was, would ignore him. (Oh, rose-red Technician's patch!)

But the sound of steps halted and a voice said, "Technician Harlan?"

Harlan whirled. It was a Junior Computer, relatively new to the Section. Harlan raged inwardly. This was not quite the 482nd. Here he was not merely a Technician, he was Twissell's Technician, and the younger Computers, in their anxiety to ingratiate themselves with the great Twissell, would extend a minimum civility to his Technician.

The Computer said, "Do you wish to see Senior Computer Twissell?"

Harlan fidgeted and said, "Yes, sir." (The fool! What did he think anyone would be standing signalling at a man's door for? To catch a kettle?)

"I'm afraid you can't," said the Computer.

"This is important enough to wake him," said Harlan.

"Maybe so," said the other, "but he's outwhen. He's not in the 575th."

"Exactly when is he, then?" asked Harlan impatiently.

The Computer's glance became a supercilious stare. "I wouldn't know."

Harlan said, "But I have an important appointment first thing in the morning."

"*You* have," said the Computer, and Harlan was at a loss to account for his obvious amusement at the thought.

The Computer went on, even smiling now, "You're a little early, aren't you?"

"But I must see him."

"I'm sure he'll be here in the morning." The smile broadened.

"But –"

The Computer passed by Harlan, carefully avoiding any contact, even of garments.

Harlan's fists clenched and unclenched. He stared helplessly after the Computer and then, simply because there was nothing else to do, he walked slowly, and without full consciousness of his surroundings, back to his own room.

Harlan slept fitfully. He told himself he needed sleep. He tried to relax by main force, and, of course, failed. His sleep period was a succession of futile thought.

First of all, there was Noÿs.

They would not dare harm her, he thought feverishly. They could not send her back to Time without first calculating the effect on Reality and that would take days, probably weeks. As an alternative, they might do to her what Finge had threatened for him; place her in the path of an untraceable accident.

He did not take that into serious consideration. There was no necessity for drastic action such as that. They would not risk Harlan's displeasure by doing it. (In the quiet of a darkened sleeping room, and in that phase of half sleep where things often grew queerly disproportionate in thought, Harlan found nothing grotesque in his sure opinion that the Allwhen Council would not dare risk a Technician's displeasure.)

Of course, there were uses to which a woman in captivity might be put. A beautiful woman from a hedonistic Reality ...

Resolutely Harlan put the thought away as often as it returned. It was at once more likely and more unthinkable than death, and he would have none of it.

He thought of Twissell.

The old man was out of the 575th. Where was he during hours when he should have been asleep? An old man needs his sleep. Harlan was sure of the answer. There were Council consultations going on. About Harlan. About Noÿs. About what to do with an indispensable Technician one dared not touch.

Harlan's lips drew back. If Finge reported Harlan's assault of that evening, it would not affect their considerations in the least. His crimes could scarcely be worsened by it. His indispensability would certainly not be lessened.

And Harlan was by no means certain that Finge *would* report him. To admit having been forced to cringe before a Technician would put an Assistant Computer in a ridiculous light, and Finge might not choose to do so.

Harlan thought of Technicians as a group, which, of late, he had done rarely. His own somewhat anomalous position as Twissell's man and as half an Educator had kept him too far apart from other Technicians. But Technicians lacked solidarity anyway. Why should that be?

Did he have to go through the 575th and the 482nd rarely seeing or speaking to another Technician? Did they have to avoid even one another? Did they have to act as though they accepted the status into which the superstition of others forced them?

In his mind he had already forced the capitulation of the Council as far as Noÿs was concerned, and now he was making further demands. The Technicians were to be allowed an organization of their own, regular meetings – more friendship – better treatment from the others.

His final thought of himself was as a heroic social revolutionary, with Noÿs at his side, when he sank finally into a dreamless sleep. ...

The door signal awoke him. It whispered at him with hoarse impatience. He collected his thoughts to the point of being able to look at the small clock beside his bed and groaned inwardly.

111

Father Time! After all that he had overslept.

He managed to reach the proper button from bed and the view-square high on the door grew transparent. He did not recognize the face, but it carried authority whoever it was.

He opened the door and the man, wearing the orange patch of Administration, stepped in.

"Technician Andrew Harlan?"

"Yes, Administrator? You have business with me?"

The Administrator seemed in no wise discommoded at the sharp belligerence of the question. He said, "You have an appointment with Senior Computer Twissell?"

"Well?"

"I am here to inform you that you are late."

Harlan stared at him. "What's this all about? You're not from the 575th, are you?"

"The 222nd is my station," said the other frigidly. "Assistant Administrator Arbut Lemm. I'm in charge of the arrangements and I'm trying to avoid undue excitement by by-passing official notification over the Communiplate."

"What arrangements? What excitement? What's it all about? Listen, I've had conferences with Twissell before. He's my superior. There's no excitement involved."

A look of surprise passed momentarily over the studious look of expression the Administrator had so far kept on his face. "You haven't been informed?"

"About what?"

"Why, that a subcommittee of the Allwhen Council is holding session here at the 575th. This place, I am told, has been alive with the news for hours."

"And they want to see me?" As soon as he asked that, Harlan thought: Of course they want to see me. What else could the session be about but me?

And he understood the amusement of the Junior Computer last night outside Twissell's room. The Computer knew of the projected committee meeting and it amused him to think that a Technician could possibly expect to see Twissell at a time like that. Very amusing, thought Harlan bitterly.

The Administrator said, "I have my orders. I know nothing more." Then, still surprised, "You've heard nothing of this?"

"Technicians," said Harlan sarcastically, "lead sheltered lives."

112

Five besides Twissell! Senior Computers all, none less than thirty-five years an Eternal.

Six weeks earlier Harlan would have been overwhelmed by the honour of sitting at lunch with such a group, tongue-tied by the combination of responsibility and power they represented. They would have seemed twice life-size to him.

But now they were antagonists of his, worse still, judges. He had no time to be impressed. He had to plan his strategy.

They might not know that he was aware they had Noÿs. They could not know unless Finge told them of his last meeting with Harlan. In the clear light of day, however, he was more than ever convinced that Finge was not the man to broadcast publicly the fact that he had been browbeaten and insulted by a Technician.

It seemed advisable, then, for Harlan to nurse this possible advantage for the time being, to let *them* make the first move, say the first sentence that would join actual combat.

They seemed in no hurry. They stared at him placidly over an abstemious lunch as though he were an interesting specimen spread-eagled against a plane of force by mild repulsors. In desperation Harlan stared back.

He knew all of them by reputation and by trimensional reproduction in the physiomonthly orientation films. The films co-ordinated developments throughout the various Sections of Eternity and were required viewing for all Eternals with rating from Observer up.

August Sennor, the bald one (not even eyebrows or eyelashes), of course attracted Harlan most. First, because the odd appearance of those dark, staring eyes against bare eyelids and forehead was remarkably greater in person than it had ever seemed in trimension. Second, because of his knowledge of past collisions of view between Sennor and Twissell. Finally, because Sennor did not confine himself to watching Harlan. He shot questions at him in a sharp voice.

For the most part his questions were unanswerable, such as: "How did you first come to be interested in Primitive times, young man?" "Do you find the study rewarding, young man?"

Finally, he seemed to settle himself in his seat. He pushed his plate casually on to the disposal chute and clasped his thick fingers lightly before him. (There was no hair on the back of the hands, Harlan noticed.)

Sennor said, "There is something I have always wanted to

113

know. Perhaps you can help me."

Harlan thought. All right, now, this is it.

Aloud he said, "If I can, sir."

"Some of us here in Eternity – I won't say all, or even enough" (and he cast a quick glance at Twissell's tired face, while the others drew closer to listen) "but some, at any rate – are interested in the philosophy of Time. Perhaps you know what I mean."

"The paradoxes of Time-travel, sir?"

"Well, if you want to put it melodramatically, yes. But that's not all, of course. There is the question of the true nature of Reality, the question of the conservation of mass-energy during Reality Change and so on. Now we in Eternity are influenced in our consideration of such things by knowing the facts of Time-travel. Your creatures of the Primitive era, however, knew nothing of time-travel. What were *their* views on the matter?"

Twissell's whisper carried the length of the table. "Cobwebs!"

But Sennor ignored that. He said, "Would you answer my question, Technician?"

Harlan said, "The Primitives gave virtually no thought to Time-travel, Computer."

"Did not consider it possible, eh?"

"I believe that's right."

"Did not even speculate?"

"Well, as to that," said Harlan uncertainly, "I believe there were speculations of sorts in some types of escape literature. I am not well acquainted with these, but I believe a recurrent theme was that of the man who returned in Time to kill his own grandfather as a child."

Sennor seemed delighted. "Wonderful! Wonderful! After all, that is at least an expression of the basic paradox of Time-travel, if we assume an indeviant Reality, eh? Now your Primitives, I'll venture to state, never assumed anything *but* an indeviant Reality. Am I right?"

Harlan waited to answer. He did not see where the conversation was aiming or what Sennor's deeper purposes were, and it unnerved him. He said, "I don't know enough to answer you with certainty, sir. I believe there may have been speculations as to alternate paths of time or planes of existence. I don't know."

Sennor thrust out a lower lip. "I'm sure you're wrong. You may have been misled by reading your own knowledge into

114

various ambiguities you may have come across. No, without actual experience of Time-travel, the philosophic intricacies of Reality would be quite beyond the human mind. For instance, why does Reality possess inertia? We all know that it does. Any alteration in its flow must reach a certain magnitude before a Change, a true Change, is effected. Even then, Reality has a tendency to flow back to its original position.

"For instance, suppose a Change here in the 575th. Reality will change with increasing effects to perhaps the 600th. It will change, but with continually lesser effects to perhaps the 650th. Thereafter, Reality will be unchanged. We all know this is so, but do any of us know why it is so? Intuitive reasoning would suggest that any Reality Change would increase its effects without limit as the Centuries pass, yet that is not so.

"Take another point. Technician Harlan, I'm told, is excellent at selecting the exact Minimum Change Required for any situation. I'll wager he cannot explain how he arrives at his own choice.

"Consider how helpless the Primitives must be. They worry about a man killing his own grandfather because they do not understand the truth about Reality. Take a more likely and a more easily analysed case and let's consider the man who in his travels through time meets himself –"

Harlan said sharply, "What about a man who meets himself?"

The fact that Harlan interrupted a Computer was a breach of manners in itself. His tone of voice worsened the breach to a scandalous extent, and all eyes turned reproachfully on the Technician.

Sennor harumphed, but spoke in the strained tone of one determined to be polite despite nearly insuperable difficulties. He said, continuing his broken sentence and thus avoiding the appearance of answering directly the unmannerly question addressed to him, "And the four subdivisions into which such an act can fall. Call the man earlier in physiotime, A, and the one later, B. Subdivision one A and B may not see one another, or do anything that will significantly affect one another. In that case, they have not really met and we may discuss this case as trivial.

"Or B, the later individual, may see A while A does not see B. Here, too, no serious consequences need be expected. B, seeing A, seems him in a position and engaged in activity of which he already has knowledge. Nothing new is involved.

"The third and fourth possibilities are that A sees B, while B does not see A, and that A and B see one another. In each possibility, the serious point is that A has seen B; the man at an earlier stage in his physiological existence sees himself at a later stage. Observe that he has learned he will be alive at the apparent age of B. He knows he will live long enough to perform the action he has witnessed. Now a man in knowing his own future in even the slightest detail can act on that knowledge and therefore change his future. It follows that Reality must be changed to the extent of not allowing A and B to meet or, at the very least, of preventing A from seeing B. Then, since nothing in a Reality made un-Real can be detected, A never has met B. Similarly, in every apparent paradox of Time-travel, Reality always changes to avoid the paradox and we come to the conclusion that there are no paradox and we come to the conclusion that there are no paradoxes in Time-travel and that there can be none."

Sennor looked well pleased with himself and his exposition, but Twissell rose to his feet.

Twissell said, "I believe, gentlemen, that time presses."

Far more suddenly than Harlan would have thought the lunch was over. Five of the subcommittee members filed out, nodding at him, with the air of those whose curiosity, mild at best, had been assuaged. Only Sennor held out a hand and added a gruff "Good day, young man" to the nod.

With mixed feelings Harlan watched them go. What had been the purpose of the luncheon? Most of all, why the reference to men meeting themselves? They had made no mention of Noÿs. Were they there, then, only to study him? Survey him from top to bottom and leave him to Twissell's judging?

Twissell returned to the table, empty now of food and cutlery. He was alone with Harlan now, and almost as though to symbolize that he wielded a new cigarette between his fingers.

He said, "And now to work, Harlan. We have a great deal to do."

But Harlan would not, could not, wait longer. He said flatly, "Before we do anything, I have something to say."

Twissell looked surprised. The skin of his face puckered up about his faded eyes, and he tamped at the ash end of his cigarette thoughtfully.

He said, "By all means, speak if you wish, but first, sit down, sit down, boy."

Technician Andrew Harlan did not sit down. He strode up and back the length of the table, biting off his sentences hard to keep them from boiling and bubbling into incoherence. Senior Computer Laban Twissell's age-yellowed pippin of a head turned back and forth as he followed the other's nervous stride.

Harlan said, "For weeks now I've been going through films on the history of mathematics. Books from several Realities of the 575th. The Realities don't matter much. Mathematics doesn't change. The order of its development doesn't change either. No matter how else the Realities shifted, mathematical history stayed about the same. The mathematicians changed; different ones switched discoveries, but the end results – Anyway, I pounded a lot of it into my head. How does that strike you?"

Twissell frowned and said, "A queer occupation for a Technician?"

"But I'm not just a Technician," said Harlan. "You know that."

"Go on," said Twissell and he looked at the timepiece he wore. The fingers that held his cigarette played with it with unwonted nervousness.

Harlan said, "There was a man named Vikkor Mallansohn who lived in the 24th Century. That was part of the Primitive era, you know. The thing he is known best for is the fact that he first successfully built a Temporal Field. That means, of course, that he invented Eternity, since Eternity is only one tremendous Temporal Field short-circuiting ordinary Time and free of the limitations of ordinary Time."

"You were taught this as a Cub, boy."

"But I was not taught that Vikkor Mallansohn could not possibly have invented the Temporal Field in the 24th Century. Nor could anyone have. The mathematical basis for it didn't exist. The fundamental Lefebvre equations did not exist; nor could they exist until the researches of Jan Verdeer in the 27th Century."

If there was one sign by which Senior Computer Twissell could indicate complete astonishment, it was that of dropping his cigarette. He dropped it now. Even his smile was gone.

He said, "Were you taught the Lefebvre equations, boy?"

"No. And I don't say I understand them. But they're necessary for the Temporal Field. I've learned that. And they weren't discovered till the 27th. I know that, too."

Twissell bent to pick up his cigarette and regarded it dubiously. "What if Mallansohn had stumbled on the Temporal Field without being aware of the mathematical justification? What if it were simply an empirical discovery? There have been many such."

"I've thought of that. But after the Field was invented, it took three centuries to work out its implications and at the end of that time there was no way in which Mallansohn's Field could be improved on. That could not be coincidence. In a hundred ways, Mallansohn's design showed that he must have used the Lefebvre equations. If he knew them or had developed them without Verdeer's work, which is impossible, why didn't he say so?"

Twissell said, "You insist on talking like a mathematician. Who told you all this?"

"I've been viewing films."

"No more?"

"And thinking."

"Without advanced mathematical training? I've watched you closely for years, boy, and would not have guessed that particular talent of yours. Go on."

"Eternity could never have been established without Mallansohn's discovery of the Temporal Field. Mallansohn could never have accomplished this without a knowledge of mathematics that existed only in his future. That's number one. Meanwhile, here in Eternity at this moment, there is a Cub who was selected as an Eternal against all the rules, since he was overage and married, to boot. You are educating him in mathematics and in Primitive sociology. That's number two."

"Well?"

"I say that it is your intention to send him back into Time somehow, back past the downwhen terminus of Eternity, back to the 24th. It is your intention to have the Cub, Cooper, teach the Lefebvre equations to Mallansohn. You see, then," Harlan added with tense passion, "that my own position as expert in the Primitive and my knowledge of that position entitles me to special treatment. *Very* special treatment."

"Father Time!" muttered Twissell.

"It's true, isn't it? We come full circle, *with my help*. Without it . . ." He let the sentence hang.

"You come so close to the truth," said Twissell. "Yet I could swear there was nothing to indicate – " He fell into a study in which neither Harlan nor the outside world seemed to play a part.

Harlan said quickly, "Only close to the truth? It *is* the truth." He could not tell why he was so certain of the essentials of what he said, even quite apart from the fact that he so desperately wanted it to be so.

Twissell said, "No, no, not the exact truth. The Cub, Cooper, is not going back to the 24th to teach Mallansohn anything."

"I don't believe you."

"But you must. You must see the importance of this. I want your co-operation through what is left of the project. You see, Harlan, the situation is more full circle than you imagine. Much more so, boy. Cub Brinsley Sheridan Cooper *is* Vikkor Mallansohn!"

CHAPTER TWELVE

THE BEGINNING OF ETERNITY

HARLAN would not have thought that Twissell could have said anything at that moment that could have surprised him. He was wrong.

He said, "Mallansohn. He – "

Twissell, having smoked his cigarette to a stub, produced another and said, "Yes, Mallansohn. Do you want a quick summary of Mallansohn's life? Here it is. He was born in the 78th, spent some time in Eternity, and died in the 24th."

Twissell's small hand placed itself lightly on Harlan's elbow and his gnomish face broke into a wrinkled extension of his usual smile. "But come, boy, physiotime passes even for us and we are not completely masters of ourselves this day. Won't you come with me to my office?"

He led the way and Harlan followed, not entirely aware of the opening doors and the moving ramps.

He was relating the new information to his own problem and plan of action. With the passing of the first moment of disorientation his resolution returned. After all, how did this change things except to make his own importance to Eternity still more crucial, his value higher, his demands more sure to be met, Noÿs more certain to be bartered back to him.

Noÿs!

Father Time, they must not harm her! She seemed the only real part of his life. All Eternity beside was only a filmy fantasy, and not a worth-while one, either.

When he found himself in Computer Twissell's office, he could not clearly recall how it had come about that he had passed from the dining area here. Though he looked about and tried to make the office grow real by sheer force of the mass of its contents, it still seemed but another part of a dream that had outlived its usefulness.

Twissell's office was a clean, long room of porcelain asepsis. One wall of the office was crowded from floor to ceiling and wall to distant wall with the computing micro-units which, together, made up the largest privately operated Computaplex in Eternity and, indeed, one of the largest altogether. The opposite wall was crammed with reference films. Between the two what was left of the room was scarcely more than a corridor, broken by a desk, two chairs, recording and projecting equipment, and an unusual object the like of which Harlan was not familiar with and which did not reveal its use until Twissell flicked the remnants of a cigarette into it.

It flashed noiselessly and Twissell, in his usual prestidigitational fashion, held another in his hands.

Harlan thought: To the point, now.

He began, a trifle too loudly, a bit too truculently, "There is a girl in the 482nd – "

Twissell frowned, waved one hand quickly as though brushing an unpleasant matter hastily to one side. "I know, I know. She will not be disturbed, nor you. All will be well. I will see to it."

"Do you mean – "

"I tell you I know the story. If the matter has troubled you, it need trouble you no more."

Harlan stared at the old man, stupefied. Was this all? Though he had thought intently of the immensity of his power, he had not expected to clear a demonstration.

But Twissell was talking again.

"Let me tell you a story," he began, with almost the tone he would have used in addressing a newly inducted Cub. "I had not thought this would be necessary, and perhaps it still isn't, but your own researches and insight deserve it."

He stared at Harlan quizzically and said, "You know, I still

120

can't quite believe that you worked this out on your own," and then went on:

"The man most of Eternity knows as Vikkor Mallansohn left the record of his life behind him after he died. It was not quite a diary, not quite a biography. It was more of a guide, bequeathed to the Eternals he knew would someday exist. It was enclosed in a volume of Time-stasis which could be opened only by the Computers of Eternity, and which therefore remained untouched for three Centuries after his death, until Eternity was established and Senior Computer Henry Wadsman, the first of the great Eternals, opened it. The document has been passed along in strictest security since, along a line of Senior Computers ending with myself. It is referred to as the Mallansohn memoir.

"The memoir tells the story of a man named Brinsley Sheridan Cooper, born in the 78th, inducted as a Cub into Eternity at the age of twenty-three, having been married for a little over a year, but having been, as yet, childless.

"Having entered Eternity, Cooper was trained in mathematics by a Computer named Laban Twissell and in Primitive sociology by a Technician named Andrew Harlan. After a thorough grounding in both disciplines, and in such matters as temporal engineering as well, he was sent back to the 24th to teach certain necessary techniques to a Primitive scientist named Vikkor Mallansohn.

"Once having reached the 24th, he embarked first on a slow process of adjusting himself to the society. In this he benefited a great deal from the training of Technician Harlan and the detailed advice of Computer Twissell, who seemed to have an uncanny insight into some of the problems he was to face.

"After the passage of two years, Cooper located one Vikkor Mallansohn, an eccentric recluse in the California backwoods, relationless and friendless but gifted with a daring and unconventional mind. Cooper made friends slowly, acclimated the man to the thought of having met a traveller from the future still more slowly, and set about teaching the man the mathematics he must know.

"With the passage of time, Cooper adopted the other's habits, learned to shift for himself with the help of a clumsy Diesel-oil electric generator and with wired electrical appliances which freed them of dependence on power beams.

"But progress was slow and Cooper found himself something less than a marvellous teacher. Mallansohn grew morose and unco-operative and then one day died, quite suddenly, in a fall down a canyon of the wild, mountainous country in which they lived. Cooper, after weeks of despair, with the ruin of his life-work and, presumably, of all Eternity, staring him in the eye, decided on a desperate expedient. He did not report Mallansohn's death. Instead, he slowly took to building, out of the materials at hand, a Temporal Field.

"The details do not matter. He succeeded after mountains of drudgery and improvisation and took the generator to the California Institute of Technology, just as years before he had expected the real Mallansohn to do.

"You know the story from your own studies. You know of the disbelief and rebuffs he first met, his period under observation, his escape and the near-loss of his generator, the help he received from the man at the lunch counter whose name he never learned, but who is now one of Eternity's heroes, and of the final demonstration for Professor Zimbalist, in which a white mouse moved backwards and forwards in time. I won't bore you with any of that.

"Cooper used the name of Vikkor Mallansohn in all this because it gave him a background and made him an authentic product of the 24th. The body of the real Mallansohn was never recovered.

"In the remainder of his life, he cherished his generator and co-operated with the Institute scientists in duplicating it. He dared do no more than that. He could not teach them the Lefebvre equations without outlining three Centuries of Mathematical development that was to come. He could not, dared not hint at his true origin. He dared not do more than the real Vikkor Mallansohn had, to his knowledge, done.

"The men who worked with him were frustrated to find a man who could perform so brilliantly and yet was unable to explain the whys of his performance. And he himself was frustrated, too, because he foresaw, without in any way being able to quicken, the work that would lead, step by step, to the classic experiments of Jan Verdeer, and how from that the great Antoine Lefebvre would construct the basic equations of Reality. And how, after that, Eternity would be constructed.

"It was only towards the end of his long life that Cooper, staring into a Pacific sunset (he describes the scene in some detail in his memoir) came to the great realization that he was

122

Vikkor Mallansohn; he was not a substitute but the man himself. The name might not be his, but the man history called Mallansohn was really Brinsley Sheridan Cooper.

"Fired with that thought, and with all that implied, anxious that the process of establishing Eternity be somehow quickened, improved, and made more secure, he wrote his memoir and placed it in a cube of Time-stasis in the living-room of his house.

"And so the circle was closed. Cooper-Mallansohn's intentions in writing the memoir were, of course, disregarded. Cooper must go through his life exactly as he had gone through it. Primitive Reality allows of no changes. At this moment in physiotime, the Cooper you know is unaware of what lies ahead of him. He believes he is only to instruct Mallansohn and to return. He will continue to believe so until the years teach him differently and he sits down to write his memoir.

"The intention of the circle in Time is to establish the knowledge of Time-travel and of the nature of Reality, to build Eternity, ahead of its natural Time. Left to itself, mankind would not have learned the truth about Time before their technological advances in other directions had made racial suicide inevitable."

Harlan listened intently, caught up in the vision of a mighty circle in Time, closed upon itself, and traversing Eternity in part of its course. He came as close to forgetting Noÿs, for the moment, as he ever could.

He asked, "Then you knew all along everything you were to do, everything I was to do, everything I *have* done."

Twissell, who seemed lost in his own telling of the tale, his eyes peering through a haze of bluish tobacco smoke, came slowly to life. His old, wise eyes fixed themselves on Harlan and he said reproachfully, "No, of course not. There was a lapse of decades of physiotime between Cooper's stay in Eternity and the moment when he wrote his memoir. He could remember only so much, and only what he himself had witnessed. You should realize that."

Twissell sighed and he drew a gnarled finger through a line of updrafting smoke, breaking it into little turbulent swirls. "It worked itself out. First, I was found and brought to Eternity. When, in the fullness of physiotime, I became a Senior Computer, I was given the memoir and placed in charge. I had been described as in charge, so I was placed in charge. Again in the fullness of physiotime, you appeared in the chang-

123

ing of a Reality (we had watched your earlier analogues carefully), and then Cooper.

"I filled in the details by using my common sense and the services of the Computaplex. How carefully, for instance, we instructed Educator Yarrow in his part while betraying none of the significant truth. How carefully, in his turn, he stimulated your interest in the Primitive.

"How carefully we had had to keep Cooper from learning anything he did not prove he had learned by reference in the memoir." Twissell smiled sadly. "Sennor amuses himself with matters such as this. He calls it the reversal of cause and effect. Knowing the effect, one adjusts the cause. Fortunately, I am not the cobweb spinner Sennor is.

"I was pleased, boy, to find you so excellent an Observer and Technician. The memoir had not mentioned that since Cooper had no opportunity to observe your work or evaluate it. This suited me. I could use you in a more ordinary task that would make your essential one less noticeable. Even your recent stay with Computer Finge fitted in. Cooper mentioned a period of your absence during which his mathematical studies were so sharpened that he longed for your return. Once, though, you frightened me."

Harlan said, at once, "You mean the time I took Cooper along the kettle ways."

"How do you come to guess that?" demanded Twissell.

"It was the one time you were really angry with me. I suppose now it went against something in the Mallansohn memoir."

"Not quite. It was just that the memoir did not speak of the kettles. It seemed to me that to avoid mention of such an outstanding aspect of Eternity meant he had little experience with it. It was my intention therefore to keep him away from the kettles as much as possible. The fact that you had taken him upwhen in one disturbed me greatly, but nothing happened afterwards. Things continued as they should, so all is well."

The old Computer rubbed one hand slowly over the other, staring at the young Technician with a look compounded of surprise and curiosity. "And all along you've been guessing this. It simply astonishes me. I would have sworn that even a fully trained Computer could not have made the proper deductions, given only the information you had. For a Technician to do it is uncanny." He leaned forward, tapped Harlan's knee lightly. "The Mallansohn memoir says nothing about your life after

Cooper's leaving, of course."

"I understand, sir," said Harlan.

"We will be free then, in a manner of speaking, to do as we please with it. You show a surprising talent that must not be wasted. I think you are meant for something more than a Technician. I promise nothing now, but I presume that you realize that Computership is a distinct possibility."

It was easy for Harlan to keep his dark face expressionless. He had had years of practice for that.

He thought: An additional bribe.

But nothing must be left to conjecture. His guesses, wild and unsupported at the start, arrived at by a freak of insight in the course of a very unusual and stimulating night, had become reasonable as the result of directed library research. They had become certainties now that Twissell had told him the story. Yet in one way at least there had been a deviation. Cooper was Mallansohn.

That had simply improved his position, but, wrong in one respect, he might be wrong in another. He must leave nothing to chance, then. Have it out! Make certain!

He said levelly, almost casually, "The responsibility is great for me, also, now that I know the truth."

"Yes, indeed?"

"How fragile is the situation? Suppose something unexpected were to happen and I were to miss a day when I ought to have been teaching Cooper something vital."

"I don't understand you."

(Was it Harlan's imagination, or had a spark of alarm sprung to life in those old, tired eyes?)

"I mean, can the circle break? Let me put it this way. If an unexpected blow on the head puts me out of action at a time when the memoir distinctly states I am well and active, is the whole scheme disrupted? Or suppose, for some reason, I deliberately choose not to follow the memoir. What then?"

"But what puts all this in your mind?"

"It seems a logical thought. It seems to me that by a careless or wilful action, I could break the circle, and well, what? Destroy Eternity? It seems to be so. If it *is* so," Harlan added composedly, "I ought to be told that I may be careful to do nothing unfitting. Though I imagine it would take a rather unusual circumstance to drive me to such a thing."

Twissell laughed, but the laughter rang false and empty in

Harlan's ear. "This is all purely academic, my boy. Nothing of this will happen since it hasn't happened. The full circle will not break."

"It might," said Harlan. "The girl of the 482nd – "

"Is safe," said Twissell. He rose impatiently. "There's no end to this kind of talk and I have quite enough of logic-chopping from the rest of the subcommittee in charge of the project. Meanwhile, I have yet to tell *you* what I originally called you here to hear and physiotime is still passing. Will you come with me?"

Harlan was satisfied. The situation was clear and his power unmistakable. Twissell knew that Harlan could say, at will, "I will no longer have anything to do with Cooper." Twissell knew Harlan could at any moment destroy Eternity by giving Cooper significant information concerning the memoir.

Harlan had known enough to do this yesterday. Twissell had thought to overwhelm him with the knowledge of the importance of his task, but if the Computer had thought to force Harlan into line in that way, he was mistaken.

Harlan had made his threat very clear with respect to Noÿs's safety, and Twissell's expression as he had barked, "Is safe," showed he realized the nature of the threat.

Harlan rose and followed Twissell.

Harlan had never been in the room they now entered. It was large and looked as though walls had been knocked down for its sake. It had been entered through a narrow corridor which had been blocked off by a force-screen that did not go down until after a pause sufficient for Twissell's face to be scanned thoroughly by automatic machinery.

The largest part of the room was filled by a sphere that reached nearly to the ceiling. A door was open, showing four small steps leading to a well-lit platform within.

Voices sounded from inside and even as Harlan watched, legs appeared in the opening and descended the steps. A man emerged and another pair of legs appeared behind him. It was Sennor of the Allwhen Council and behind him was another of the group at the breakfast table.

Twissell did not look pleased at this. His voice, however, was restrained. "Is the subcommittee still here?"

"Only we two," said Sennor casually, "Rice and myself. A

126

beautiful instrument we have here. It has the level of complexity of a spaceship."

Rice was a paunchy man with the perplexed look of one who is accustomed to being right yet finds himself unaccountably on the losing side of an argument. He rubbed his bulbous nose and said, "Sennor's mind is running on space-travel lately."

Sennor's bald head glistened in the light. "It's a neat point, Twissell," he said. "I put it to you. Is space-travel a positive factor or a negative in the calculus of Reality?"

"The question is meaningless," said Twissell impatiently. "What type of space-travel in what society under what circumstances?"

"Oh, come. Surely there's something to be said concerning space-travel in the abstract."

"Only that it is self-limiting, that it exhausts itself and dies out."

"Then it is useless," said Sennor with satisfaction, "and therefore it is a negative factor. My view entirely."

"If you please," said Twissell, "Cooper will be here soon. We will need the floor clear."

"By all means." Sennor hooked an arm under that of Rice and led him away. His voice declaimed clearly as they departed. "Periodically, my dear Rice, all the mental effort of mankind is concentrated on space-travel, which is doomed to a frustrated end by the nature of things. I would set up the matrices except that I am certain this is obvious to you. With minds concentrated on space, there is neglect of the proper development of things earthly. I am preparing a thesis now for submission to the Council recommending that Realities be changed to eliminate all space-travel eras as a matter of course."

Rice's treble sounded. "But you can't be that drastic. Space-travel is a valuable safety-valve in some civilizations. Take Reality 54 of the 290th, which I happen to recall offhand. Now there – "

The voices cut off and Twissell said, "A strange man, Sennor. Intellectually, he's worth two of any of the rest of us, but his worth is lost in leapfrog enthusiasms."

Harlan said, "Do you suppose he can be right? About space-travel, I mean."

"I doubt it. We'd have a better chance of judging if Sennor would actually submit the thesis he mentioned. But he won't.

He'll have a new enthusiasm before he's finished and drop the old. But never mind – " He brought the flat of his hand against the sphere so that it rang resoundingly, then brought his hand back so that he could remove a cigarette from his lip. He said, "Can you guess what this is, Technician?"

Harlan said, "It looks like an outsize kettle with a top."

"Exactly. You're right. You've got it. Come on inside."

Harlan followed Twissell into the sphere. It was large enough to hold four or five men, but the interior was absolutely featureless. The floor was smooth, the curved wall was broken by two windows. That was all.

"No controls?" asked Harlan.

"Remote controls," said Twissell. He ran his hand over the smoothness of the wall and said, "Double walls. The entire interwall volume is given over to a self-contained Temporal Field. This instrument is a kettle that is not restricted to the kettle shafts but can pass beyond the downwhen terminus of Eternity. Its design and construction were made possible by valuable hints in the Mallansohn memoir. Come with me."

The control room was a cut-off corner of the large room. Harlan stepped in and stared somberly at immense bus bars.

Twissell said, "Can you hear me, boy?"

Harlan started and looked about. He had not been aware that Twissell had not followed him inside. He stepped automatically to the window and Twissell waved to him. Harlan said, "I can hear you, sir. Do you want me outside?"

"Not at all. You are locked in."

Harlan sprang to the door and his stomach turned into a series of cold, wet knots. Twissell was correct and what in Time was going on?

Twissell said, "You will be relieved to know, boy, that your responsibility is over. You were worried about that responsibility; you asked searching questions about it; and I think I know what you meant. This should not be your responsibility. It is mine alone. Unfortunately, we must have you in the control room, since it is stated that you were there and handled the controls. It is stated in the Mallansohn memoir. Cooper will see you through the window and that will take care of that.

"Furthermore, I will ask you to make the final contact accordingly to instructions I will give you. If you feel that that, too, is too great a responsibility, you may relax. Another contact in parallel with yours is in charge of another man. If, for any reason, you are unable to operate the contact, he will do so. Furthermore, I will cut off radio transmission from within the control room. You will be able to hear us but not speak to us. You need not fear, therefore, that some involuntary exclamation from you will break the circle."

Harlan stared helplessly out of the window.

Twissell went on, "Cooper will be here in moments and his trip to the Primitive will take place within two physiohours. After that, boy, the project will be over and you and I will be free."

Harlan was plunging chokingly through the vortex of a waking nightmare. Had Twissell tricked him? Had everything he had done been designed only to get Harlan quietly into a locked control room? Having learned that Harlan knew his own importance, had he improvised with diabolical cleverness, keeping him engaged in conversation, drugging his emotions with words, leading him here, leading him there, until the time was ripe for locking him in?

That quick and easy surrender over Noÿs. She wont be hurt, Twissell had said. All will be well.

How could he have believed that! If they were not going to harm her, or touch her, why the temporal barrier across the kettleways at the 100,000th? That alone should have given Twissell completely away.

But because he (fool) wanted to believe, he allowed himself to be led through those last physiohours blindly, placed inside a locked room where he was no longer needed, even to close the final contact.

In one stroke he had been robbed of his essentiality. The trumps in his hand had been neatly manoeuvred into deuces and Noÿs was out of his reach forever. What punishment might lie in wait for him did not concern him. Noÿs was out of his reach forever.

It had never occurred to him that the project would be so close to its end. That, of course, was what had really made his defeat possible.

Twissell's voice sounded dimly. "You'll be cut off now, boy."

Harlan was alone, helpless, useless....

CHAPTER THIRTEEN

BEYOND THE DOWNWHEN TERMINUS

BRINSLEY COOPER entered. Excitement flushed his thin face and made it almost youthful, despite the heavy Mallansohn moustache that draped its upper lip.

(Harlan could see him through the window, hear him clearly over the room's radio. He thought bitterly: A Mallansohn moustache! Of course!)

Cooper strode towards Twissell. "They wouldn't let me in till now, Computer."

"Very right," said Twissell. "They had their instructions."

"Now's the time, though? I'll be heading out?"

"Almost the time."

"And I'll be coming back? I'll be seeing Eternity again?" Despite the straightness Cooper gave his back, there was an edge of uncertainty in his voice.

(Within the control room Harlan brought his clenched hands bitterly to the reinforced glass of the window, longing to break through somehow, to shout: "Stop it! Meet my terms, or I'll – " What was the use?)

Cooper looked about the room, apparently unaware that Twissell had refrained from answering his question. His glance fell on Harlan at the control-room window.

He waved his hand excitedly. "Technician Harlan! Come on out. I want to shake your hand before I go."

Twissell interposed. "Not now, boy, not now. He's at the controls."

Cooper said, "Oh? You know, he doesn't look well."

Twissell said, "I've been telling him the true nature of the project. I'm afraid that's enough to make anyone nervous."

Cooper said, "Great Time, yes! I've known about it for weeks now and I'm not used to it yet." There was a trace of near-hysteria in his laugh. "I still haven't got it through my thick head that it is really my show. I – I'm a little scared."

"I scarcely blame you for that."

"It's my stomach, mostly, you know. It's the least happy part of me."

Twissell said, "Well, it's very natural and it will pass. Meanwhile, your time of departure on Standard Intertemporal has been set and there is still a certain amount of orientation to be gone through, For instance, you haven't actually seen the kettle you will use."

In the two hours that passed Harlan heard it all, whether they were in sight or not. Twissell lectured Cooper in an oddly stilted manner, and Harlan knew the reason. Cooper was being informed of just those things that he was to mention in Mallansohn's memoir.

(Full circle. Full circle. And no way for Harlan to break that circle in one, last defiant Samson-smash of the temple – round and round the circle goes; round and round it goes.)

"Ordinary kettles," he heard Twissell say, "are both pushed and pulled, if we can use such terms in the case of Intertemporal forces. In travelling from Century X to Century Y within Eternity there is a fully powered initial point and a fully powered final point.

"What we have here is a kettle with a powered initial point but an unpowered destination point. It can only be pushed, not pulled. For that reason, it must utilize energies at a level whole orders of magnitude higher than those used by ordinary kettles. Special power-transfer units have had to be laid down along the kettleways to siphon in sufficient concentrations of energy from Nova Sol.

"This special kettle, its controls and power supply, are a composite structure. For physiodecades, the passing Realities have been combed for special alloys and special techniques. The 13th Reality of the 222nd was the key. It developed the Temporal Pressor and without that, this kettle could not have been built. The 13th Reality of the 222nd."

He pronounced that with elaborate distinctness.

(Harlan thought: Remember that, Cooper! Remember the 13th Reality of the 222nd so you can put it into the Mallansohn memoir so that the Eternals will know where to look so they will know what to tell you so you can put it.... Round and round the circle goes....)

Twissell said, "The kettle has not been tested past the down-when terminus, of course, but it has taken numerous trips within Eternity. We are convinced there will be no bad effects."

"There can't be, can there?" said Cooper. "I mean I did

get there or Mallansohn could not have succeeded in building the field and he *did* succeed."

Twissell said, "Exactly. You will find yourself in a protected and isolated spot in the sparsely populated southwestern area of the United States of Amellika – "

"America," corrected Cooper.

"America, then. The Century will be the 24th; or, to put it to nearest hundredth, the 23.17th. I suppose we can even call it the year 2317, if we wish. The kettle, as you saw, is large, much larger than necessary for you. It is being filled now with food, water, and the means of shelter and defence. You will have detailed instructions that will, of course, be meaningless to anyone but you. I must impress upon you now that your first task will be to make certain that none of the indigenous inhabitants discovers you before you are ready for them. You will have force-diggers with which you will be able to burrow well into a mountain to form a cache. You will have to remove the contents of the kettle rapidly. They will be stacked so as to facilitate that."

(Harlan thought: Repeat! Repeat! He must have been told all this before, but repeat what must go into the memoir. Round and round. . . .)

Twissell said, "You will have to unload in fifteen minutes. After that, the kettle will return automatically to starting point, carrying with it all tools that are too advanced for the Century. You will have a list of those. After the kettle returns, you will be on your own."

Cooper said, "Must the kettle return so quickly?"

Twissell said, "A quick return increases the probabilities of success."

(Harlan thought: The kettle *must* return in fifteen minutes because it *did* return in fifteen minutes. Round and . . .)

Twissell hurried on. "We cannot attempt to counterfeit their medium of exchange of any of their negotiable scrip. You will have gold in the form of small nuggets. You will be able to explain its possession according to your detailed instructions. You will have native clothing to wear or at least clothing that will pass for native."

"Right," said Cooper.

"Now, remember. Move slowly. Take weeks, if necessary. Work your way into the era, spiritually. Technician Harlan's instructions are a good basis but they are not enough. You will have a wireless receiver built on the principles of the 24th which will enable you to come abreast of the current events and, more important, learn the proper pronunciation and intonation of the language of the times. Do that thoroughly. I'm sure that Harlan's knowledge of English is excellent, but nothing can substitute for native pronunciation on the spot."

Cooper said, "What if I don't end up in the right spot? I mean, not in the 23.17?"

"Check on that very carefully, of course. But it will be right. It will be right."

(Harlan thought: It will be right because it was right. Round . . .)

Cooper must have looked unconvinced, though, for Twissell said, "The accuracy of focus was carefully worked out. I intended to explain our methods and now is a good time. For one thing, it will help Harlan understand the controls."

(Suddenly Harlan turned away from the windows and fixed his gaze on the controls. A corner of the curtain of despair lifted. What if –)

Twissell still lectured Cooper with the anxious overprecise tone of the schoolteacher, and with part of his mind Harlan still listened.

Twissell said, "Obviously a serious problem was that of determining how far into the Primitive an object is sent after the application of a given energy thrust. The most direct method would have been to send a man into the downwhen via this kettle using carefully graduated thrust levels. To do that, however, would have meant a certain lapse of time in each case while the man determined the Century to its nearest hundredth through astronomical observation or by obtaining appropriate information over the wireless. That would be slow and also dangerous since the man might well be discovered by the native inhabitants with probably catastrophic effects on our project.

"What we did then instead was this: We sent back a known mass of the radioactive isotope, niobium-94, which decays by beta-particle emission to the stable isotope, molybdenum-94. The process has a half-life of almost exactly 500 Centuries. The original radiation intensity of the mass was known. That intensity decreases with time according to the simple relationship involved in first-order kinetics, and, of course, the intensity can be measured with great precision.

133

"When the kettle reaches its destination in Primitive times, the ampule containing the isotope is discharged into the mountainside and the kettle then returns to Eternity. At the moment in physiotime that the ampule is discharged, it simultaneously appears at all future Times growing progressively older. At the place of discharge in the 575th (in actual Time and not in Eternity) a Technician detects the ampule by its radiation and retrieves it.

"The radiation intensity is measured, the time it has remained in the mountainside is then known, the Century to which the kettle travelled is also known to two decimal places. Dozens of ampules were thus sent back at various thrust levels and a calibration curve set up. The curve was a check against ampules sent not all the way into the Primitive but into the early Centuries of Eternity where direct observation could also be made.

"Naturally, there were failures. The first few ampules were lost until we learned to allow for the not too major geological changes between the late Primitive and the 575th. Then, three of the ampules later on never showed up in the 575th. Presumably, something went wrong with the discharge mechanism and they were buried too deeply in the mountain for detection. We stopped our experiments when the level of radiation grew so high that we feared that some of the Primitive inhabitants might detect and wonder what radioactive artifacts might be doing in the region. But we had enough for our purposes and we are certain we can send back a man to any hundredth of a Century of the Primitive that is desired."

"You follow all this, Cooper, don't you?"

Cooper said, "Perfectly, Computer Twissell. I have seen the calibration curve without understanding the purpose at the time. It is quite clear now."

But Harlan was exceedingly interested now. He stared at the measured arc marked off in centuries. The shining arc was porcelain on metal and the fine lines divided it into Centuries, Decicenturies and Centicenturies. Silvery metal gleamed thinly through the porcelain-penetrating lines, marking them clearly. The figures were as finely done and, bending close, Harlan could make out the Centuries from 17 to 27. The hairline was fixed at the 23.17 Century mark.

He had seen similar time-gauges and almost automatically he reached to the pressure-control lever. It did not respond to his grasp. The hairline remained in place.

134

He nearly jumped when Twissell's voice suddenly addressed him.

"Technician Harlan!"

He cried, "Yes, Computer," then remembered that he could not be heard. He stepped to the window and nodded.

Twissell said, almost as though chiming in with Harlan's thoughts, "The time-gauge is set for a thrust back to the 23.17th. That requires no adjustment. Your only task is to pour energy through at the proper moment in physiotime. There is a chronometer to the right of the gauge. Nod if you see it."

Harlan nodded.

"It will reach zero-point backwards. At the minus-fifteen-second point, align the contact points. It's simple. You see how?"

Harlan nodded again.

Twissell went on, "Synchronization is not vital. You can do it at minus fourteen or thirteen or even minus five seconds, but please make every effort to stay this side of minus ten for safety's sake. Once you've closed contact, a synchronized force-gear will do the rest and make certain that the final energy thrust will occur precisely at time zero. Understood?"

Harlan nodded still again. He understood more than Twissell said. If he himself did not align the points by minus ten, it would be taken care of from without.

Harlan thought grimly: There'll be no need for outsiders.

Twissell said, "We have thirty physiominutes left. Cooper and I will leave to check on the supplies."

They left. The door closed behind them, and Harlan was left alone with the thrust control, the time (already moving slowly backwards towards zero) – and a resolute knowledge of what must be done.

Harlan turned away from the window. He put his hand inside his pocket and half withdrew the neuronic whip it still contained. Through all this he had kept the whip. His hand shook a little.

An earlier thought recurred: a Samson-smash of the temple!

A corner of his mind wondered sickly: How many Eternals have ever heard of Samson? How many know how he died?

There were only twenty-five minutes left. He was not certain how long the operation would take. He was not really certain it would work at all.

But what choice had he? His damp fingers almost dropped

the weapon before he succeeded in unhinging the butt.

He worked rapidly and in complete absorption. Of all the aspects of what he planned, the possibility of his own passage into nonexistence occupied his mind the least and bothered him not at all.

At minus one minute Harlan was standing at the controls.

Detachedly he thought: The last minute of life?

Nothing in the room was visible to him but the backward sweep of the red hairline that marked the passing seconds.

Minus thirty seconds.

He thought: It will not hurt. It is not death.

He tried to think only of Noÿs.

Minus fifteen seconds.

Noÿs!

Harlan's left hand moved a switch down towards contact. Not hastily!

Minus twelve seconds.

Contact!

The force-gear would take over now. Thrust would come at zero time. And that left Harlan one last manipulation. The Samson-smash!

His right hand moved. He did not look at his right hand.

Minus five seconds.

Noÿs!

His right hand mo – ZERO – ved again, spasmodically. He did not look at it.

Was this nonexistence?

Not yet. Nonexistence not yet.

Harlan stared out the window. He did not move. Time passed and he was unaware of its passage.

The room was empty. Where the giant, enclosed kettle had been was nothing. Metal blocks that had served as its base sat emptily, lifting their huge strength against air.

Twissell, strangely small and dwarfed in the room that had become a waiting cavern, was the only thing that moved as he tramped edgily this way and that.

Harlan's eyes followed him for a moment and then left him.

Then, without any sound or stir, the kettle was back in the spot it had left. Its passage across the hairline from time past to time present did not as much as disturb a molecule of air.

Twissell was hidden from Harlan's eyes by the bulk of the kettle, but then he rounded it, came into view. He was running.

A flick of his hand was enough to activate the mechanism that opened the door of the control room. He hurtled inside, shouting with an almost lyrical excitement. "It's done. It's done. We've closed the circle." He had breath to say no more.

Harlan made no answer.

Twissell stared out of the window, his hands flat against the glass. Harlan noted the blotches of age upon them and the way in which they trembled. It was as though his mind no longer had the ability or the strength to filter the important from the inconsequential, but were selecting observational material in a purely random manner.

Wearily he thought: What does it matter? What does anything matter now?

Twissell said (Harlan heard him dimly), "I'll tell you now that I've been more anxious than I cared to admit. Sennor used to say once that this whole thing was impossible. He insisted something must happen to stop it – What's the matter?"

He had turned to Harlan's odd grunt.

Harlan shook his head, managed a choked, "Nothing."

Twissell left it at that and turned away. It was doubtful whether he spoke to Harlan or to the air. It was as though he were allowing years of pent-up anxieties to escape in words.

"Sennor," he said, "was the doubter. We reasoned with him and argued. We used mathematics and presented the results of generations of research that had preceded us in the physiotime of Eternity. He put it all to one side and presented his case by quoting the man-meets-himself paradox. You heard him talk about it. It's his favourite.

"We knew our own future, Sennor said. I, Twissell, knew, for instance, that I would survive, despite the fact that I would be quite old, until Cooper made his trip past the downwhen terminus. I knew other details of my future, the things I would do.

"Impossible, he would say. Reality must change to correct your knowledge, even if it meant the circle would never close and Eternity never be established.

"Why he argued so, I don't know. Perhaps he honestly believed it, perhaps it was an intellectual game with him, perhaps it was just the desire to shock the rest of us with an unpopular viewpoint. In any case, the project proceeded and some of the memoir began to be fulfilled. We located Cooper, for instance, in the Century and Reality that the memoir gave us. Sennor's case was exploded by that alone, but it didn't bother him. By that time, he had grown interested in something else.

"And yet, and yet" – he laughed gently, with more than a trace of embarrassment, and let his cigarette, unnoticed, burn down nearly to his fingers – "you know I was never quite easy in my mind. Something *might* happen. The Reality in which Eternity was established *might* change in some way in order to prevent what Sennor called a paradox. It would have to change to one in which Eternity would not exist. Sometimes, in the dark of a sleeping period, when I couldn't sleep, I could almost persuade myself that that was indeed so ... and now it's all over and I laugh at myself as a senile fool."

Harland said in a low voice, "Computer Sennor was right."

Twissell whirled. "What?"

"The project failed." Harlan's mind was coming out of the shadows (why, and into what, he was not sure). "The circle is not complete."

"What are you talking about?" Twissell's old hands fell on Harlan's shoulders with surprising strength. "You're ill, boy. The strain."

"Not ill. Sick of everything. You. Me. Not ill. The gauge. See for yourself."

"The gauge?" The hairline on the gauge stood at the 27th Century, hard against the right-hand extreme. "What happened?" The joy was gone from his face. Horror replaced it.

Harlan grew matter-of-fact. "I melted the locking mechanism, freed the thrust control."

"How could you – "

"I had a neuronic whip. I broke it open and used its micropile energy source in one flash, like a torch. There's what's left of it." He kicked at a small heap of metal fragments in one corner.

Twissell wasn't taking it in. "In the 27th? You mean Cooper's in the 27th – "

"I don't know where he is," said Harlan dully. "I shifted the thrust control downwhen, further down than the 24th. I don't know where. I didn't look. Then I brought it back. I still didn't look."

Twissell stared at him, his face a pale, unhealthy yellowish colour, his lower lip trembling.

"I don't know where he is now," said Harlan. "He's lost in the Primitive. The circle is broken. I thought everything would end when I made the stroke. At zero time. That's silly. We've got to wait. There'll be a moment in physiotime when Cooper will realize he's in the wrong Century, when he'll do something against the memoir, when he – " He broke off, then broke into a forced and creaky laughter. "What's the difference? It's only a delay till Cooper makes the final break in the circle. There's no way of stopping it. Minutes, hours, days. What's the difference? When the delay is done, there will be no more Eternity. Do you hear me? It will be the end of Eternity."

CHAPTER FOURTEEN

THE EARLIER CRIME

"WHY? Why?"

Twissell looked helplessly from the gauge to the Technician, his eyes mirroring the puzzled frustration in his voice.

Harlan lifted his head. He had only one word to say. "Noÿs!"

Twissell said, "The woman you took into Eternity?"

Harlan smiled bitterly, said nothing.

Twissell said, "What has she to do with this? Great Time, I don't understand, boy."

"What is there to understand?" Harlan burned with sorrow. "Why do you pretend ignorance? I had a woman. I was happy and so was she. We harmed no one. She did not exist in the new Reality. What difference would it have made to anyone?"

Twissell tried vainly to interrupt.

Harlan shouted. "But there are rules in Eternity, aren't there? I know them all. Liaisons require permission; liaisons require computations, liaisons require status; liaisons are tricky things. What were you planning for Noÿs when all this was over. A seat in a crashing rocket? Or a more comfortable position as community mistress for worthy Computers? You won't make any plans *now*, I think."

He ended in a kind of despair and Twissell moved quickly to the Communiplate. Its function as a transmitter had obviously been restored.

The Computer shouted into it till he aroused an answer. Then he said, "This is Twissell. No one is to be allowed in here. No one. No one. Do you understand? ... Then see to it. It goes for members of the Allwhen Council. It goes for them particularly."

He turned back to Harlan, saying abstractedly, "They'll do it because I'm old and senior member of the Council and because they think I'm cranky and queer. They give in to me because I'm cranky and queer." For a moment he fell into a ruminative silence. Then he said, "Do you think I'm queer?" and his face turned swiftly up to Harlan's like that of a seamed monkey.

Harlan thought: Great Time, the man's mad. The shock has driven him mad.

He took a step backward, automatically aghast at being trapped with a madman. Then he steadied. The man, be he ever so mad, was feeble, and even madness would end soon.

Soon? Why not at once? What delayed the end of Eternity?

Twissell said (he had no cigarette in his fingers; his hand made no move to take one) in a quiet insinuating voice, "You haven't answered me. *Do* you think I'm queer? I suppose you do. Too queer to talk to. If you had thought of me as a friend instead of as a crotchety old man, whimsical and unpredictable, you would have spoken openly to me of your doubts. You would have taken no such action as you did."

Harlan frowned. The man thought *Harlan* was mad. That was it!

He said angrily, "My action was the right one. I'm quite sane."

Twissell said, "I told you the girl was in no danger, you know."

"I was a fool to believe that even for a while. I was a fool to believe the Council would be just to a Technician."

"Who told you the Council knew of any of this?"

"Finge knew of it and sent in a report concerning it to the Council."

"And how do you know that?"

"I got it out of Finge at the point of a neuronic whip. The business end of a whip abolishes comparative status."

"The same whip that did this?" Twissell pointed to the gauge with its blob of molten metal perched wryly above the face of the dial.

"Yes."

140

"A busy whip." Then, sharply, "Do you know why Finge took it to the Council instead of handling the matter himself?"

"Because he hated me and wanted to make certain I lost all status. He wanted Noÿs."

Twissell said, "You're naïve! If he had wanted the girl, he could easily have arranged liaison. A Technician would not have been in his way. The man hated *me*, boy." (Still no cigarette. He looked odd without one and the stained finger he lay on his chest as he spoke the last pronoun looked almost indecently bare.)

"You?"

"There's such a thing, boy, as Council politics. Not every Computer is appointed to the Council. Finge wanted an appointment. Finge is ambitious and wanted it badly. I blocked it because I thought him emotionally unstable. Time, I never fully appreciated how right I was ... Look, boy. He knew you were a protégé of mine. He had seen me take you out of a job as an Observer and make you a master Technician. He saw you working for me steadily. How better could he get back at me and destroy my influence? If he could prove my pet Technician guilty of a terrible crime against Eternity, it would reflect on me. It might force my resignation from the Allwhen Council, and who do you suppose would then be a logical successor?"

His empty hands moved to his lips and when nothing happened, he looked at the space between finger and thumb blackly.

Harlan thought: He's not as calm as he's trying to sound. He can't be. But why does he talk all this nonsense *now*? With Eternity ending?

Then in agony: But why doesn't it *end* then? Now!

Twissell said, "When I allowed you to go to Finge just recently, I more than half suspected danger. But Mallansohn's memoir *said* you were away the last month and no other natural reason for your absence offered itself. Fortunately, Finge underplayed his hand."

"In what way?" asked Harlan wearily. He didn't really care, but Twissell talked and talked and it was easier to take part than to try to shut the sound out of his ears.

Twissell said, "Finge labelled his report: '*In re* unprofessional conduct of Technician Adrew Harlan.' He was being the faithful Eternal, you see, being cool, impartial, unexcited. He was leaving it to the Council to rage and throw itself at me. Unfortunately for himself, he did not know of your real importance.

141

He did not realize that any report concerning you would be instantly referred to me, unless its supreme importance were made perfectly clear on the very face of things."

"You never spoke to me of this?"

"How could I? I was afraid to do anything that would disturb you with the crisis of the project at hand. I gave you every opportunity to bring your problem to me."

Every opportunity? Harlan's mouth twisted in disbelief, but then he thought of Twissell's weary face on the Communiplate asking him if he had nothing to say to him. That was yesterday. Only yesterday.

Harlan shook his head, but turned his face away now.

Twissell said softly. "I realized at once that he had deliberately goaded you into your – rash action."

Harlan looked up. "You know that?"

"Does that surprise you? I knew Finge was after my neck. I've known it for a long time. I am an old man, boy. I know these things. But there are ways in which doubtful Computers can be checked upon. There are some protective devices, culled out of Time, that are not placed in the museums. There are some that are known to the Council alone."

Harlan thought bitterly of the time-block at the 100,000th.

"From the report and from what I knew independently, it was easy to deduce what must have happened."

Harlan asked suddenly, "I suppose Finge suspected you of spying?"

"He might have. I wouldn't be surprised."

Harlan thought back to his first days with Finge when Twissell first showed his abnormal interest in the young Observer. Finge had known nothing of the Mallansohn project, and he had been interested in Twissell's interference. "Have you ever met Senior Computer Twissell?" he had once asked, and, thinking back, Harlan could recall the exact tone of sharp uneasiness in the man's voice. As early as that Finge must have suspected Harlan of being Twissell's finger-man. His enmity and hate must have begun that early.

Twissell was speaking, "So if you had come to me –"

"Come to *you*?" cried Harlan. "What of the Council?"

"Of the entire Council, only I know."

"You never told them?" Harlan tried to be mocking.

"I never did."

Harlan felt feverish. His clothes were choking him. Was this nightmare to go on forever. Foolish, irrelevant chatter! *For what? Why?*

Why didn't Eternity end? Why didn't the clean peace of non-Reality reach out for them? *Great Time, what was wrong?*

Twissell said, "Don't you believe me?"

Harlan shouted, "Why should I? They came to look at me, didn't they? At that breakfast? Why should they have done that if they didn't know of the report? They came to look at the queer phenomenon who had broken the laws of Eternity but who couldn't be touched for one more day. One more day and then the project would be over. They came to gloat for the tomorrow they were expecting."

"My boy, there was nothing of that. They wanted to see you only because they were human. Councilmen are human, too. They could not witness the final kettle drive because the Mallansohn memoir did not place them at the scene. They could not interview Cooper since the memoir made no mention of that either. Yet they wanted something. Father Time, boy, don't you see they would want something. You were as close as they could get, so they brought you close and stared at you."

"I don't believe you."

"It's the truth."

Harlan said, "Is it? And while we ate, Councilman Sennor talked of a man meeting himself. He obviously knew about my illegal trips into the 482nd and my nearly meeting myself. It was his way of poking at me, enjoying himself cutely at my expense."

Twissell said, "Sennor? You worried about Sennor? Do you know the pathetic figure he is? His homewhen is the 803rd, one of the few cultures in which the human body is deliberately disfigured to meet the aesthetic requirements of the time. It is rendered hairless at adolescence.

"Do you know what that means in the continuity of man? Surely you do. A disfigurement sets men apart from their ancestors and descendants. Men of the 803rd are poor risks as Eternals; they are too different from the rest of us. Few are chosen. Sennor is the only one of his Century ever to sit on the Council.

"Don't you see how that affects him? Surely you understand what insecurity means. Did it ever occur to you that a Councilman could be insecure? Sennor has to listen to discussions in-

143

volving the eradication of his Reality for the very characteristic that makes him so conspicuous among us. And eradicating it would leave him one of a very few in all the generation to be disfigured as he is. Someday it will happen.

"He finds refuge in philosophy. He overcompensates by taking the lead in conversation, by deliberately airing unpopular or unacceptable viewpoints. His man-meeting-himself paradox is a case in point. I told you that he used it to predict disaster for the project and it was we, the Councilmen, that he was attempting to annoy, not you. It had nothing to do with you. Nothing!"

Twissell had grown heated. In the long emotion of his words he seemed to forget where he was and the crisis that faced them, for he slipped back into the quick-gestured, uneasily motioned gnome that Harlan knew so well. He even slipped a cigarette from his sleeve pouch and had all but frictioned it into combustion.

But then he stopped, wheeled, and looked at Harlan again, reaching back through all his own words to what Harlan had last said, as though until that moment he had not heard them properly.

He said, "What do you mean, you almost met yourself?"

Harlan told him briefly and went on, "You didn't know that?"

"No."

There was a few moments of silence that were as welcome to the feverish Harlan as water would have been.

Twissell said, "Is that it? What if you *had* met yourself?"

"I didn't."

Twissell ignored that. "There is always room for random variation. With an infinite number of Realities there can be no such thing as determinism. Suppose that in the Mallansohn Reality, in the previous turn of the cycle –"

"The circles go on forever?" asked Harlan with what wonder he could still find in himself.

"Do you think only twice? Do you think two is a magic number? It's a matter of infinite turns of the circle infinite physiotime. Just as you can draw a pencil round and round the circumference of a circle infinitely yet enclose a finite area. In previous turns of the cycle, you had not met yourself. This one time, the statistical uncertainty of things made it possible for you to meet yourself. Reality had to change to prevent the

144

meeting and in the new Reality, you did not send Cooper back to the 24th but –"

Harlan cried, "What's all this talk about? What are you getting at? It's all done. Everything. Let me alone now! *Let me alone!*"

"I want you to know you've done wrong. I want you to realize you did the wrong thing."

"I didn't. And even if I did, *it's done.*"

"But it's *not* done. Listen just a little while longer." Twissell was wheedling, almost crooning with an agonized gentleness. "You will have your girl. I promised that. I still promise it. She will not be harmed. You will not be harmed. I promise you this. It is my personal guarantee."

Harlan stared at him wide-eyed. "But it's too late. What's the use?"

"It is *not* too late. Things are *not* irreparable. With your help, we can succeed yet. I must have your help. You must realize that you did wrong. I am trying to explain this to you. You must want to undo what you have done."

Harlan licked his dry lips with a dry tongue and thought: He *is* mad. His mind can't accept the truth – or, does the Council know more?

Did it? Did it? Could it reverse the verdict of the Changes? Could they halt Time or reverse it?

He said, "You locked me in the control room, kept me helpless, you thought, till it was all over."

"You said you were afraid something might go wrong with you; that you might not be able to carry on with your part."

"That was meant to be a threat."

"I took it literally. Forgive me. I must have your help."

It came to that. Harlan's help must be had. Was he mad? Was Harlan mad? Did madness have meaning? Or anything at all, for that matter?

The Council needed his help. For that help they would promise him anything. Noÿs. Computership. What would they not promise him? And when his help was done with, what would he *get*? He would not be fooled a second time.

"No!" he said.

"You'll have Noÿs."

"You mean the Council will be willing to break the laws of Eternity once the danger is safely gone? I don't believe it." How could the danger safely be passed, a sane scrap of his mind demanded. What was this all about?

"The Council will never know."

"Would *you* be willing to break the laws? You're the ideal Eternal. With the danger gone, you would obey the law. You couldn't act otherwise."

Twissell reddened blotchily, high on each cheekbone. From the old face all shrewdness and strength drained away. There was left only a strange sorrow.

"I will keep my word to you and break the law," said Twissell, "for a reason you don't imagine. I don't know how much time is left us before Eternity disappears. It could be hours; it could be months. But I have spent so much time in the hope of bringing you to reason that I will spend a little more. Will you listen to me? Please?"

Harlan hesitated. Then, out of a conviction of the uselessness of all things as much as out of anything else said wearily, "Go on."

I have heard (began Twissell) that I was born old, that I cut my teeth on a Micro-Computaplex, that I keep my hand computer in a special pocket of my pyjamas when I sleep, that my brain is made up of little force-relays in endless parallel hookups and that each corpuscle of my blood is a microscopic spatio-temporal chart floating in computer oil.

All these stories come to me eventually, and I think I must be a little proud of them. Maybe I go around believing them a bit. It's a foolish thing for an old man to do, but it makes life a little easier.

Does that surprise you? That I must find a way to make life easier? I, Senior Computer Twissell, senior member of the Allwhen Council?

Maybe that's why I smoke. Ever think of that? I have to have a reason, you know. Eternity is essentially an unsmoking society, and most of Time is, too. I've thought of that often. I sometimes think it's a rebellion against Eternity. Something to take the place of a greater rebellion that failed....

No, it's all right. A tear or two won't hurt me, and it isn't pretence, believe me. It's just that I haven't thought about this for a long time. It isn't pleasant.

It involved a woman, of course, as your affair did. That's not coincidence. It's almost inevitable, if you stop to think of it. An Eternal, who must sell the normal satisfactions of family life for a handful of perforations on foil, is ripe for infection.

146

That's one of the reasons Eternity must take the precautions it does. And, apparently, that's also why Eternals are so ingenious in evading the precautions once in a while.

I remember my woman. It's foolish of me to do so, perhaps. I can't remember anything else about that physiotime. My old colleagues are only names in the record books; the Changes I supervised – all but one – are only items in the Computaplex memory pools. I remember her, though, very well. Perhaps you can undestand that.

I had had a long-standing request for liaison in the books; and after I achieved status as a Junior Computer, she was assigned to me. She was a girl of this very Century, the 575th. I didn't see her until after the assignment, of course. She was intelligent and kind. Not beautiful or even pretty, but then, even when young (yes, I was young, never mind the myths) I was not noted for my own looks. We were well suited to one another by temperament, she and I, and if I were a Timed man, I would have been proud to have her as my wife. I told her that many times. I believe it pleased her. I know it was the truth. Not all Eternals, who must take their women as and how Computing permits, are that fortunate.

In that particular Reality, she was to die young, of course, and none of her analogues was available for liaison. At first, I took that philosophically. After all, it was her short lifetime which made it possible for her to live with me without deleteriously affecting Reality.

I am ashamed of that now, of the fact that I was glad she had a short time to live. Just at first, that is. Just at first.

I visited her as often as spatio-temporal charting allowed. I squeezed every minute out of it, giving up meals and sleep when necessary, shifting my labour load shamelessly whenever I could. Her amiability passed the heights of my expectations, and I was in love. I put it bluntly. My experience of love is very small, and understanding it through Observation in Time is a shaky matter. As far as my understanding went, however, I was in love.

What began as the satisfaction of an emotional and physical need became a great deal more. Her imminent death stopped being a convenience and became a calamity. I Life-Plotted her. I didn't go to the Life-Plotting departments, either. I did it myself. That surprises you, I imagine. It was a misdemeanour, but it was nothing compared to the crimes I committed later.

Yes, I, Laban Twissell. Senior Computer Twissell.

Three separate times, a point in physiotime came and passed, during which some simple action of my own might have altered her personal Reality. Naturally, I knew that no such personally motivated Change could possibly be authorized by the Council. Still, I began to feel personally responsible for her death. That was part of my motivation later on, you see.

She became pregnant. I took no action, though I should have. I had worked her Life-Plot, modified to include her relationship with me, and I knew pregnancy to be a high-probability consequence. As you may or may not know, Timed women are occasionally made pregnant by Eternals despite precautions. It is not unheard of. Still, since no Eternal may have a child, such pregnancies as do occur are ended painlessly and safely. There are many methods.

My Life-Plotting had indicated she would die before delivery, so I took no precautions. She was happy in her pregnancy and I wanted her to remain so. So I only watched and tried to smile when she told me she could feel life stirring within her.

But then something happened. She gave birth prematurely –

I don't wonder you look that way. I had a child. A real child of my own. You'll find no other Eternal, perhaps, who can say that. That was more than a misdemeanour. That was a serious felony, but it was still nothing.

I hadn't expected it. Birth and its problems were an aspect of life with which I had had little experience.

I went back to the Life-Plot in panic and found the living child, in an alternate solution to a low-probability forklet I had overlooked. A professional Life-Plotter would not have overlooked it and I had done wrong to trust my own abilities that far.

But what could I do now?

I couldn't kill the child. The mother had two weeks to live. Let the child live with her till then, I thought. Two weeks of happiness is not an exorbitant gift to ask.

The mother died, as foreseen, and in the manner foreseen. I sat in her room, for all the time permitted by the spatio-temporal chart, aching with a sorrow all the keener for my having waited for death, in full knowledge, for over a year. In my arms, I held my son and hers.

– Yes, I let it live. Why do you cry out so? Are *you* going to condemn me?

You cannot know what it means to hold a little atom of your own life in your arms. I may have a Computaplex for nerves and spatio-temporal charts for a bloodstream, but I do know.

I let it live. I committed that crime, too. I put it in the charge of an appropriate organization and returned when I could (in strict temporal sequence, held even with physiotime) to make necessary payments and to watch the boy grow.

Two years went by that way. Periodically, I checked the boy's Life-Plot (I was used to breaking that particular rule, by now) and was pleased to find that there were no signs of deleterious effects on the then-current Reality at probability levels over 0.0001. The boy learned to walk and mispronounced a few words. He was not taught to call me "daddy". Whatever speculations the Timed people of the child-care institution might have made concerning me I don't know. They took their money and said nothing.

Then, when the two years had passed, the necessities of a Change that included the 575th at one wing was brought up before the Allwhen Council. I, having been lately promoted to Assistant Computer, was placed in charge. It was the first Change ever left to my sole supervision.

I was proud, of course, but also apprehensive. My son was an intruder in the Reality. He could scarcely be expected to have analogues. Thought of his passage into nonexistence saddened me.

I worked at the Change and I flatter myself even yet that I did a flawless job. My first one. But I succumbed to a temptation. I succumbed to it all the more easily because it was becoming an old story now for me. I was a hardened criminal, a habitué of crime. I worked out a new Life-Plot for my son under the new Reality, certain of what I would find.

But then for twenty-four hours, without eating or sleeping, I sat in my office striving with the completed Life-Plot, tearing at it in a despairing effort to find an error.

There was no error.

The next day, holding back my solution to the Change, I worked out a spatio-temporal chart, using rough methods of approximation (after all, the Reality was not to last long) and entered Time at a point more than thirty years upwhen from the birth of my child.

He was thirty-four years old, as old as I myself. I introduced myself as a distant relation, making use of my knowledge of his

149

mother's family, to do so. He had no knowledge of his father, no memory of my visits to him in his infancy.

He was an aeronautical engineer. The 575th was expert in half a dozen varieties of air travel (as it still is in the current Reality, and my son was a happy and successful member of his society. He was married to an ardently enamoured girl, but would have no children. Nor would the girl have married at all in the Reality in which my son had not existed. I had known that from the beginning. I had known there would be no deleterious effect in Reality. Otherwise, I might not have found it in my heart to let the boy live. I am not *completely* abandoned.

I spent the day with my son. I spoke to him formally, smiled politely, took my leave coolly, when the spatio-temporal chart dictated. But underneath all that, I watched and absorbed every action, filling myself with him, and trying to live one day at least out of a Reality that the next day (by physiotime) would no longer have existed.

How I longed to visit my wife one last time, too, during that portion of Time in which she lived, but I had used every second that had been available to me. I dared not even enter Time to see her, unseen.

I returned to Eternity and spent one last horrible night wrestling futilely against what must be. The next morning I handed in my computations together with my recommendations for Change.

Twissell's voice had lowered to a whisper and now it stopped. He sat there with his shoulders bent, his eyes fixed on the floor between his knees, and his fingers twisting slowly into and out of a knotted clasp.

Harlan, waiting vainly for another sentence out of the old man, cleared his throat. He found himself pitying the man, pitying him despite the many crimes he had committed. He said, "And that's all?"

Twissell whispered, "No, the worst – the worst – An analogue of my son did exist. In the new Reality, he existed – as a paraplegic from the age of four. Forty-two years in bed, under circumstances that barred me from arranging to have the nerve-regenerating techniques of the 900's applied to his case, or even for arranging to have his life ended painlessly.

"That new Reality still exists. My son is still out there in the appropriate portion of the Century. *I* did that to him. It was

150

my mind and my Computaplex that discovered this new life for him, and my word that ordered the Change. I had committed a number of crimes for his sake and for his mother's, but that one last deed, though strictly in accordance with my oath as an Eternal, has always seemed to me to be my great crime, *the* crime."

There was nothing to say, and Harlan said nothing.

Twissell said, "But you see now why I understand your case, why I will be willing to let you have your girl. It would not harm Eternity and, in a way, it would be expiation for my crime."

And Harlan believed. All in one change of mind, he believed!

Harlan sank to his knees and lifted his clenched fists to his temples. He bent his head and rocked slowly as savage despair beat through him.

He had thrown Eternity away, and lost Noÿs – when, except for his Samson-smash, he might have saved one and kept the other.

CHAPTER FIFTEEN

SEARCH THROUGH THE PRIMITIVE

TWISSELL was shaking Harlan's shoulders. The old man's voice urgently called his name.

"Harlan! Harlan! For Time's sake, man."

Harlan emerged only slowly from the slough. "What are we to do?"

"Certainly not *this*. Not despair. To begin with, listen to me. Forget your Technician's view of Eternity and look at it through a Computer's eyes. The view is more sophisticated. When you alter something in Time and create a Reality Change, the Change may take place at once. Why should that be?"

Harlan said shakily, "Because your alteration has made the Change inevitable?"

"Has it? You could go back and reverse your alteration, couldn't you?"

"I suppose so. I never did, though. Or anyone that I heard of."

"Right. There is no intention of reversing an alteration, so it goes through as planned. But here we have something else. An unintentional alteration. You sent Cooper into the wrong Century and now I firmly intend to reverse that alteration and bring Cooper back here."

"For Time's sake, how?"

"I'm not sure yet, but there *must* be a way. If there were no way, the alteration would be irreversible; Change would come at once. But Change has not come. We are still in the Reality of the Mallansohn memoir. That means the alteration is reversible and *will* be reversed."

"What?" Harlan's nightmare was expanding and swirling, growing murkier and more engulfing.

"There must be some way of knitting the circle in Time together again and our ability to find the way to do it must be a high-probability affair. As long as our Reality exists, we can be certain that the solution remains high-probability. If at any moment, you or I make the wrong decision, if the probability of healing the circle falls below some crucial magnitude, Eternity disappears. Do you understand?"

Harlan was not sure that he did. He wasn't trying very hard. Slowly he got to his feet and stumbled his way into a chair.

"You mean we can get Cooper back –"

"And send him to the right place, yes. Catch him at the moment he leaves the kettle and he may end up in his proper place in the 24th no more than a few physiohours older; physiodays, at the most. It would be an alteration, of course, but undoubtedly not enough of one. Reality would be rocked, boy, but not upset."

"But how do we get him?"

"We know there's a way, or Eternity wouldn't be existing this moment. As to what that way is, that is why I need you, why I've fought to get you back on my side. You're the expert on the Primitive. Tell me."

"I can't," groaned Harlan.

"You can," insisted Twissell.

There was suddenly no trace of age or weariness in the old man's voice. His eyes were ablaze with the light of combat and he wielded his cigarette like a lance. Even to Harlan's regret-drugged senses the man seemed to be enjoying himself, actually enjoying himself, now that battle had been joined.

"We can reconstruct the event," said Twissell. "Here is the thrust control. You're standing at it, waiting for the signal. It comes. You make contact and at the same time squeeze the power thrust in the downwhen direction. How far?"

"I don't know, I tell you. I don't know."

"*You* don't know, but your muscles do. Stand there and take the controls in your hand. Get hold of yourself. Take them, boy. You're waiting for the signal. You're hating me. You're hating the Council. You're hating Eternity. You're wearying your heart out for Noÿs. Put yourself back at that moment. Feel what you felt then. Now I'll set the clock in motion again. I'll give you one minute, boy, to remember your emotions and force them back into your thalamus. Then, at the approach of zero, let your right hand jerk the control as it had done before. Then take your hand away! Don't move it back again. Are you ready?"

"I don't think I can do it."

"You don't think – Father Time, you have no choice. Is there another way you can get back your girl?"

There wasn't. Harlan forced himself back to the controls, and as he did so emotion flooded back. He did not have to call on it. Repeating the physical movements brought them back. The red hairline on the clock started moving.

Detachedly he thought: The last minute of life?

Minus thirty seconds.

He thought: It will not hurt. It is not death.

He tried to think only of Noÿs.

Minus five seconds.

Noÿs!

Harlan's left hand moved a switch down towards contact.

Minus twelve seconds.

Contact!

His right hand moved.

Minus five seconds.

Noÿs!

His right hand mo – ZERO – ved spasmodically.

He jumped away, panting.

Twissell came forward, peering at the dial. "Twentieth Century," he said. "Nineteen point three eight, to be exact."

Harlan choked out, "I don't know. I tried to feel the same, but it was different. I knew what I was doing and that made it different."

Twissell said, "I know, I know. Maybe it's all wrong. Call it a first approximation." He paused a moment in mental calculation, took a pocket computer half out of its container and thrust it back without consulting it. "To Time with the decimal points. Say the probability is 0.99 that you sent him back to the second quarter of the 20th. Somewhere between 19.25 and 19.50. All right?"

"I don't know."

"Well, now, look. If I make a firm decision to concentrate on that part of the Primitive to the exclusion of all else and if I am wrong, the chances are that I will have lost my chance to keep the circle in time closed and Eternity will disappear. The decision itself will be the crucial point, the Minimum Necessary Change, the M.N.C., to bring about the Change. I now make the decision. I decide, definitely —"

Harlan looked about cautiously, as though Reality had grown so fragile that a sudden head movement might shatter it.

Harlan said, "I'm thoroughly conscious of Eternity." (Twissell's normality had infected him to the point where his voice sounded firm in his own ears.)

"Then Eternity still exists," said Twissell in a blunt, matter-of-fact manner, "and we have made the right decision. Now there's nothing more to do here for a while. Let's go to my office and we can let the subcommittee of the Council swarm over this place, if that will make them any happier. As far as they are concerned, the project has ended successfully. If it doesn't, they'll never know. Nor we."

Twissell studied his cigarette and said, "The question that now confronts us is this: What will Cooper do when he finds himself in the wrong Century?"

"I don't know."

"One thing is obvious. He's a bright lad, intelligent, imaginative, wouldn't you say?"

"Well, he's Mallansohn."

"Exactly. And he wondered if he would end up wrong. One of his last questions was: What if I don't end up in the right spot? Do you remember?"

"Well?" Harlan had no idea where this was leading.

"So he is mentally prepared for being displaced in Time. He will do something. Try to reach us. Try to leave traces for us. Remember, for part of his life he was an Eternal. That's an important thing." Twissell blew a smoke ring, hooked it with a finger, and watched it curl and break up. "He's used to the

154

notion of communication across Time. He is not likely to surrender to the thought of being marooned in Time. He'll know that we're looking for him."

Harlan said, "Without kettles and with no Eternity in the 20th, how would he go about communicating with us?"

"With *you*, Technician, with *you*. Use the singular. You're our expert on the Primitive. You taught Cooper about the Primitive. You're the one he would expect to be capable of finding his traces."

"*What* traces, Computer?"

Twissell's shrewd old face stared up at Harlan, its lines crinkling. "It was intended to leave Cooper in the Primitive. He is without the protection of an enclosing shield of physiotime. His entire life is woven into the fabric of Time and will remain so until you and I reverse the alteration. Likewise woven into the fabric of Time is any artifact, sign, or message he may have left us. Surely there must be particular sources you used in studying the 20th Century. Documents, archives, films, artifacts, reference works. I mean primary sources, dating from the Time itself."

"Yes."

"And he studied them with you?"

"Yes."

"And is there any particular reference that was your favourite, one that he knew you were intimately acquainted with, so that you would recognize in it some reference to himself?"

"I see what you're driving at, of course," said Harlan. He grew thoughtful.

"Well?' asked Twissell with an edge of impatience.

Harlan said, "My news magazines, almost surely. News magazines were a phenomenon of the early 20's. The one of which I have nearly a complete set dates from early in the 20th and continues well into the 22nd."

"Good. Now is there any way, do you suppose, in which Cooper could make use of that news magazine to carry a message? Remember, he'd know you'd be reading the periodical, that you'd be acquainted with it, that you'd know your way about in it."

"I don't know." Harlan shook his head. "The magazine affected an artificial style. It was selective rather than inclusive and quite unpredictable. It would be difficult or even impossible to rely on its printing something you would plan to have it print. Cooper couldn't very well create news and be sure of its appearance. Even if Cooper managed to get a position on its editorial staff, which is very unlikely, he couldn't be certain that his exact writing would pass the various editors. I don't see it, Computer."

Twissell said, "For Time's sake, think! Concentrate on that news magazine. You're in the 20th and you're Cooper with his education and background. You taught the boy, Harlan. You moulded his thinking. Now what would he do? How would he go about placing something in the magazine; something with the exact wording he wants?"

Harlan's eyes widened. "An advertisement!"

"What?"

"An advertisement. A paid notice which they would be compelled to print exactly as requested. Cooper and I discussed them occasionally."

"Ah, yes. They have that sort of thing in the 186th," said Twissell.

"Not like the 20th. The 20th is peak in that respect. The cultural milieu –"

"Considering the advertisement now," interposed Twissell hastily, "what kind would it be?"

"I wish I knew."

Twissell stared at the lighted end of his cigarette as though seeking inspiration. "He can't say anything directly. He can't say: 'Cooper of the 78th, stranded in the 20th and calling Eternity –' "

"How can you be sure?"

"Impossible! To give the 20th information we know they did not have would be as damaging to the Mallansohn circle as would wrong action on our part. We're still here, so in his whole lifetime in the current Reality of the Primitive he's done no harm of that sort."

"Besides which," said Harlan, retreating from the contemplation of the circular reasoning which seemed to bother Twissell so little, "the news magazine is not likely to agree to publish anything which seems mad to it or which it cannot understand. It would suspect fraud or some form of illegality and would not wish to be implicated. So Cooper couldn't use Standard Intertemporal for his message."

"It would have to be something subtle," said Twissell. "He would have to use indirection. He would have to place an advertisement that would seem perfectly normal to the men of the Primitive. Perfectly normal! And yet something that is obvious to us, once we know what we were searching for. Very obvious. Obvious at a glance because it would have to be found among uncounted individual items. How big do you suppose it would be, Harlan? Are those advertisements expensive?"

"Quite expensive, I believe."

"And Cooper would have to hoard his money. Besides which, to avoid the wrong kind of attention, it would have to be small, anyway. Guess, Harlan. How large?"

Harlan spread his hands. "Half a column?"

"Column?"

"They were printed magazines, you know. On paper. With print arranged in columns."

"Oh yes, I can't seem to separate literature and film somehow.... Well, we must have a first approximation of another sort now. We must look for a half-column advertisement which will, practically at a glance, give evidence that the man who placed it came from another Century (in the upwhen direction, of course) and yet which is so normal an advertisement that no man of that Century would see anything suspicious in it."

Harlan said, "What if I don't find it?"

"You will. Eternity exists, doesn't it? As long as it does, we're on the right track. Tell me, can you recall such an advertisement in your work with Cooper? Anything which struck you, even momentarily, as odd, queer, unusual, subtly wrong."

"No."

"I don't want an answer so quickly. Take five minutes and think."

"No point. At the time I was going over the news magazines with Cooper, he hadn't been in the 20th."

"Please, boy. Use your head. Sending Cooper to the 20th has introduced an alteration. There's no Change; it isn't an irreversible alteration. But there have been some changes with a small 'c', or micro-changes, as it is usually referred to in Computation. At the instant Cooper was sent to the 20th, the advertisement appeared in the appropriate issue of the magazine. Your own Reality has micro-changed in the sense that you may have looked at the page with that advertisement on it rather than one without that advertisement as you did in the previous Reality. Do you understand?"

Harlan was again bewildered, almost as much at the ease

with which Twissell picked his way through the jungle of temporal logic, as at the "paradoxes" of Time. He shook his head. "I remember nothing of the sort."

"Well, then, where do you keep the files of that periodical?"

"I had a special library built on Level Two, using the Cooper priority."

"Good enough," said Twissell. "Let's go there. *Now!*"

Harlan watched Twissell stare curiously at the old, bound volumes in the library and then take one down. They were so old that the fragile paper had to be preserved by special methods and they creaked under Twissell's insufficiently gentle handling.

Harlan winced. In better times he would have ordered Twissell away from the books, Senior Computer though he was.

The old man peered through the crinkling pages and silently mouthed the archaic words. "This is the English the linguists are always talking about, isn't it?" he asked, tapping a page.

"Yes. English," muttered Harlan.

Twissell put the volume back. "Heavy and clumsy."

Harlan shrugged. To be sure, most of the Centuries of Eternity were film eras. A respectable minority were molecular-recording eras. Still, print and paper were not unheard of.

He said, "Books don't require the investment in technology that films do."

Twissell rubbed his chin. "Quite. Shall we get started?"

He took another volume down from the shelf, opening it at random and staring at the page with odd intentness.

Harlan thought: Does the man think he's going to hit the solution by a lucky stab?

The thought might have been correct, for Twissell, meeting Harlan's appraising eyes, reddened and put the book away.

Harlan took the first volume of the 19.25th Centicentury and began turning the pages regularly. Only his right hand and his eyes moved. The rest of his body remained at rigid attention.

At what seemed aeonic intervals to himself Harlan rose, grunting, for a new volume. On those occasions there would be the coffee break or the sandwich break or the other breaks.

Harlan said heavily, "It's useless your staying."

Twissell said, "Do I bother you?"

"No."

"Then I'll stay," muttered Twissell. Throughout he wandered occasionally to the bookshelves, staring helplessly at the bindings. The sparks of his furious cigarettes burned his finger ends at times, but he disregarded them.

A physioday ended.

Sleep was poor and sparse. Midmorning, between two volumes, Twissell lingered over his last sip of coffee and said, "I wonder sometimes why I didn't throw up my Computership after the matter of my – You know."

Harlan nodded.

"I felt like it," he old man went on. "I felt like it. For physiomonths, I hoped desperately that no Changes would come in my way. I got morbid about it. I began to wonder if Changes were right. Funny, the tricks emotions will play on you.

"*You* know Primitive history, Harlan. You know what it was like. Its Reality flowed blindly along the line of maximum probability. If that maximum probability involved a pandemic, or ten Centuries of slave economy, a breakdown of technology, or even a – a – let's see, what's really bad – even an atomic war if one had been possible then, why, by Time – it *happened*. There was nothing to stop it.

"But where Eternity exists, that's been stopped. Upwhen from the 28th, things like that don't happen. Father Time, we've lifted our Reality to a level of well-being far beyond anything Primitive times could imagine; to a level which, but for the interference of Eternity, would have been very low probability indeed."

Harlan thought in shame: What's he trying to do? Get me to work harder? I'm doing my best.

Twissell said, "If we miss our chance now, Eternity disappears, probably through all of physiotime. And in one vast Change all Reality reverts to maximum probability with, I am positive, atomic warfare and the end of man."

Harlan said, "I'd better get on to the next volume."

At the next break Twissell said helplessly, "There's so much to do. Isn't there a faster way?"

Harlan said, "Name it. To me it seems that I must look at every single page. And look at every part of it, too. How can I do it faster?"

Methodically he turned the pages.

"Eventually," said Harlan, "the print starts blurring and that means it's time for sleep."

A second physioday ended.

At 10:22 A.M., Standard Physiotime, of the third physioday of the search Harlan stared at a page in quiet wonder and said, "This is it!"

Twissell didn't absorb the statement. He said, "What?"

Harlan looked up, his face twisted with astonishment. "You know, I didn't believe it. By Time, I never really believed it, even while you were working out all that rigmarole about news magazines and advertisements."

Twissell had absorbed it now. "*You've found it!*"

He leaped at the volume Harlan was holding it, clutching at it with shaking fingers.

Harlan held it out of reach and slammed the volume shut. "Just a moment. *You* won't find it, even if I showed you the page."

"What are you doing?" shrieked Twissell. "You've lost it."

"It's not lost. I know where it is. But first –"

"First what?"

Harlan said. "There's one point remaining, Computer Twissell. You say I can have Noÿs. Bring her to me, then. Let me see her."

Twissell stared at Harlan, his thin white hair in disarray. "Are you joking?"

"No," said Harlan sharply, "I'm not joking. You assured me that you would make arrangements – Are *you* joking? Noÿs and I would be together. You promised that."

"Yes I did. That part's settled."

"Then produce her alive, well, and untouched."

"But I don't understand you. I don't have her. No one has. She's still in the far upwhen, where Finge reported her to be. No one has touched her. Great Time, I told you she was safe."

Harlan stared at the old man and grew tense. He said, chokingly, "You're playing with words. All right, she's in the far upwhen, but what good is that to me? Take down the barrier at the 100,000th –"

"The what?"

"The barrier. The kettle won't pass it."

"You never said anything of this," said Twissell wildly.

"I haven't?" said Harlan with sharp surprise. Hadn't he? He had thought of it often enough. He had never said a word about it? He couldn't recall, at that. But then he hardened.

He said, "All right. I tell you *now*. Take it down."

"But the thing is impossible. A barrier against the kettle? A

160

temporal barrier?"

"Are you telling me you didn't put one up?"

"I didn't. By Time, I swear it."

"Then – then –" Harlan felt himself grow pale. "Then the Council did it. They know of all this and they've taken action independently of you and – and by all of Time and Reality, they can whistle for their ad and for Cooper, for Mallansohn and all of Eternity. They'll have none of it. None of it."

"Wait. Wait." Twissell yanked despairingly at Harlan's elbow. "Keep hold of yourself. Think, boy, think. The Council put up no barrier."

"It's there."

"But they can't have put up such a barrier. No one could have. It's theoretically impossible."

"You don't know it all. It's there."

"I know more than anyone else on the Council and such a thing is impossible."

"But it's there."

"But if it is –"

And Harlan grew sufficiently aware of his surroundings to realize that there was a kind of abject fear in Twissell's eyes; a fear that had not been there even when he first learned of Cooper's misdirection and of the impending end of Eternity.

CHAPTER SIXTEEN

THE HIDDEN CENTURIES

ANDREW HARLAN watched the men at work with abstracted eyes. They ignored him politely because he was a Technician. Ordinarily they were Maintenance men. But now he watched them and, in his misery, he even caught himself envying them.

They were service personnel from the Department of Intertemporal Transportation, in dun-grey uniforms with shoulder patches showing a red, double-headed arrow against a black background. They used intricate force-field equipment to test the kettle motors and the degrees of hyper-freedom among the kettleways. They had, Harlan imagined, little theoretical knowledge of temporal engineering, but it was obvious that they had a vast practical knowledge of the subject.

Harlan had not learned much concerning Maintenance when he was a Cub. Or, to put it more accurately, he had not really wished to learn. Cubs who did not make the grade were put into Maintenance. The "unspecialized profession" (as the euphemism had it) was the landmark of failure and the average Cub automatically avoided the subject.

Yet now, as he watched the Maintenance men at work, they seemed to Harlan to be quietly, tensionlessly efficient, reasonably happy.

Why not? They outnumbered the Specialists, the "true Eternals", ten to one. They had a society of their own, residential levels devoted to them, pleasures of their own. Their labour was fixed at so many hours per physioday and there was no social pressure in their case to make them relate their sparetime activity to their profession. They had time, as Specialists did not, to devote to the literature and film dramatizations culled out of the various Realities.

It was they, after all, who probably had the better-rounded personalities. It was the Specialist's life which was harried and affected, artificial in comparison with the sweet and simple life of Maintenance.

Maintenance was the foundation of Eternity. Strange that such an obvious fact had not struck him earlier. They supervised the importation of food and water from Time, the disposal of waste, the functioning of the power plants. They kept all the machinery of Eternity running smoothly. If every Specialist were to die of a stroke on the spot, Maintenance could keep Eternity going indefinitely. Yet were Maintenance to disappear, the Specialists would have to abandon Eternity in days or die miserably.

Did Maintenance men resent the loss of their homewhens, of their womanless, childless lives? Was security from poverty, disease, and Reality Change sufficient compensation? Were their views ever consulted on any matter of importance? Harlan felt some of the fire of the social reformer within him.

Senior Computer Twissell broke Harlan's train of thought by bustling in at a half run, looking even more haunted than he had an hour before, when he had left, with Maintenance already at work.

Harlan thought: How does he keep it up? He's an old man.

Twissell glanced about him with birdlike brightness as the men automatically straightened up to respectful attention.

He said, "What about the kettleways?"

One of the men responded, "Nothing wrong, sir. The ways are clear, the fields mesh."

"You've checked everything?"

"Yes, sir. As far upward as the Department stations go."

Twissell said, "Then go."

There was no mistaking the brusque insistence of his dismissal. They bowed respectfully, turned, and hastened out briskly.

Twissell and Harlan were alone in the kettleways.

Twissell turned to him. "You'll stay here. Please."

Harlan shook his head. "I must go."

Twissell said, "Surely you understand. If anything happens to me, you still know how to find Cooper. If anything happens to you, what can I or any Eternal or any combination of Eternals do alone?"

Harlan shook his head again.

Twissell put a cigarette between his lips. He said, "Sennor is suspicious. He's called me several times in the past two physiodays. Why am I in seclusion, he wants to know. When he finds out I've ordered a complete overhaul of the kettleway machinery ... I must go now, Harlan. I can't delay."

"I don't want to delay. I'm ready."

"You insist on going?"

"If there's no barrier, there'll be no danger. Even if there is, I've been there already and come back. What are you afraid of, Computer?"

"I don't want to risk anything I don't have to."

"Then use your logic, Computer. Make the decision that I'm to go with you. If Eternity still exists after that, then it means that the circle can still be closed. It means we'll survive. If it's a wrong decision, then Eternity will pass into nonexistence, but it will anyway if I don't go, because without Noÿs, I'll make no move to get Cooper. I swear it."

Twissell said, "I'll bring her back to you."

"If it's so simple and safe, there will be no harm if I come along."

Twissell was in an obvious torture of hesitation. He said gruffly, "Well, then, come!"

And Eternity survived.

Twissell's haunted look did not disappear once they were

within the kettle. He stared at the skimming figures of the temporometer. Even the scaler gauge, which measured in units of Kilocenturies, and which the men had adjusted for this particular purpose, was clicking at minute intervals.

He said, "You should not have come."

Harlan shrugged. "Why not?"

"It disturbs me. No sensible reason. Call it a long-standing superstition of mine. It makes me restless." He clasped his hands together, holding them tightly.

Harlan said, "I don't understand you."

Twissell seemed eager to talk, as though to exorcize some mental demon. He said, "Maybe you'll appreciate this, at that. You're the expert on the Primitive. How long did man exist in the Primitive?"

Harlan said, "Ten thousand Centuries. Fifteen thousand, maybe."

"Yes. Beginning as a kind of primitive apelike creature and ending as Homo sapiens. Right?"

"It's common knowledge. Yes."

"Then it must be common knowledge that evolution proceeds at a fairly rapid pace. Fifteen thousand Centuries from ape to Homo sapiens."

"Well?"

"Well, I'm from a Century in the 30,000's –"

(Harlan could not help starting. He had never know Twissell's homewhen or known of anyone who did.)

"I'm from a Century in the 30,000's," Twissell said again, "and you're from the 95th. The time between our homewhens is twice the total length of time of man's existence in the Primitive, yet what change is there between us? I was born with four fewer teeth than you, and without an appendix. The physiological differences about end with that. Our metabolism is almost the same. The major difference is that your body can synthesize the steroid nucleus and my body can't, so that I require cholesterol in my diet and you don't. I was able to breed with a woman of the 575th. That's how undifferentiated with time the species is."

Harlan was unimpressed. He had never questioned the basic identity of man throughout the Centuries. It was one of those things you lived with and took for granted. He said, "There have been cases of species living unchanged through millions of Centuries."

164

"Not many, though. And it remains a fact that the cessation of human evolution seems to coincide with the development of Eternity. Just coincidence? It's not a question which is considered, except by a few here and there like Sennor, and I've never been a Sennor. I didn't believe speculation was proper. If something couldn't be checked by a Computaplex, it had no business taking up the time of a Computer. And yet, in my younger days, I sometimes thought –"

"Of what?" Harlan thought: Well, it's something to listen to, anyway.

"I sometimes thought about Eternity as it was when it was first established. It stretched over just a few Centuries in the 30's and 40's, and its function was mostly trade. It interested itself in the reforestation of denuded areas, shipping topsoil back and forth, fresh water, fine chemicals. Those were simple days.

"But then we discovered Reality Changes. Senior Computer Henry Wadsman, in the dramatic manner with which we are all acquainted, prevented a war by removing the safety brake of a Congressman's ground vehicle. After that, more and more, Eternity shifted its centre of gravity from trade to Reality Change. Why?"

Harlan said, "The obvious reason. Betterment of humanity."

"Yes. Yes. In normal times, I think so, too. But I'm talking of my nightmare. What if there were another reason, an unexpressed one, an unconscious one. A man who can travel into the indefinite future may meet man as far advanced over himself as he himself is over an ape. Why not?"

"Maybe. But men are men –"

"– even in the 70,000th. Yes, I know. And have our Reality Changes had something to do with it? We bred out the unusual. Even Sennor's homewhen with its hairless creatures is under continual question and that's harmless enough. Perhaps in all honesty, in all sincerity, we've prevented human evolution because we don't *want* to meet the supermen."

Still no spark was struck. Harlan said, "Then it's done. What does it matter?"

"But what if the superman exists just the same, further up-when than we can reach? We control only to the 70,000th. Beyond that are the Hidden Centuries! Why are they hidden? Because evolved man does not want to deal with us and bars us from his time? Why do we allow them to remain hidden? Because we don't want to deal with them and, having failed to enter in our first attempts, we refuse even to make additional attempts? I don't say it's our conscious reason, but conscious or unconscious, it's a reason."

"Grant everything," said Harlan sullenly. "They're out of our reach and we're out of theirs. Live and let live."

Twissell seemed struck by the phrase. "Live and let live. But we don't. We make Changes. The Changes extend only through a few Centuries before temporal inertia causes its effects to die out. You remember Sennor brought that up as one of the unanswered problems of Time at our breakfast. What he might have said was that it's all a matter of statistics. Some Changes affect more Centuries than others. Theoretically, any number of Centuries can be affected by the proper Change; a hundred Centuries, a thousand, a hundred thousand. Evolved man of the Hidden Centuries may know that. Suppose he is disturbed by the possibility that someday a Change may reach him clear by the 200,000th."

"It's useless to worry about such things," said Harlan with the air of a man who had much greater worries.

"But, suppose," went on Twissell in a whisper, "they were calm enough as long as we left the Sections of the Hidden Centuries empty. It meant we weren't aggressing. Suppose this truce, or whatever you wish to call it, were broken, and someone appeared to have established permanent residence upwhen from the 70,000th. Suppose they thought it might mean the first of a serious invasion? They can bar us from their Time, so their science is that far advanced beyond ours. Suppose they may further do what seems impossible to us and throw a barrier across the kettleways, cutting us off –"

And now Harlan was on his feet, in full horror, "*They* have Noÿs?"

"I don't know. It's speculation. Maybe there is no barrier. Maybe there was something wrong with your ket –"

"There was a barrier!" yelled Harlan. "What other explanation is there? Why didn't you tell me this before."

"I didn't believe it," groaned Twissell. "I still don't. I shouldn't have said a word of this foolish dreaming. My own fears – the question of Cooper – everything – But wait, just a few minutes."

He pointed at the temporometer. The scaler indicated them to be between the 95,000th and the 96,000th Centuries.

Twissell's hand on the control slowed the kettle. The 99,000th was passed. The scaler's motions stopped. The individual Centuries could be read.

99,726, – 99, 727, – 99,728 –

"What will we do?" muttered Harlan.

Twissell shook his head in a gesture that spoke eloquently of patience and hope, but perhaps also of helplessness.

99,851 – 99,852 – 99,853 –

Harlan steeled himself for the shock of the barrier and thought desperately: Would preserving Eternity be the only means of finding time to fight back at the creatures of the Hidden Centuries? How else recover Noÿs? Dash back, back to the 575th and work like fury to –

99,938, – 99,939, – 99,940 –

Harlan held his breath. Twissell slowed the kettle further, let it creep. It responded perfectly to the controls.

"No, now, now," said Harlan in a whisper, unaware that he had made any sound at all.

99,998 – 99,999 – 100,000 – 100,001 – 100,002 –

The numbers mounted and the two men watched them continue to mount in paralytic silence.

Then Twissell cried, "There *is* no barrier."

And Harlan answered, "There was! There was!" Then, in agony, "Maybe they've got her, and need a barrier no longer."

111,394th!

Harlan leaped from the kettle, and raised his voice. "Noÿs! Noÿs."

The echoes bounced off the walls of the empty Section in hollow syncopation.

Twissell, climbing out more sedately, called after the younger man, "Wait, Harlan –"

That was useless. Harlan, at a run, was hurtling along the corridors towards that portion of the Section they had made a kind of home.

He thought vaguely of the possibility of meeting one of Twissell's "evolved men" and momentarily his skin prickled, but then that was drowned in his urgent need to find Noÿs.

"Noÿs!"

And all at once, so quickly that she was in his arms before he was sure he had seen her at all, she was there and with him, and her arms were around him and clutching him and her cheek

167

was against his shoulder and her dark hair was soft against his chin.

"Andrew?" she said, her voice muffled by the pressure of his body. "Where were you? It's been days and I was getting frightened."

Harlan held her out at arm's length, staring at her with a kind of hungry solemnity. "Are you all right?"

"*I'm* all right. I thought something might have happened to you. I thought –" She broke off, terror springing into her eyes and grasped, "Andrew!"

Harlan whirled.

It was only Twissell, panting.

Noÿs must have gained confidence from Harlan's expression. She said more quietly, "Do you know him, Andrew? Is it all right?"

Harlan said, "It's all right. This is my superior, Senior Computer Laban Twissell. He knows of you."

"A Senior Computer?" Noÿs shrank away.

Twissell advanced slowly. "I will help you my child. I will help you both. The Technician has my promise, if he would only believe it."

"My apologies, Computer," said Harlan stiffly, and not yet entirely repentant.

"Forgiven," said Twissell. He held out his hand, took the girl's reluctant one. "Tell me, girl, has it been well with you here?"

"I've been worried."

"There's been no one here, since Harlan last left you."

"N – no, sir."

"No one at all? Nothing?"

She shook her head. Her dark eyes sought Harlan's. "Why do you ask?"

"Nothing, girl. A foolish nightmare. Come, we will take you back to the 575th."

On the kettle back Andrew Harlan sank, by degrees, into a troubled and deepening silence. He did not look up when the 100,000th was passed in the downwhen direction and Twissell had snorted an obvious sigh of relief as though he had half expected to be trapped on the upwhen side.

He scarcely moved when Noÿs's hand stole into his, and the manner in which he returned the pressure of her fingers was almost mechanical.

Noÿs slept in another room and now Twissell's restlessness reached a peak of devouring intensity.

"The advertisement, boy! You have your woman. My part of the agreement is done."

Silently, still abstracted, Harlan turned the pages of the volume on his desk. He found his page.

"It's simple enough," he said, "but it's in English. I'll read it to you and then translate it."

It was a small advertisement in the upper left-hand corner of a page numbered 30. Against an irregular line drawing as background were the unadorned words, in block letters:

ALL THE
TALK
OF THE
MARKET

Underneath, in smaller letters, it said: 'Investments News-Letter, P.O. Box 14, Denver, Colorado."

Twissell listened painstakingly to Harlan's translation and was obviously disappointed. He said, "What is the market? What do they mean by that?"

"The stock market," said Harlan impatiently. "A system by which private capital was invested in business. But that's not the point at all. Don't you see the line drawing against which the advertisement is set?"

"Yes. The mushroom cloud of an A-bomb blast. An attention getter. What about it?"

Harlan exploded. "Great Time, Computer, what's wrong with you? Look at the date of the magazine issue."

He pointed to the top heading, just to the left of the page number. It read March 28, 1932.

Harlan said, "That scarcely needs translation. The numbers are about those of Standard Intertemporal and you see it's the 19.32nd Century. Don't you know that at that time no human being who had ever lived had seen the mushroom cloud? No one could possibly reproduce it so accurately, except –"

"Now, wait. It's just a line pattern," said Twissell, trying to retain his equilibrium. "It might resemble the mushroom cloud only coincidentally."

"Might it? Will you look at the wording again?" Harlan's fingers punched out the short lines: "All the – Talk – Of the – Market. The initials spell out ATOM, which is English for atom.

Is that coincidence, too? Not a chance.

"Don't you see, Computer, how this advertisement fits the conditions you yourself set up? It caught my eye instantly. Cooper knew it would out of sheer anachronism. At the same time, it has no meaning other than its face value, no meaning at all, for any man of the 19.32nd.

"So it must be Cooper. That's his message. We have the date to the nearest week of Centicentury. We have his mailing address. It is only necessary to go after him and I'm the only one with enough knowledge of the Primitive to manage that."

"And you'll go?" Twissell's face was ablaze with relief and happiness.

"I'll go – on one condition."

Twissell frowned in a sudden reversal of emotion. "Again conditions?"

"The same condition. I'm not adding new ones. Noÿs must be safe. She must come with me. I will not leave her behind."

"You *still* don't trust me? In what way have I failed you? What can there be that still disturbs you?"

"One thing, Computer," said Harlan solemnly. "One thing still. There *was* a barrier across the 100,000th. Why? That is what still disturbs me."

CHAPTER SEVENTEEN

THE CLOSING CIRCLE

It did not stop disturbing him. It was a matter that grew in his mind as the days of preparation sped by. It interposed itself between him and Twissell; then between him and Noÿs. When the day of departure came, he was only distantly aware of the fact.

It was all he could do to rouse a shadow of interest when Twissell returned from a session with the Council subcommittee. He said, "How did it go?"

Twissell said wearily, "It wasn't exactly the most pleasant conversation I've ever had."

Harlan was almost willing to let it go at that, but he broke his moment's silence with a muttered "I suppose you said nothing about –"

"No, no," was the testy response. "I said nothing about the girl or about your part in the misdirection of Cooper. It was an unfortunate error, a mechanical failure. I took full responsibility."

Harlan's conscience, burdened as it was, could find room for a twinge. He said, "That won't affect you well."

"What can they do? They must wait for the correction to be made before they can touch me. If we fail, we're all beyond help or harm. If we succeed, success itself will probably protect me. And if it doesn't –" The old man shrugged. "I plan to retire from active participation in Eternity's affairs thereafter anyway." But he fumbled his cigarette and disposed of it before it was half burned away.

He sighed. "I would rather not have brought them into this at all, but there would have been no way, otherwise, of using the special kettle for further trips past the downwhen terminus."

Harlan turned away. His thoughts moved round and about the same channels that had been occupied to the increasing exclusion of all else for days. He heard Twissell's further remark dimly, but it was only at its repetition that he said with a start, "Pardon me?"

"I say, is your woman ready, boy? Does she understand what she's to do?"

"She's ready. I've told her everything."

"How did she take it?"

"What ... Oh, yes, uh, as I expected her to. She's not afraid."

"It's less than three physiohours now."

"I know."

That was all for the moment, and Harlan was left alone with his thoughts and a sickening realization of what he must do.

With the kettle loading done and the controls adjusted Harlan and Noÿs appeared in a final change of costume, approximating that of an urbanized area of the early 20th.

Noÿs had modified Harlan's suggestion for her wardrobe, according to some instinctive feeling she claimed women had when it came to matters of clothing and aesthetics. She chose thoughtfully from pictures in the advertisements of the appropriate volumes of the news magazine and had minutely scrutinized items imported from a dozen different Centuries.

Occasionally she would say to Harlan, "What do you think?"

He would shrug. "If it's instinctive knowledge, I'll leave it to you."

"That's a bad sign, Andrew," she said, with a lightness that did not quite ring true. "You're too pliable. What's the matter, anyway? You're just not yourself. You haven't been for days."

"I'm all right," Harlan said in a monotone.

Twissell's first sight of them in the role of natives of the 20th elicited a feeble attempt at jocularity. "Father Time," he said, "what ugly costumes in the Primitive, and yet how it fails to hide your beauty, my – my dear."

Noÿs smiled warmly at him, and Harlan, standing there impassively silent, was forced to admit that Twissell's rust-choked vein of gallantry had something of truth in it. Noÿs's clothing encompassed her without accentuating her as clothing should. Her make-up was confined to unimaginative dabs of colour on lips and cheeks and an ugly arrangement of the eyebrow line. Her lovely hair (this had been the worst of it) had been cut ruthlessly. Yet she was beautiful.

Harlan himself was already growing accustomed to his own uncomfortable belt, the tightness of fit under armpits and in the crotch and the mousy lack of colour about his rough-textured clothing. Wearing strange costumes to suit a Century was an old story to him.

Twissell was saying, "Now what I really wanted to do was to install hand controls inside the kettle, as we discussed, but there isn't any way, apparently. The engineers simply must have a source of power large enough to handle temporal displacement and that isn't available outside Eternity. Temporal tension while occupying the Primitive is all that can be managed. However, we have a return level."

He led them into the kettle, picking his way among the piled supplies, and pointed out the obtruding finger of metal that now marred the smooth inner wall of the kettle.

"It amounts to the installation of a simple switch," he said. "Instead of returning automatically to Eternity, the kettle will remain in the Primitive indefinitely. Once the lever is plunged home, however, you will return. There will then be the matter of the second and, I hope, final trip –"

"A second trip?" asked Noÿs at once.

Harlan said, "I haven't explained that. Look, this first trip is intended merely to fix the time of Cooper's arrival precisely. We don't know how long a Time-lapse exists between his arrival and the placing of the advertisement. We'll reach him by the post-office box, and learn, if possible, the exact minute of his arrival, or as close as we can, anyway. We can then return to that moment plus fifteen minutes to allow for the kettle to have left Cooper –"

Twissell interposed, "Couldn't have the kettle in the same place at the same time in two different physiotimes, you know," and tried to smile.

Noÿs seemed to absorb it. "I see," she said, not too definitely.

Twissell said to Noÿs, "Picking up Cooper at the time of his arrival will reverse all micro-changes. The A-bomb advertisement will disappear again and Cooper will know only that the kettle, having disappeared as we told him it would, had unexpectedly appeared again. He will not know that he was in the wrong Century and he will not be told. We will tell him that there was some vital instruction we had forgotten to give him (we'll have to manufacture some) and we can only hope that he will regard the matter as so unimportant that he won't mention being sent back twice when he writes his memoir."

Noÿs lifted her plucked eyebrows. "It's very complicated."

"Yes. Unfortunately." He rubbed his hands together and looked at the others as though nursing an inner doubt. Then he straightened, produced a fresh cigarette, and even managed a certain jauntiness as he said, "And now, boy, good luck."

Twissell touched hands briefly with Harlan, nodded to Noÿs, and stepped out of the kettle.

"Are we leaving now?" asked Noÿs of Harlan when they were alone.

"In a few minutes," said Harlan.

He glanced sideways at Noÿs. She was looking up at him, smiling, unfrightened. Momentarily his own spirits responded to that. But that was emotion, not reason, he councilled himself; instinct, not thought. He looked away.

The trip was nothing, or almost nothing; no different from an ordinary kettle ride. Midway there was a kind of internal jar that might have been the downwhen terminus and might have been purely psychomatic. It was barely noticeable.

And then they were in the Primitive and they stepped into craggy, lonely world brightened by the splendour of an afternoon sun. There was a soft wind with a chilly edge to it and, most of all, silence.

The bare rocks were tumbled and mighty, coloured into dull rainbows by compounds of iron, copper, and chromium. The grandeur of the manless and all but lifeless surroundings dwarfed and shrivelled Harlan. Eternity, which did not belong to the world of matter, had no sun and none but imported air. His memories of his own homewhen were dim. His Observations in the various Centuries had dealt with men and their cities. He had never experienced *this*.

Noÿs touched his elbow.

"Andrew! I'm cold."

He turned to her with a start.

She said, "Hadn't we better set up the Radiant?"

He said, "Yes. In Cooper's cavern."

"Do you know where it is?"

"It's right here," he said shortly.

He had no doubt of that. The memoir had located it and first Cooper, now he, had been pin-pointed back to it.

He had not doubted precision pin-pointing in time-travel since his Cubhood days. He remembered himself then, facing Educator Yarrow seriously, saying, "But Earth moves about the Sun, and the Sun moves about the Galactic Centre and the Galaxy moves, too. If you started from some point on Earth, and move downwhen a hundred years, you'll be in empty space, because it will take a hundred years for Earth to reach that point." (Those were the days when he still referred to a Century as a "hundred years".)

And Educator Yarrow had snapped back, "You don't separate Time from Space. Moving through Time, you share Earth's motions. Or do you believe that a bird flying through the air whiffs out into space because the Earth is hurrying around the Sun at eighteen miles a second and vanishes from under the creature?"

Arguing from analogy is risky, but Harlan obtained more rigorous proof in later days and, now, after a scarcely pre-cedented trip into the Primitive, he could turn confidently and feel no surprise at finding the opening precisely where he had been told it would be.

He moved the camouflage of loose rubble and rock to one side and entered.

He probed the darkness within, using the white beam of his flash almost like a scalpel. He scoured the walls, ceiling, floor, every inch.

Noÿs remaining close behind him, whispered, "What are you looking for?"

He said, "Something. Anything."

He found his something, anything, at the very rear of the cave in the shape of a flattish stone covering greenish sheets like a paperweight.

Harlan threw the stone aside and flipped the sheets past one thumb.

"What are they?" asked Noÿs.

"Bank notes. Medium of exchange. Money."

"Did you know they were there?"

"I knew nothing. I just hoped."

It was only a matter of using Twissell's reserve logic, of calculating cause from effect. Eternity existed, so Cooper must be making correct decisions, too. In assuming the advertisement would pull Harlan into the correct Time, the cave was an obvious additional means of communication.

Yet this was almost better than he had dared hope. More than once during the preparations for his trip into the Primitive, Harlan had thought that making his way into a town with nothing but bullion in his possession would result in suspicion and delay.

Cooper had managed, to be sure, but Cooper had had time. Harlan hefted the sheaf of bills. And he must have used time to accumulate this much. He had done well, the youngster, marvellously well.

And the circle was closing!

The supplies had been moved into the cave, in the increasingly ruddy glow of the westering sun. The kettle had been covered by a diffuse reflecting film which would hide it from any but the closest of prying eyes, and Harlan had a blaster to take care of those, if need be. The Radiant was set up in the cave and the flash was wedged into a crevice, so that they had heat and light.

Outside it was a chill March night.

Noÿs stared thoughtfully into the smooth paraboloid interior of the Radiant as it slowly rotated. She said, "Andrew, what are your plans?"

"Tomorrow morning," he said, "I'll leave for the nearest town. I know where it is – or should be." (He changed it back to "is" in his mind. There would be no trouble. Twissell's logic again.)

"I'll come with you, won't I?"

He shook his head. "You can't speak the language, for one thing, and the trip will be difficult enough for one to negotiate."

Noÿs looked strangely archaic in her short hair and the sudden anger in her eyes made Harlan look away uneasily.

She said, "I'm no fool, Andrew. You scarcely speak to me. You don't look at me. What is it? Is your homewhen morality taking hold? Do you feel you have betrayed Eternity and are you blaming me for that? Do you feel I have corrupted you? What is it?"

He said, "You don't know what I feel."

She said, "Then describe it. You might as well. You'll never have a chance as good as this one. Do you feel love? For me? You couldn't or you wouldn't be using me as a scapegoat. Why did you bring me here? Tell me. Why not have left me in Eternity since you have no use for me here and since it seems you can hardly bear the sight of me?"

Harlan muttered, "There's danger."

"Oh, come now."

"It's more than danger. It's a nightmare. Computer Twissell's nightmare," said Harlan. "It was during our last panicky flash upwhen into the Hidden Centuries that he told me of thoughts he had had concerning those Centuries. He speculated on the possibility of evolved varieties of man, new species, supermen perhaps, hiding in the far upwhen, cutting themselves off from our interference, plotting to end our tamperings with Reality. He thought it was they who built the barrier across the 100,000th. Then we found you, and Computer Twissell abandoned his nightmare. He decided there had never been a barrier. He returned to the more immediate problem of salvaging Eternity.

"But I, you see, had been infected by his nightmare. I had experienced the barrier, so I knew it existed. No Eternal had built it, for Twissell said such a thing was theoretically impossible. Maybe Eternity's theories didn't go far enough. The barrier was there. Someone had built it. Or something.

"Of course," he went on thoughtfully, "Twissell was wrong in some ways. He felt that man *must* evolve, but that's not so. Paleontology is not one of the sciences that interests Eternals, but it interested the late Primitives, so I picked up a bit of it myself. I know this much: species evolve only to meet the pressures of new environments. In a stable environment, a species

176

may remain unchanged for millions of Centuries. Primitive man evolved rapidly because his environment was a harsh and changing one. Once, however, mankind learned to create his own environment, he created a pleasant and stable one, so he just naturally stopped evolving."

"I don't know what you're talking about," said Noÿs, sounding not the least mollified, "and you're not saying anything about us, which is what I want to talk about."

Harlan managed to remain outwardly unmoved. He said, "Now why the barrier at the 100,000th? What purpose did it serve? You weren't harmed. What other meaning could it have? I asked myself: What happened because of its presence that would not have happened had it been absent?"

He paused, looking at his clumsy and heavy boots of natural leather. It occurred to him that he could add to his comfort by removing them for the night, but not now, not now ...

He said, "There was only one answer to that question. The existence of that barrier sent me raving back downwhen to get a neuronic whip, to assault Finge. It fired me to the thought of risking Eternity to get you back and smashing Eternity when I thought I had failed. Do you see?"

Noÿs stared at him with a mixture of horror and disbelief. "Do you mean the people in the upwhen wanted you to do all that? They planned it?"

"*Yes.* Don't look at me like that. *Yes!* And don't you see how it makes everything different? As long as I acted on my own, for reasons of my own, I'll take all the consequences, material and spiritual. But to be *fooled* into it, to be *tricked* into it, by people handling and manipulating my emotions as though I were a Computaplex on which it was only necessary to insert the properly perforated foils –"

Harlan realized suddenly that he was shouting and stopped abruptly. He let a few moments pass, then said, "That is impossible to take. I've got to undo what I was marionetted into doing. And when I undo it, I will be able to rest again."

And he would – perhaps. He could feel the coming of an impersonal triumph, dissociated from the personal tragedy which lay behind and ahead. The circle was closing!

Noÿs's hand reached out uncertainly as though to take his own rigid, unyielding one.

Harlan drew away, avoiding her sympathy. He said, "It had all been arranged. My meeting with you. Everything. My

177

emotional make-up had been analyzed. Obviously. Action and response. Push this button and the man will do that. Push that button and he will do this."

Harlan was speaking with difficulty, out of the depths of shame. He shook his head, trying to shake the horror of it away as a dog would water, then went on. "One thing I didn't understand at first. How did I come to guess that Cooper was to be sent back into the Primitive? It was a most unlikely thing to guess. I had no basis. Twissell didn't understand it. More than once he wondered how I could have done it with so little understanding of mathematics.

"Yet I had. The first time was that – that night. You were asleep, but I wasn't. I had the feeling then that there was something I must remember; some remark, some thought, *something* that I had caught sight of in the excitement and exhilaration of the evening. When I thought long, the whole significance of Cooper sprang into my mind, and along with it the thought entered my mind that I was in a position to destroy Eternity. Later I checked through histories of mathematics, but it was unnecessary really. I already knew. I was certain of it. How? How?"

Noÿs stared at him intently. She didn't try to touch him now. "Do you mean the men of the Hidden Centuries arranged that too? They put it all in your mind, then manoeuvred you properly?"

"Yes. Yes. Nor are they done. There is still work for them to do. The circle may be closing, but it is not yet closed."

"How can they do anything now? They're not here with us."

"No?" He said the word in so hollow a voice that Noÿs paled.

"Invisible superthings?" she whispered.

"Not superthings. Not invisible. I told you man would not evolve while he controlled his own environment. The people of the Hidden Centuries are Homo sapiens. Ordinary people."

"Then they're certainly not here."

Harlan said sadly, "You're here, Noÿs."

"Yes. And you. And no one else."

"You and I," agreed Harlan. "No one else. A woman of the Hidden Centuries and I ... Don't act any more, Noÿs. Please."

She stared at him with horror. "What are you saying, Andrew?"

"What I must say. What were *you* saying that evening, when

178

you gave me the peppermint drink? You were talking to me. Your soft voice – soft words ... I heard nothing, not consciously, but I remember your delicate voice whispering. About what? The downwhen journey of Cooper; the Samson-smash of Eternity. Am I right?"

Noÿs said, "I don't even know what Samson-smash means."

"You can guess very accurately, Noÿs. Tell me, when did you enter the 482nd? Whom did you replace? Or did you just – squeeze in? I had your Life-Plot worked out by an expert in the 2456th. In the new Reality, you had no existence at all. No analogue. Strange for such a small Change, but not impossible. And then the Life-Plotter said one thing which I heard with my ears but not with my mind. Strange that I should remember it. Perhaps even then, something clanged in my mind, but I was too full of – you to listen. He said: *'with the combination of factors you handed me, I don't quite see how she fits in the old Reality.'*

'He was right. You didn't fit in. You were an invader from the far upwhen, manipulating me and Finge, too, to suit yourself."

Noÿs said urgently, "Andrew –"

"It all fits in, if I had the eyes to look. A book-film in your house entitled *Social and Economic History*. It surprised me when I first saw it. You needed it, didn't you, to teach you how best to be a woman of the Century? Another item. Our first trip into the Hidden Centuries, remember? *You* stopped the kettle at the 111,394th. You stopped it with finesse, without fumbling. Where did you learn to control a kettle? If you were what you seemed to be, that would have been your first trip in a kettle. Why the 111,394th anyway? Was it your homewhen?"

She said softly, "Why did you bring me to the Primitive, Andrew?"

He shouted suddenly, "To protect Eternity. I could not tell what damage you might do there. Here you are helpless, because I know you. Admit that all I say is true! Admit it!"

He rose in a paroxysm of wrath, arm upraised. She did not flinch. She was utterly calm. She might have been modelled out of warm, beautiful wax. Harlan did not complete his motion.

He said, "Admit it!"

She said, "Are you so uncertain, after all your deductions? What will it matter to you whether I admit it or not?"

Harlan felt the wildness mount. "Admit it, anyway, so that I need feel no pain at all. None at all."

"Pain?"

"Because I have a blaster, Noÿs, and it is my intention to kill you."

CHAPTER EIGHTEEN

THE BEGINNING OF INFINITY

THERE was a crawling uncertainty inside Harlan, an irresolution that was consuming him. He had the blaster in his hand. It was aimed at Noÿs.

But why did she say nothing? Why did she persist in this impassive attitude?

How could he kill her?

How could he not kill her?

He said hoarsely, "Well?"

She moved, but it was only to clasp her hands loosely in her lap, to look more relaxed, more aloof. When she spoke her voice seemed scarcely that of a human being. Facing the muzzle of a blaster, it yet gained assurance and took on an almost mystic quality of impersonal strength.

She said, "You cannot wish to kill me only in order to protect Eternity. If that were your desire, you could stun me, tie me firmly, pin me within this cave and then take to your travels in the dawn. Or you might have asked Computer Twissell to keep me in solitary confinement during your absence in the Primitive. Or you might take me with you at dawn, lose me in the wastes. If it is only killing that will satisfy you, it is only because you think that I have betrayed you, that I have tricked you into love first in order that I might trick you into treason later. This is murder out of wounded pride and not at all the just retribution you tell yourself it is."

Harlan squirmed. "Are you from the Hidden Centuries? Tell me."

Noÿs said, "I am. Will you now blast?"

Harlan's finger trembled on the blaster's contact point. Yet he hesitated. Something irrational within him could still plead her case and point up the remnants of his own futile love and longing. Was she desperate at his rejection of her? Was she deliberately courting death by lying? Was she indulging in foolish heroics born of despair at his doubts of her?

No!

The book-films of the sickly-sweet literary traditions of the 289th might have it so, but not a girl like Noÿs. She was not one to meet her death at the hands of a false lover with the joyful masochism of a broken, bleeding lily.

Then was she scornfully denying his ability to kill her for any reason whatever? Was she confidently relying on the attraction she knew she had for him even now, certain that it would immobilize him, freeze him in weakness and shame.

That hit too closely. His finger clamped a bit harder on the contact.

Noÿs spoke again. "You're waiting. Does that mean you expect me to enter a brief for the defence?"

"What defence?" Harlan tried to make that scornful, yet he welcomed the diversion. It could postpone the moment when he must look down upon her blasted body, upon whatever remnants of bloody flesh might remain, and know that what had been done to his beautiful Noÿs had been done by his own hand.

He found excuses for his delay. He thought feverishly: Let her talk. Let her tell what she can about the Hidden Centuries. So much better protection for Eternity.

It put a front of firm policy on his action and for the moment he could look at her with as calm a face, almost, as she looked at him.

Noÿs might have read his mind. She said, "Do you want to know about the Hidden Centuries? If that will be a defence, it is easily done. Would you like to know, for instance, why Earth is empty of mankind after the 150,000th? Would you be interested?"

Harlan wasn't going to plead for knowledge, nor was he going to buy knowledge. He had the blaster. He was very intent on no show of weakness.

He said, "Talk!" and flushed at the little smile which was her first response to his exclamation.

She said, "At a moment in physiotime before Eternity had reached very far upwhen, before it had reached even the 10,000th, we of our Century – and you're right, it was the 111,394th – learned of Eternity's existence. We, too, had Time-travel, you see, but it was based on a completely different set of postulates than yours, and we preferred to view Time, rather

181

than shifting mass. Furthermore, we dealt with our past only, our downwhen.

"We discovered Eternity indirectly. First, we developed the calculus of Realities and tested our own Reality through it. We were amazed to find we lived in a Reality of rather low probability. It was a serious question. Why such an improbable Reality? ... You seem abstracted, Andrew! Are you interested at all?"

Harlan heard her say his name with all the intimate tenderness she had used in weeks past. It should grate on him now, anger him with its cynical faithlessness. And yet it didn't.

He said desperately, "Go on and get it over with, woman."

He tried to balance the warmth of her "Andrew" with the chill anger of his "woman" and yet she only smiled again, pallidly.

She said, "We searched back through time and came across the growing Eternity. It seemed obvious to us almost at once that there had been at one point in physiotime (a conception we have also, but under another name) another Reality. The other Reality, the one of maximum probability we call the Basic State. The Basic State had encompassed us once, or had encompassed our analogues, at least. All the time we could not say what the nature of the Basic State was. We could not possibly know.

"We did know, however, that some Change initiated by Eternity in the far downwhen had managed, through the workings of statistical chance, to alter the Basic State all the way up to our Century and beyond. We set about determining the nature of the Basic State, intending to undo the evil, if evil it was. First we set up the quarantined area you call the Hidden Centuries, isolating the Eternals on the downwhen side of the 70,000th. This armour of isolation would affect us from all but a vanishingly small percentage of the Changes being made. It wasn't absolute security but it gave us time.

'We next did something our culture and ethics did not ordinarily allow us to do. We investigated our own future, our upwhen. We learned the destiny of man in the Reality that actually existed in order that we might compare it eventually with Basic State. Somewhere past the 125,000th, mankind solved the secret of the interstellar drive. They learned how to manage the Jump through hyperspace. Finally, mankind could reach the stars."

Harlan was listening in growing absorption to her measured

182

words. How much truth was there in all this? How much was a calculated attempt to deceive him? He tried to break the spell by speaking, by breaking the smooth flow of her sentences. He said:

"And once they could reach the stars, they did so and left the Earth. Some of us have guessed that."

"Then some of you have guessed wrong. Man *tried* to leave Earth. Unfortunately, however, we are not alone in the Galaxy. There are other stars with other planets, you know. There are even other intelligences. None, in this Galaxy at least, are as ancient as mankind, but in the 125,000 Centuries man remained on Earth, younger minds caught up and passed us, developed the interstellar drive, and colonized the Galaxy.

"When we moved out into space, the signs were up. *Occupied! No Trespassing! Clear out!* Mankind drew back its exploratory feelers, remained at home. But now he knew Earth for what it was: a prison surrounded by an infinity of freedom ... And mankind died out!"

Harlan said, "Just died out. Nonsense."

"They didn't *just* die out. It took thousands of Centuries. There were ups and downs but, on the whole, there was a loss of purpose, a sense of futility, a feeling of hopelessness that could not be overcome. Eventually there was one last decline of the birth rate and finally, extinction. Your Eternity did that."

Harlan could defend Eternity now, the more intensely and extravagantly for having so shortly before attacked it so keenly. He said, "Let us at the Hidden Centuries and we will correct that. We have not failed yet to achieve the greatest good in those Centuries we could reach."

"The greatest good?" asked Noÿs in a detached tone that seemed to make a mockery of the phrase. "What is that? Your machines tell you. Your Computaplexes. But who adjusts the machines and tells them what to weigh in the balance? The machines do not solve problems with greater insight than men do, only faster. Only faster! Then what is it the Eternals consider good? I'll tell you. Safety and security. Moderation. Nothing in excess. No risks without overwhelming certainty of an adequate return."

Harlan swallowed. With sudden force he remembered Twissell's words in the kettle while talking about the evolved men of the Hidden Centuries. He said: *"We bred out the unusual."*

183

And wasn't it so?

"Well," said Noÿs, "you seem to be thinking. Think of this, then. In the Reality that now exists, why is it that man is continually attempting space-travel and continually failing? Surely each space-travel era must know its previous failures. Why try again, then?"

Harlan said, "I haven't studied the matter." But he thought uneasily of the colonies on Mars, established again and again, always failing. He thought of the odd attraction that space-flights always had, even for Eternals. He could hear Sociologist Kantor Voy of the 2456th, sighing at the loss of electro-gravitic space-flight in one Century, and saying longingly: *It had been very beautiful.* And Life-Plotter Neron Feruque, who had sworn bitterly at its passing and had launched into a fit of railing at Eternity's handling of anti-cancer serums to ease his spirit.

Was there such a thing as an instinctive yearning on the part of intelligent beings to expand outward, to reach the stars, to leave the prison of gravity behind? Was it that which forced man to develop interplanetary travel dozens of times, forced him to travel over and over again to the dead worlds of a solar system in which only Earth was liveable? Was it the eventual failure, the knowledge that one must return to the home prison, that brought about the maladjustments that Eernity was forever fighting. Harlan thought of the drug addiction in those same futile Centuries of the electro-gravitics.

Noÿs said, "In ironing out the disasters of Reality, Eternity rules out the triumphs as well. It is in meeting the great tests that mankind can most successfully rise to great heights. Out of danger and restless insecurity comes the force that pushes mankind to newer and loftier conquests. Can you understand that? Can you understand that in averting the pitfalls and miseries that beset man, Eternity prevents men from finding their own bitter and better solutions, the real solutions that come from conquering difficulty, not avoiding it."

Harlan began woodenly, "The greatest good of the greatest number –"

Noÿs cut in. "Suppose Eternity had never been established?"

"Well?"

"I'll tell you what would have happened. The energies that went into temporal engineering would have gone into nucleonics instead. Eternity would not have come but the interstellar drive

184

would. Man would have reached the stars more than a hundred thousand Centuries before he did in this current Reality. The stars would then have been untenanted and mankind would have established itself throughout the Galaxy. *We* would have been first."

"And what would have been gained?" asked Harlan doggedly. 'Would we be happier?"

"Whom do you mean by 'we'? Man would not be a world but a million worlds, a billion worlds. We would have the infinite in our grasp. Each world would have its own stretch of the Centuries, each its own values, a chance to seek happiness after ways of its own in an environment of its own. There are many happinesses, many goods, infinite variety.... *That* is the Basic State of mankind."

"You're guessing," said Harlan, and he was angry at himself for feeling attraction for the picture she had conjured. "How can you tell what would have happened?"

Noÿs said, "You smile at the ignorance of the Timers who know only one Reality. We smile at the ignorance of the Eternals who think there are many Realities but that only one exists at a time."

"What does that gibberish mean?"

"We don't calculate alternate Realities. We view them. We see them in their state of non-Reality."

"A kind of ghostly never-never land where the might-have-beens play with the ifs."

"Without the sarcasm, yes."

"And how do you do that?"

Noÿs paused, then said, "How can I explain that, Andrew? I have been educated to know certain things without really understanding all about them, just as you have. Can you explain the workings of a Computaplex? Yet you know it exists and works."

Harlan flushed. "Well, then?"

Noÿs said, "We learned to view Realities and we found Basic State to be as I have described. We found, too, the Change that had destroyed Basic State. It was not any Change that Eternity had initiated; it was the establishment of Eternity itself – the mere fact of its existence. Any system like Eternity, which allows men to choose their own future, will end by choosing safety and mediocrity, and in such a Reality the stars are out of reach. The mere existence of Eternity at once wiped out the

185

Galactic Empire. To restore it, Eternity must be done away with.

"The number of Realities is infinite. The number of any sub-class of Realities is also infinite. For instance, the number of Realities containing Eternity is infinite; the number in which Eternity does not exist is infinite; the number in which Eternity does exist but is abolished is also infinite. But my people chose from among the infinite a group that involved me.

"I had nothing to do with that. They educated me for my job as Twissell and yourself educated Cooper for his job. But the number of Realities in which I was the agent in destroying Eternity was also infinite. I was offered a choice among five Realities that seemed least complex. I chose this one, the one Reality system involving you."

Harlan said, "Why did you choose it?"

Noÿs looked away. "Because I loved you, you see. I loved you long before I met you."

Harlan was shaken. She said it with such depths of sincerity. He thought, sickly: She's an actress —

He said, "That's rather ridiculous."

"Is it? I studied the Realities at my disposal. I studied the Reality in which I went back to the 482nd, met first Finge, then you. The one in which you came to me and loved me, in which you took me into Eternity and the far upwhen of my own Century, in which you misdirected Cooper, and in which you and I, together, returned to the Primitive. We lived in the Primitive for the rest of our days. I saw our lives together and they were happy and I loved you. So it's not ridiculous at all. I chose this alternative so that our love might be true."

Harlan said, "All this is false. It's false. How can you expect me to believe you?" He stopped, then said suddenly, "Wait! You say you knew all this in advance? All that would happen?"

"Yes."

"Then you're obviously lying. You would have known that I would have you here at blaster point. You would have known you would fail. What is your answer to that?"

She sighed lightly, "I told you there are an infinite number of any subclass of Realities. No matter how finely we focus on a given Reality it always represents an infinite number of very similar Realities. There are fuzzy spots. The finer we focus, the less fuzzy, but perfect sharpness cannot be obtained. The less fuzzy, the lower the probability of chance variation spoiling the result, but the probability is never absolutely zero. One fuzzy spot spoiled things."

"Which?"

"You were to have come back to the far upwhen after the barrier at the 100,000th had been lowered and you did. But you were to have come back alone. It is for that reason that I was momentarily so startled at seeing Computer Twissell with you."

Again Harlan was troubled. How she made things fit in!

Noÿs said, "I would have been even more startled had I realized the significance of that alteration in full. Had you come alone, you would have brought me back to the Primitive as you did. Then, for love of humanity, for love of me, you would have left Cooper untouched. Your circle would have been broken, Eternity ended, our life together here safe.

"But you came with Twissell, a chance variation. While coming, he talked to you of his thoughts about the Hidden Centuries and started you on a train of deductions that ended with your doubting *my* good faith. It ended with a blaster between us. . . . And now, Andrew, that's the story. You may blast me. There is nothing to stop you."

Harlan's hand ached from its spastic grasp on the blaster. He shifted it dizzily to the other hand. Was there no flaw in her story? Where was the resolution he was to have gained from knowing certainly that she was a creature of the Hidden Centuries? He was more than ever tearing at himself in conflict and dawn was approaching.

He said, "Why two efforts to end Eternity? Why couldn't Eternity have ended once and for all when I sent Cooper back to the 20th? Things would have ended then and there would not have been this agony of uncertainty."

"Because," said Noÿs, "ending this Eternity is not enough. We must reduce the probability of establishing any form of Eternity to as near zero as we can manage. So there is one thing we must do here in the Primitive. A small Change, a little thing. You know what a Minimum Necessary Change is life. It is only a letter to a peninsula called Italy here in the 20th. It is now the 19.32nd. In a few Centicenturies, provided I send the letter, a man of Italy will begin experimenting with the neutronic bombardment of uranium."

Harlan found himself horrified. "You will alter Primitive history?"

"Yes. It is our intention. In the new Reality, the final Reality, the first nuclear explosion will take place not in the 30th Century but in the 19.45th."

"But do you know the danger? Can you possibly estimate the danger?"

"We know the danger. We have viewed the sheaf of resulting Realities. There is a probability, not a certainty, of course, that Earth will end with a largely radioactive crust, but before that –"

"You mean there can be compensation for that?"

"A Galactic Empire. An actual intensification of the Basic State."

"Yet you accuse the Eternals of interfering –"

"We accuse them of interfering many times to keep mankind safely at home and in prison. We interfere once, *once*, to turn him prematurely to nucleonics so that he might never, *never*, establish an Eternity."

"No," said Harlan desperately. "There must be an Eternity."

"If you choose. It is yours to choose. If you wish to have psychopaths dictate the future of man –"

"*Psychopaths!*" exploded Harlan.

"Aren't they? You know them. Think!"

Harlan stared at her in outraged horror, yet he could not help thinking. He thought of Cubs learning the truth about Reality and Cub Latourette trying to kill himself as a result. Latourette had survived to become an Eternal, with what scars on his personality none could say, yet helping to decide on alternate Realities.

He thought of the caste system in Eternity, of the abnormal life that turned guilt feelings into anger and hatred against Technicians. He thought of Computers, struggling against themselves, of Finge intriguing against Twissell and Twissell spying on Finge. He thought of Sennor, fighting his bald head by fighting all the Eternals.

He thought of himself.

Then he thought of Twissell, the great Twissell, also breaking the laws of Eternity.

It was as though he had always known Eternity to be all this. Why else should he have been so willing to destroy it? Yet he had never admitted it to himself fully; he had never looked it clearly in the face, until, suddenly, now.

And he saw Eternity with great clarity as a sink of deepening

188

psychoses, a writing pit of abnormal motivation, a mass of desperate lives torn brutally out of context.

He looked blankly at Noÿs.

She said softly, "Do you see? Come to the mouth of the cave with me, Andrew?"

He followed her, hypnotized, appalled at the completeness with which he had gained a new viewpoint. His blaster fell away from the line connecting it and Noÿs's heart for the first time.

The pale streaking of dawn greyed the sky, and the bulking kettle just outside the cave was an oppressive shadow against the pallor. Its outlines were dulled and blurred by the film thrown over it.

Noÿs said, "This is Earth. Not the eternal and only home of mankind, but only a starting point of an infinite adventure. All you need do is make the decision. It is yours to make. You and I and the contents of this cave will be protected by a physio-time field against the Change. Cooper will disappear along with his advertisement; Eternity will go and the Reality of my Century, but *we* will remain to have children and grandchildren, and mankind will remain to reach the stars."

He turned to look at her, and she was smiling at him. It was Noÿs, as she had been, and his own heart beating as it had used to.

He wasn't even aware that he had made his decision until the greyness suddenly invaded all the sky as the hulk of the kettle disappeared from against it.

With that disappearance, he knew, even as Noÿs moved slowly into his arms, came the end, the final end of Eternity.

– And the beginning of Infinity.

Isaac Asimov, Grand Master of Science Fiction, in Panther Books

Panther Science Fiction – A Selection from the World's Best S.F. List

All these book are available at your local bookshop or newsagent, or can be ordered direct from the publisher. Just tick the titles you want and fill in the form below.

Name ....

Address ....

....

Write to Panther Cash Sales, PO Box 11, Falmouth, Cornwall TR10 9EN.

Please enclose remittance to the value of the cover price plus:

UK: 22p for the first book plus 10p per copy for each additional book ordered to a maximum charge of 82p.

BFPO and EIRE: 22p for the first book plus 10p per copy for the next 6 books, thereafter 3p per book.

OVERSEAS: 30p for the first book and 10p for each additional book.

Granada Publishing reserve the right to show new retail prices on covers, which may differ from those previously advertised in the text or elsewhere.